Praise for bestselling author

LORI
FOSTER

"Lori Foster delivers the goods."
—*Publishers Weekly*

"Lori Foster is a master at creating likable
characters and placing them in situations that tug
at the heart and set your pulse racing..."
—*Romance Reviews Today*

"Lori Foster's stories are raw excitement!"
—Stella Cameron

"Author Lori Foster has a reputation
for warm, engaging characters
combined with sizzling sexual tension...."
—Lois Dyer, Amazon.com Editorial Reviews

"When it comes to writing outstanding family
stories, especially about brothers, no one does it
like Lori Foster."
—*Romance Reviews Today*

"Foster outwrites most of her peers..."
—*Library Journal*

"For outstanding steamy romance entertainment,
Lori Foster can't be beat!"
—*Romantic Times*

Lori Foster was first published in January 1996 and since then has sold over thirty books with six different houses, including series romance, novellas, online books, special projects and, most recently, single titles. Lori's second book launched the Harlequin Temptation Blaze subseries, and her twenty-fifth book launched the new Temptation Heat series.

Lori has brought a sensitivity and sensibility to erotic romances by combining family values and sizzling yet tender love. Though Lori enjoys writing, her first priority will always be her family. Her husband and three sons keep her on her toes.

Watch for Lori's story in the Men of Courage *anthology coming out in May 2003, and also her spin-off book in Temptation due out in June 2003.*

LORI FOSTER

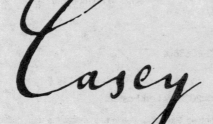

Casey

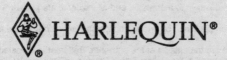

HARLEQUIN®

TORONTO • NEW YORK • LONDON
AMSTERDAM • PARIS • SYDNEY • HAMBURG
STOCKHOLM • ATHENS • TOKYO • MILAN • MADRID
PRAGUE • WARSAW • BUDAPEST • AUCKLAND

To all my very special friends on the bookjunkies list.
You keep me smiling from one book to the next. Sharing with you,
knowing you, having your support and friendship, has meant
the world to me. Thank you! I'd also like to give a special thanks
to these bookjunkies gals: Lois, Ann, Donna and Kristin. It was fun
teasing you about Casey, and using your first names. The characters,
however, are strictly from my imagination. No pretend characters
could ever be as wonderful as each of you.
And to Jana Taylor and Cyn Witkus
for all the research help on massage therapy.
Smooches to both of you!

ISBN 0-373-83568-X

CASEY

Copyright © 2002 by Lori Foster.

Visit us at www.eHarlequin.com

Printed in U.S.A.

Dear Readers,

After the release of my four-book Temptation series THE BUCKHORN BROTHERS, Casey Hudson became my most popular male character ever—and he was only a teenager! I've been overwhelmed and delighted with all the notes and posts and e-mails requesting, begging for and sometimes demanding Casey's story. Thank you! What fun it's been watching his popularity grow. He was a great kid—but now he's a man, and writing his story has been loads of fun. I hope you approve.

Many of you also became enthralled with Ceily, the woman who owned the diner. I liked her as well, so Ceily has a secondary romance in this book that I think will make you laugh, and maybe sigh just a little.

Please let me know what you think of Casey and Emma, and I'll keep my fingers crossed that you close this book, the last in the series, with a huge smile of satisfaction. You can reach me at Lori Foster, P.O. Box 854, Ross OH 45061 or check out my Web page at www.lorifoster.com.

My best to all of you!

Lori Foster

THE BUCKHORN BROTHERS

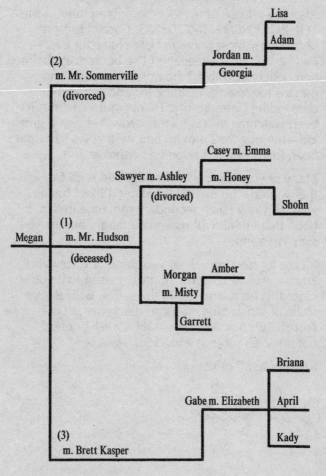

PROLOGUE

THE FAMILY PICNIC had lasted all day, and Casey had a feeling everything that should have been accomplished had been. In fact, even more had developed than he'd expected—like his present uncomfortable situation.

He hadn't exactly meant to pair up with Emma Clark. She had few friends, none of them female, and Casey had just naturally defended her when the others had started sniping.

So now, with nearly every girl in town chasing after him, he found himself behind the garage at the far end of the house with a girl—the one girl he'd been doing his best to avoid—snuggled up to his side. No one else in the yard could see them. They had complete privacy.

How the hell was a guy supposed to deal with that?

His father and his uncles had been the most eligible bachelors in Buckhorn, Kentucky. It had been fun for Casey growing up in an all-male household and watching his uncles and his dad deal with all that female adoration. Casey had been proud of their popularity and amused by it all. And pleased by the situation, since he'd gained his own share of adoration as he'd matured. He'd learned a lot from watching them—but he hadn't learned how to deal with Emma.

Like his father and his uncles, Casey loved and respected women, most especially his grandmother and his new stepmother and aunts. But then, they were all so different from Emma.

And that thought had him frowning.

Emma was...well, she had a reputation that could rival his Uncle Gabe's, and that said something since Gabe had been a complete and total hedonist when it came to his sexuality. By all accounts, Gabe had started young; from what Casey knew, Emma had started even younger.

At seventeen, she flaunted herself with all the jaded expertise of a woman twice her age. Her bleached-blond hair and overdone makeup advertised her status of being on the make.

Lately she'd been on the make for Casey. For the most part, he'd been able to resist her.

For the most part.

Emma's small soft hand began trailing over Casey's chest. His heart thumped hard, his body hardened. Very gently, doing his best to hide his reaction from her, he eased her away. "We should join the others."

In fact, he thought, all too aware of the heat of her young body so close to his own, he never should have been alone with her in the first place. Thanks to his stepmother and her father, he had a great business opportunity coming up. But before he could take advantage of that, he had several years of college to get through. Emma, with her hard-to-resist curves and open sensuality, would be nothing but trouble.

"No." She stroked down his bare chest, but Casey caught her hand before she reached the fly to his jeans. He liked her more than he should have, and wanted her more than that. Hell, to be truthful, he was crazy nuts with wanting her, not that he'd ever even hinted as much. His plans for the future did not include Emma. They couldn't.

Emma had led a very different life from him. Tangling the two up wouldn't be good for either of them.

His head understood that, but his body did not.

It took more control than he knew he had to turn her away this time.

"Emma," Casey chided, hoping that she couldn't hear the shaking of his voice. He'd only wanted to champion her, but Emma wanted more. She was so blatant about it, so brazen, that it took all his concentration not to give in. Besides, more than anything else, Emma needed a friend not another conquest. And beyond that, Casey didn't share.

"Are you a virgin?" she taunted, not giving a single inch, and Casey laughed outright at her ploy. She was determined, he'd give her that. But then, so was he.

Flicking a finger over her soft cheek, he said, "That's none of your business."

Her incredible brown eyes widened, reflecting the moonlight and a femininity that went bone deep. She shook her head in wonder. "You're the only guy I know who wouldn't have denied it right away."

"I'm not denying or confirming."

"I know," she whispered, still sounding amazed, "but most guys'd lie if they had to, rather than let a girl think—"

"What?" Casey cupped her face and despite his resolve, he kissed her. Damn, it was hard fighting both himself and her. "I don't care what anyone thinks, Emma. You should know that by now. Besides, what I've done or with who isn't the point."

"No," she agreed, her tone suddenly so sad it nearly broke his heart. "It's what I've done, isn't it?"

Thinking about that, about the guys she'd probably been with and the notoriety of her reputation, filled Casey with possessive rage. So many guys had bragged. Too damn many. Ruthlessly, Casey tamped down the urges he refused to acknowledge, and repeated his own thoughts out loud. "I don't share."

"Casey," she said, shyly peeking up at him, her expression tinted with hope, "what if I promised not to—"

"Shh." He couldn't bear for Emma to start pleading, to make promises he doubted she could keep and that wouldn't matter in the long run anyway. He couldn't let them matter. "Don't do that, Emma. Don't make it harder than it already is. Summer break is almost over and I'll be leaving for school. You know that. I won't be around, so there's no point in us even discussing this."

Big tears welled in her eyes, causing his guts to cramp. One of her hands fisted in his shirt. "I'm leaving too, Casey." Her breathing was choppy, the words broken.

Emma leaving? That surprised him. As gently as possible, Casey stroked the tears from her cheeks and then, because he couldn't help himself, he kissed her forehead. "And where do you think to go, Em?" She hadn't finished high school yet, had no real prospects that he knew of, no opportunities. Her home life was crap, and that bothered him too. He wanted...

No, he couldn't even think that way.

"It doesn't matter," she said. "I just wanted you to know."

He didn't like the sound of that, but had no idea what to say. He could see her soft mouth trembling, could smell her hot, sweet scent carried on the evening breeze. Unlike the other girls he knew, Emma didn't wear fragrances. But then, she didn't need to.

Her warm palm touched his jaw. "You're all that matters to me right now, Case. You and the fact that we might not ever see each other again."

Boldly, she took his hand and pressed it to her breast. Casey shuddered. She was so damn soft.

His resolve weakened, then cracked. With a muttered curse, he pulled her closer and kissed her again, this time giving his hunger free rein. Her mouth opened under his, accepted his tongue, gave him her own. It didn't matter, he promised himself, filling his hand with her firm breast, finding her puckered nipple and stroking with his thumb.

She gave a startled, hungry purr of relief, her fingers clenching on his shoulders, her hips snuggling closer to his, stroking his erection, driving him insane.

Casey gave in with a growl of frustration and overwhelming need. He was damned if he did, and damned if he didn't. And sometimes Emma was just too much temptation to resist.

But it wouldn't change anything. He told her so in a muted whisper, and her only reply was a groan.

Two Months Later
CASEY SAT BACK in his seat and watched them all with an indulgent smile. Family gatherings had be-

come a common event now that everyone had married and started families of their own. He missed having everyone so close, but they visited often, and it was obvious his father and uncles had found the perfect women for them.

The girl beside Casey cleared her throat, uncomfortable in the boisterous crowd of his family. It didn't matter because he doubted he'd see her again anyway. Donna was beautiful, sexy and anxious to please him—but she wasn't perfect for him. He knew it was dumb, considering he wasn't quite nineteen yet, but Casey couldn't help wondering if he'd ever meet the perfect girl.

An image of big brown eyes, filled with sexual curiosity, sadness, and finally rejection, formed in his mind. With a niggling dread that wouldn't ease up, Casey wondered if he'd already found the perfect girl—but had sent her away.

Then he heard his aunt talking to Donna, and he pulled himself out of his reverie. No, she wasn't perfect, but she didn't keep him awake nights either. And that was good, because no matter what, no matter how he felt now, he would not let his plans get off track. He decided to forget all about women and the future and simply enjoy the night with his family.

It was late when the family get-together ended and Casey finally got home after dropping off his date. He'd just pulled off his shirt when a fist started pounding on the front door. He and his father, Sawyer, met in the hall, both of them frowning. Sawyer was the town doctor and out of necessity, patients sometimes came this late at night, but as a rule they called first—unless there was an emergency. Casey's stepmother, Honey, pulled on her robe and hustled after them.

When Sawyer got the door open, they found themselves confronted with Emma's father, Dell Clark. Beyond furious, Dell had a tight grip on his daughter's upper arm. His gaunt face was flushed, his eyes red, the tendons in his neck standing out.

Casey's first startled thought was that even though he hadn't seen her in two months, Emma hadn't gone after all. She was right here in Buckhorn.

Then he got a good look at her ravaged face, and he erupted in rage.

He'd been wrong. His plans were changed after all.

In a big way.

CHAPTER ONE

ENRAGED AND UNCERTAIN what he planned to do, Casey started forward. Before he reached Dell, Sawyer caught his arm and drew him up short. "Take it easy, Case."

Emma covered her mouth with a shaking hand, crying while trying not to cry, held tight by her father's grip even as she attempted to inch away from him. She wouldn't look at any of them, her narrow shoulders hunched in embarrassment—and possibly pain.

Casey's heart hurt, and his temper roiled. Emma's pretty brown eyes, usually so warm and sexy, were downcast, circled by ruined makeup and swollen from her tears. There was a bruise on her cheek, just visible in the glow of the porch light.

Casey felt tight enough to break as a kind of animal outrage that he'd never before experienced struggled to break free. Every night he'd thought about seeing Emma again, and every night he'd talked himself out of it.

Not once had he considered that he'd see her like this.

His vision nearly blurred as he heard Emma sniff and watched her wipe her eyes with a shaking hand.

With unnecessary roughness, her father shoved her forward and she stumbled across the wide porch before righting herself and turning her back to Casey. Without a word, she held on to the railing, staring out at the moonlit yard. Her broken breathing was audible over the night sounds of wind and crickets and rustling leaves.

"Do you know what your damn son did?" Dell demanded.

Casey felt Sawyer look at him but he ignored the unasked questions and instead went to Emma, taking her arm and pulling her close. It didn't matter why she was here; he wanted to hold her, to tell her it'd be all right.

Drawn into herself, Emma sidled away from him, whispering a broken apology again and again. She hugged her arms around herself. Casey realized the night was cool, and while Dell wore a jacket, Emma wore only a T-shirt and jeans, as if she'd been pulled away without having time to grab her coat. Since he was shirtless, he couldn't offer her anything. He tried to think, to figure out what to do, but he couldn't get his brain to work. He felt glued to the spot, unable to take his gaze off her.

She needed his help.

Honey came to the same realization. "Why don't we all go inside and talk?"

Looking horrified by that proposition, Emma backed up. "No. That's not—"

"Be quiet, girl!" Her father reached for her again, his anger and his intent obvious.

Casey stepped in front of him, bristling, coiled. "Don't even try it." No way in hell would he let Dell touch her again.

Face mottled with rage, her father shouted, "You

think you get some say-so, boy? You think what
you've done to her gives you that right?''

Without moving his gaze from the man in front of
him, Casey said, ''Honey, will you take Emma inside?''

Honey looked at her husband, who nodded. Casey
hadn't had a single doubt what his father would do
or say. Not once in his entire life had he ever had to
question his father's support.

Never in his life had he been more grateful for it.

Again, Emma tried to back away, moving into the
far shadows of the big porch. Casey snapped his gaze
to hers, so attuned to her it seemed he felt her every
shuddering breath. ''Go inside, Emma.''

She bit her lip, big tears spilling over her blotchy
cheeks and clinging to her long lashes. Her mouth
trembled. ''Casey, I...''

''It's all right.'' He struggled to keep his voice soft,
comforting, but it wasn't easy—not while he could
see the hurt in her eyes and feel her very real distress.
''We'll talk in a little bit.''

Speaking low and gentle, Honey put her arm
around Emma, and reluctantly, Emma allowed herself
to be led away. The front door closed quietly behind
them.

With his daughter out of sight, Dell seemed more
incensed than ever. He took two aggressive steps forward. ''You'll do more than talk. You'll damn well
marry her.''

Casey gave him a cool look of disdain. That Dell
could treat a female so callously made him sick to his
stomach, but that he'd treat his own daughter that way
brought out all Casey's protective instincts. More than

anyone else he knew, Emma needed love and under-standing. Yet, her own father was throwing her out, deliberately humiliating her.

"You brought her here," Casey growled. "You've delivered her to my doorstep, to *me*. What she or I do now is no concern of yours. Go home and leave us the hell alone."

Though Casey knew it would only complicate things more, he wanted to tear Dell apart. It wouldn't strain him at all. He was taller, stronger, with raw fury adding to his edge. He deliberately provoked Dell, and waited for his reaction.

It came in a lightning flash of curses and motion. The older man erupted, lunging forward. Smiling with intent, anxious for the confrontation, Casey braced himself.

Unfortunately, Sawyer caught Dell by his jacket collar before Casey could throw his first swing.

At well over six feet tall, solid with muscle, Sawyer wasn't a man to be messed with. He slammed Dell hard into the side of the house, and held him there with his forearm braced across his throat. He leaned close enough that their noses nearly touched.

"You come onto my property," Sawyer snarled, looking meaner than Casey had ever seen him look, "treating your only daughter like garbage and threat-ening my son?" He slammed Dell again, making his head smack back against the wood siding. "Unless you want me to take you apart right now, which I'm more than willing to do, I suggest you get hold of your goddamn temper."

Dell's face turned red from Sawyer's choking hold, but he managed a weak nod. When Sawyer released him, he sagged down, gulping in air. It took him several moments, and Casey was glad that Emma had gone inside so she didn't hear her father's next words.

Wheezing, Dell eyed both Sawyer and Casey. ''You're so worried about Emma, fine. She's yours.'' He spit as he talked, his face distorted with anger and pain. ''You and your son are welcome to her, but don't think you can turn around and send her back home.''

''To you?'' Casey curled his lip. ''Hell no.''

Something in the man's eyes didn't make sense. The fury remained, no doubt about that. But Dell also looked...desperate. And a bit relieved. ''You swear?''

He should have hit the son of a bitch at least once, Casey thought. He nodded, and forced the next words out from between clenched teeth. ''You just make sure you stay the hell away from her.''

Glaring one last time, Dell stepped around Sawyer and stomped down off the porch. At the edge of the grass, he stopped, his shoulders stiff, his back expanding with deep breaths, and for a long moment he hesitated. Casey narrowed his eyes, waiting. For Emma's sake, he half hoped her father had a change of heart, that he showed even an ounce of concern or compassion.

Dell looked over his shoulder at Casey. His mouth opened twice but no words were spoken. Finally he shook his head and went to his battered truck. He didn't glance back again. His headlights came on and he left the yard, squealing his tires and spewing gravel.

Casey stood there, breathing hard, his hands curled

into fists, his whole body vibrating with tension. The enormity of the situation, of what he'd just taken on, nearly leveled him. He squeezed his eyes shut, trying to think.

Jesus, what had he done?

Sawyer's hand slipped around the back of his neck, comforting, supportive. A heavy, uncomfortable beat of silence passed.

"What do you want to do first, Case?" Sawyer spoke in a nearly soundless murmur, his voice disappearing in the dark night. "Talk to me, or talk to Emma?"

Casey looked at his dad, a man he loved and respected more than anyone else on earth. He swallowed. "Emma."

Nodding, Sawyer turned them both around and headed for the door. Casey hoped a few answers came to him before the morning light began creeping over the lake. Because, at the moment, he had no idea what the hell was going on.

EMMA HEARD the opening and the closing of the front door. She squeezed her eyes shut, horrified, ashamed, scared spitless.

And oddly relieved.

More tears leaked out, choking her, burning her cheeks and throat. What had she done? What choice had she been given?

Honey touched her arm in a motherly way. "Drink your hot chocolate. And Emma, everything will be okay. You'll see."

Shaking down deep in her soul, Emma wiped at her eyes. She felt like a child, and knew she looked more like a barroom whore. Her makeup had long since been ruined and her nose and eyes were red. Her hair was a wild mess and her T-shirt was dirty.

Though the Hudson household was cozy and warm, she still felt chilled from the inside out. In that moment, she wondered if she'd ever be warm again.

Hugging herself in self-conscious dismay, she wished she could just disappear. She didn't belong in this house with these nice respectable people. But disappearing wasn't an option. She'd gotten herself in this mess and now she had to face them all. She had to explain.

She owed Casey at least that much.

At that moment, barefoot and shirtless, Casey came around the corner into the kitchen. His muscled arms crossed over his chest as he stopped in front of the kitchen table where she sat. His light-brown eyes, filled with compassion and confusion, warmed to glittering amber as he looked her over.

Stomach churning in dread, Emma flicked her gaze away.

Casey's father, Sawyer, stood behind him. Honey sat beside her. She felt surrounded, circled by their concern and curiosity, hemmed in by their kindness.

The damn tears welled up again and she felt herself start to shudder. Oh God, if she bawled like a baby now she'd never forgive herself.

His expression solemn, Casey held out his hand. "Let's me and you talk a little, Emma."

She stared at him through a haze of tears.

Sawyer frowned. "Casey…"

"Just a few minutes, Dad. I promise."

Honey sent Sawyer a pointed look, then patted

Emma's shoulder. "You can use the family room. Sawyer and I will make sandwiches and join you in just a few minutes."

Keeping her head bowed so she wouldn't have to make eye contact with anyone, Emma left her chair. She didn't want to take Casey's hand, and tried to walk around him, but he caught her and his fingers laced into hers. His hand was big and warm, strong and steady. Reassuring.

Normally, just being near him made her feel more secure. But not this time.

To her amazement, when he reached the family room, Casey sat down and tugged her into his lap. She couldn't remember anyone ever holding her like that before. Emma was so shocked she almost bolted upright, but Casey wrapped both arms around her and pulled her so tightly to him, her head just naturally went to his shoulder. Her shaking increased.

Very gently, Casey stroked one hand up and down her back. "Em? Tell me what's going on."

Despite her resolve, she clutched at him. "I'm so sorry, Casey. So, so sorry."

He pushed her hair away from her face, then reached for a box of tissues on the end table and held them in front of her. Emma blew her nose, but it didn't help. The tears kept coming and she couldn't make them stop. "I didn't mean to get you involved, I swear."

Calmly, as if she hadn't just turned his life upside down, he said, "Involved in what?"

That was the thing about Casey. He was always calm, always so mature and sure of himself that, without thinking, she'd used his name and now... Emma grabbed for three more tissues. This was where she had to be careful. "I told my parents that I'm pregnant."

Casey went very still. Silence hung heavy in the air, broken only by her gasping breaths and awful sniffling. Casey sat there, tall and proud and strong, while she fell apart like a deranged child.

In that moment, Emma hated herself.

His hand began stroking her again. "I take it they weren't too happy about it?"

She laughed, but the humor faded into a wail. "I couldn't think of what else to do."

"So you came to me?"

He didn't seem nearly as outraged as she had expected. But then Casey was so different from any other guy she knew, she didn't know what to expect from him. He had a good handle on everything, on his life, his temper, his future.

"It's not...not what you think." This was even harder than she'd imagined. On the silent drive to his house, with her father fuming beside her, she'd tried to prepare herself, tried to make decisions. But this was the worst thing she'd ever done.

"No?" His thumb carefully smoothed over the bruise on her cheek.

God, she wished he'd say something more, maybe yell at her or throw her out. His calm destroyed what little control she'd been able to hold on to. "No." She shook her head and leaned away from the gentleness of his touch. It took one breath, then another, before she could speak convincingly. "I don't need or want anything from you, Case."

The intensity of his dark gaze seeped into her and she tried to look away.

Gently, Casey brought her face back up to his. "Then why are you here, Em?"

"I just…" *I had to escape.* She drew a shaking breath and attempted to gather herself together. The last few hours had seemed endless, and the night was far from over. "I needed to get away and I couldn't think of anything else."

A rap on the door made her jerk, and she looked up to see Sawyer and Honey standing there, each carrying a tray. Sawyer held sandwiches and Honey held mugs of hot chocolate.

Emma started to groan. God, they were like Leave it to freakin' Beaver or something, so homey and together that nothing shook them for long, not even the neighborhood riffraff dropping in with a bombshell that should have disrupted the rest of their lives.

Envy formed a vise around her heart, but she knew she'd never belong to a family like theirs. They'd never want her.

Her own family didn't.

Sawyer's smile appeared strained but kind. "I think we should all do a little talking now."

He set the tray on the coffee table and settled into a chair. Honey did the same. They both seemed to ignore the fact that she'd ended up perched on Casey's lap, held in his strong arms. But the second Emma realized just how that would look, she shot to her feet. Before she could move too far away, Casey leaned forward and caught her wrist. Unlike her father's grip, his was gentle and warm.

Casey's hold offered comfort not restraint.

He came to his feet beside her, and she had the awful suspicion he wanted to provide a united front to his parents. He faced his father squarely, without an ounce of uncertainty or embarrassment. "Emma is pregnant."

Sawyer's jaw locked, and Honey looked down at her clasped hands, but not fast enough to hide her distress. When Emma started to speak, Casey squeezed her hand, silencing her. She understood what he wanted to do, and this time it was love clenching her heart. Not infatuation, not jealousy for all he had.

Real love.

There didn't exist a better man than Casey Hudson. Emma knew in that moment she'd never forget him, no matter what turns her life took in the morning.

Very slowly, her movements deliberate and unmistakable, Emma pulled herself away from Casey. She took one step, then another and another, until she stood several feet away from him.

It wasn't easy, but she managed to face his parents. This time her gaze never wavered. What she had to say was too important to leave any doubts. "Casey has never touched me."

Sawyer sat up a little straighter, and his eyebrows came down in a dark frown of bewilderment. Honey's gaze darted between them.

"Emma..." Casey took a step toward her.

She shot up a hand to ward him off. His nobility, his willingness to sacrifice himself, amazed her and made her love him that much more. She smiled at him, her first genuine smile in weeks. The time for sniffling and crying and being a fool had ended. She owed this family more than that. She owed Casey so damn much. "Casey, when I told my parents I was pregnant, I lied."

"But…"

Feeling stiff and awkward, she rolled one shoulder in a casual shrug. "I'm sorry." Her words trembled, nearly incoherent, and she cleared her throat. She wanted to beg him not to hate her, but that wouldn't be fair. "I know it was wrong. I had to say something to get away and I couldn't think of anything else."

His gaze locked on her, Sawyer rose from his chair. He looked angry, but Emma had the feeling his anger wasn't directed at her. Still, she couldn't stop herself from backing away at his approach. When she caught Casey's frown, she halted and forced herself to remain still.

With a large gentle hand on her chin, Sawyer tipped her face this way and that to examine her bruised cheek, then he carefully looked at the rest of her face. He was an imposing man, and she'd always been in awe of him. Now, with him in front of her and Casey close at her side, she almost felt faint.

"What happened to your face, Emma?" Sawyer's tone left no room for evasions. He expected an answer. He expected the truth.

He couldn't have it.

Emma touched the bruise, and winced. "I…I fell, that's all."

Casey snorted.

She cast him a quick worried look, but couldn't meet his piercing gaze for more than a few seconds. They didn't deserve to be lied to, but neither did they deserve to be drawn into her problems. If they knew, they'd never let her get away. She'd done enough to them. From here on out, she would handle things. Alone. She had to.

Sawyer again tipped up her chin, this time to regain her attention. "We can help if you'll let us."

Did every one of them take nobility in stride? Emma wiped her eyes on her crumpled tissue, wondering how to explain without telling too much. Shame bit into her, and she sighed. "Dr. Hudson, I'm so sorry—"

Casey caught her elbow and whirled her around to face him, his anger barely leashed. "Quit apologizing, damn it. It's not necessary."

Emma pulled back. "I've barged in here—"

"Your father barged in, not you." Casey's light-brown eyes burned nearly gold, and his jaw was set. "You're not responsible for what he does, Emma."

"But...this time I am," she explained gently. She was very aware of his parents' attention. "I told him I was pregnant, and I told him...I told him that you were the father."

She turned to Sawyer and Honey in a rush, stumbling over her words. "Casey hasn't ever touched me, I swear. He wouldn't. He's so much better than that. But I knew if I named any other guy..." She stalled, not sure what else to say. From the time she became a teenager, she'd been with so many boys. And yet, she'd named the only one who hadn't wanted her.

Hands on his hips, Casey dropped his head forward, staring at the floor. He made a rough sound, part growl, part sarcasm. "None of the other guys would have defended you, would have taken you in."

Relief that she hadn't had to explain, after all, made

Emma's knees weak. "I used your integrity against you, and I *am* sorry." Twisting her hands together, she faced Sawyer. "Everyone in Buckhorn knows that you and your brothers are good people. I thought that you might help me, so I used Casey's name to get here. It wasn't right and I can understand if you hate me, but it was the only thing I could think of."

"Emma," Honey murmured, her tone filled with sympathy, "no one hates you."

Impatient, Sawyer shook his head. "Why did you need to get here, Emma? That's what I want to know."

And Honey added, "But of course you're more than welcome to stay—"

"Oh, no." Appalled by the conclusions she'd led them to, Emma shook her head. "No, you're not stuck with me or anything like that." She'd made a real muddle of things, she realized. "I have no intention of imposing on you, I swear."

They met her promises with blank stares.

She started trembling again. She'd never felt more unsophisticated or more trashy than she did right at that moment, standing among them. The comparisons between herself and them made her stomach pitch. She wanted to take off running and never look back.

Soon, she promised herself. Very soon. "I have some money that I've saved up, and I know how to work. I'm going to go to Ohio first thing in the morning."

"What's in Ohio?" Casey asked, and he didn't look so even-tempered now. He looked ready to explode.

A new life, she wanted to tell him, but instead she

lied. Again. "I have a…a cousin there. She offered me a place to stay and a job."

Her expression worried, Honey glanced at Sawyer, then Casey, before tilting her head at Emma. "What kind of job?"

What kind of job? Emma blinked, taken aback by the question. She hadn't expected this. She'd thought they'd be glad to see her gone. Oh, she'd known that they would offer to let her stay the night, that they'd be kind. She wouldn't have come to them otherwise. But she figured once she told them she had a place to go they'd send her on her way with no questions asked.

Think, she told herself, and finally mumbled, "I'm not sure, actually. But she said it'd be perfect for me and I assume it'll be something…reasonable."

The way they all looked at her, they knew she was lying. Emma started backing away toward the phone. "I…I'm going to call a cab now." She dared a quick peek at Casey, then wished she hadn't. In all the time she'd known him, she'd never once seen him so enraged. "When…when I get settled, I'll write to you, okay?"

Casey again crossed his arms over his chest. "That won't be necessary."

Her heart sank and she wanted to crumble in on herself. "I understand." Why would he want to hear from her anyway? She'd offered herself to him plenty of times—and every single time he'd turned her away. And still she'd barged into his life.

"You don't understand a damn thing." Casey began striding toward her. "Emma, you're not going anywhere."

His tone frightened her. She felt locked in his gaze, unable to look away, unable to think. "Of course I am."

"No." Sawyer strode toward her too, his movements easy, nonthreatening, which didn't help Emma's panic one bit. "Casey is right. It's damn near the middle of the night and you look exhausted. You need to get some sleep. In the morning we'll all talk and figure out what's to be done."

"No…" She shook her head, dazed by their reactions.

"Yes." Sawyer took her arm, his expression gentle, his intent implacable. "For now, I want you to eat a sandwich and drink some chocolate, then you can take a warm shower and get some sleep."

In a quandary, Emma found herself reseated on the sofa. They weren't throwing her out? After what she'd done, what she'd just admitted to them?

Her own father, despite everything or maybe because of it, had used the opportunity of her supposed pregnancy to rid himself of her. And her mother… No, she wouldn't, *couldn't*, think about that right now.

Honey smiled at her. "Please don't worry so much, Emma. Everything is okay now."

"Nothing is okay." Why couldn't they understand that?

Honey's gentle smile never slipped. "I felt the same way when I first came here, but they're sincere, I swear. We're *all* sincere. We just don't want you rushing off until we know you'll be all right."

Confusion weighed heavy on her brain. She didn't know how to deal with this.

Casey sat down beside her and shoved a peanut butter and jelly sandwich into her hand. Emma stared at it, knowing she wouldn't be able to swallow a single bite without throwing up. She had to do... something. She had to get out of here before their acceptance and understanding weakened her resolve.

She would not become someone else's burden.

Her mind made up, she put the sandwich aside. "I'd really like to just take a shower if that's okay. I know I look a mess."

Using his fingertips, Casey wiped away a lingering tear she hadn't been aware of. He hesitated, but finally nodded. "All right. You can sleep in my room tonight."

Her eyes widened and her mouth fell open. Casey grinned at her, then pinched her chin. "I'll, of course, sleep on the couch."

Mortification washed over her for her asinine assumption. At her blush, Casey's grin widened. She couldn't believe the way he teased her in front of his parents.

"You could have used Morgan's old room, except that Honey's been painting it and everything is a mess in there."

Morgan was his uncle, the town sheriff. Most people thought he was a big, scary guy. He was enormous, but he'd always been kind to Emma, even when he'd caught her getting into trouble, like breaking curfew or being truant from school. Newly wed, Morgan had recently moved into his own house.

"I'll take the couch." Emma thought that would be easier, but Casey wouldn't hear of it.

"You'll take the bed."

His father and stepmother agreed with him. In the end, Emma knew she was no match for them. Exhaustion won out and she nodded. "All right." It would be strange sleeping in Casey's room, in his bed. A secret part of her already looked forward to it. "Thank you."

Casey took her down the hall to the bathroom, then got her one of his large T-shirts to sleep in. She knew it was selfish, but she accepted the shirt, holding it close to her heart. It was big and soft and it held his indescribable scent. Since she couldn't have Casey, it was the next best thing.

Their bathroom was bigger than her whole bedroom. It was clean and stylish and that damn envy threatened to get hold of her again. Emma swore to herself that someday, she'd have a house as nice as this one. Maybe not as big, but just as clean and warm and filled with happiness. Somehow, she'd make it happen.

Knowing it would take forever for it to dry, she didn't bother washing her long hair. When her opportunity arose, she had to be ready, and she didn't want to run away with wet hair. She did brush out all the tangles and tie it back with a rubber band. The shower did a lot to revive her and make her feel less pathetic.

After she'd dried off and donned the shirt, Emma glared at herself in the mirror, and cursed herself for being such a crybaby. Casey wouldn't be a whiner. If something happened in his life, he'd figure out how to deal with it. He'd do what he had to.

And so would she.

With the makeup washed away, her red nose and
eyes looked even worse. The bruise showed up more
too. It had all been necessary, she reminded herself,
but still the thought of change terrified her—just not
as much as staying.

She lifted the neckline of the shirt and brushed it
against her nose, breathing deeply of Casey's scent.
She closed her swollen eyes a moment to compose
herself.

Everyone was waiting for her when she left the
bathroom, which made her feel like a spectacle. She
was used to being ignored, not drawing attention. In
a lot of ways, she preferred being ignored to this cod-
dling. They were all just so...*kind*.

Sawyer gave her a cool compress to put over her
puffy eyes, along with two over-the-counter pills that
he said would help her relax and get some sleep.

Honey fussed over her, occasionally touching her
in that mothering way. She told Emma to help herself
if she got hungry during the night and to let her know
if she needed anything.

She'd rather die than disturb any of them further.
Emma knew she could be very quiet when she needed
to be; she'd learned that trick early in life. Like a
wraith, she could creep in and out without making a
sound. No way would she wake anyone up tonight.

Honey kissed Emma on the forehead before she
and Sawyer went down the hall, leaving her alone
with Casey so he could say good-night. Emma was
amazed anew that they'd trust her enough to leave
Casey in the room with her, especially now that they
had firsthand evidence of her character. She was a liar
and a user.

Then she realized it wasn't a matter of trusting her. They trusted Casey, and with good reason.

Casey sat on the edge of the bed and looked at her. After a moment, he even smiled.

Emma remembered how many times she'd done her best to get Casey this close. That last time at his family's picnic, she'd almost succeeded. But in the end, Casey had been too strong-willed, and too moral to get involved with her. She'd decided that night to leave him alone, and for the most part she'd stuck to that conviction. She hadn't seen him in so long.

Now he was right next to her and she was in his bed, and she could see the awful pity in his gaze. That hurt so much, she almost couldn't bear it. She'd make sure this was the last time he ever looked at her that way.

"Are you all right now, Em?"

"I'm fine," she lied, confident that it would be true soon enough. "I just wish I hadn't put your family through all this." She wished she could have thought of another way.

Rather than reply to that, Casey smoothed his hand over her head. "I've never seen your hair in a po-nytail."

Her heart started thumping too hard and her breath caught. She stared down at her hands. "That's because it looks dumb, but I figured I looked bad enough tonight that nothing could make it worse."

As if she hadn't intruded in the middle of the night, hadn't dragged him into her problems, hadn't disrupted his life, Casey chuckled. "It does not look dumb. Actually it looks kinda cute." Then, startling her further, he leaned forward and brushed his mouth over her forehead. "I'll be right out on the couch if you need anything, or if you just want to talk."

Emma said nothing to that.

"Promise me, Em." His expression was stern, with that iron determination that awed her so much in evidence. "If you need me, you'll wake me, okay?"

"Yeah, sure." *Not in a million years.*

Looking unconvinced, Casey straightened. "All right. I know it's not easy, but try not to fret, okay? I'm sure we'll be able to figure everything out."

We. This family kept saying that, as if they each really wanted to help. She'd made herself his problem by using his name, but by tomorrow he wouldn't have to worry about her ever again. "Casey? Thank you for everything."

"I haven't done anything, Em."

She lifted his large, warm hand and kissed his palm. Her heart swelled with love, threatening to break. "You're the finest person I've ever met."

THE RED HAZE OF DAWN streamed through the windows when Honey shook Casey awake early the next morning. He pushed himself up on one elbow and tried to clear away the cobwebs. He'd been in the middle of a dark, intensely erotic dream. About Emma.

His father stood behind Honey and right away Casey knew something was wrong. "What is it?"

"Emma is better than me," Honey said.

Casey frowned at that. "How so?"

"None of us heard her when she left."

Sawyer looked grim. "There's a note on your bed."

Casey threw the sheet aside and bolted upright. He wore only his boxers, but didn't give a damn. His heart threatened to punch out of his chest as he ran to his bedroom. Worry filled him, but also a strange panic.

She couldn't really be gone.

He came to a halt in the middle of his room. The covers had been neatly smoothed over the empty bed, and on the pillow lay a single sheet of paper, folded in half.

Dreading what he would read, Casey dropped onto the mattress and picked up the note. Honey and Sawyer crowded into the doorway, watching, waiting.

Dear Casey,
I know you told me not to say it, but I'm so sorry. For everything. Not just for barging into your life tonight but for trying to corrupt you and trying to interrupt your plans. It was so selfish of me. For a while there, I thought I wanted you more than anything.

Here she had drawn a small smiley face. It nearly choked Casey up, seeing her attempt at humor. He swallowed and firmed his resolve.

But that would have been really unfair to you.
I'm also sorry that I took the money you had on your dresser.

Casey glanced at his dresser. Hell, he'd forgotten all about the money, which, if he remembered right, amounted to about a hundred dollars. Not enough for her to get very far. Emotion swamped him, then tightened like a vise around his chest, making it hard to breathe.

I had some money of my own, too. I've been saving it up for a long time. I promise as soon as I get settled I'll return your money to you. I just needed it to get me away from Buckhorn, and I figured better that I borrow your money and leave tonight than to continue hanging around being a burden.

Damn it, hadn't he told her a dozen times she wasn't a bother? No. He'd told her not to apologize, but he hadn't told her that he wanted her there, that he wanted to help. That he cared about her.

Have a good life, Casey. I'll never, ever forget you.

Love,
Emma Clark

Casey crumpled the letter in his fist. He wanted to punch something, someone. He wanted to rage. It felt as though his chest had just caved in, destroying his heart. For a long moment, he couldn't speak, couldn't get words out around the lump in his throat.

Sawyer sat down beside him with a sigh. "I'll call Morgan and see if he can track her down."

As the town sheriff, Morgan had connections and legal avenues that the others didn't have. Casey looked at his father, struggling for control. "We don't know for sure where she's going."

"To Ohio, to her cousin, she told us," Honey reminded them.

"She never gave us her cousin's name."

"I'll call Dell." Sawyer clapped Casey on the shoulder, offering reassurance. "He'll know."

But half an hour later, after Sawyer had finished his conversation with Emma's surprisingly rattled father, Casey's worst suspicions were confirmed. Emma didn't have a cousin in Ohio. As far as Dell knew, there was no one in Ohio, no relative, no friend. Dell spewed accusations, blaming Casey for his little girl's problems, for her pregnancy, even going so far as to insist he should be compensated for his loss. He said his wife was sick and now his daughter was missing.

Casey suffered a vague sense of relief that Emma had gotten away from her unfeeling father. If only he knew where she'd gone.

If only he knew how to get her back.

Neither he nor Sawyer bothered to explain the full situation to Dell Clark. If Emma had wanted him to know, she would have told him herself. Eventually Dell would know there had never been a baby, that Emma had only used that as an excuse to be thrown out—to escape.

But from what?

Casey hoped she hadn't gone far, that it wouldn't take too long to find her. Damn it, he *wanted* to take care of her, dumb as that seemed.

But hours after Sawyer put in the request to Morgan, he came outside to give Casey the bad news.

Casey had been standing by a fence post, staring out at the endless stretch of wildflowers in the meadow. He'd bored the horses with his melancholy

and they'd wandered away to munch grass elsewhere.
The sun was hot, the grass sweet smelling and the sky
so blue it could blind you. Casey barely noticed any
of it.

"Case?"

At his father's voice, Casey jerked around. One
look at Sawyer's expression and fear grabbed him.
"What is it?"

Sawyer quickly shook his head. "Nothing's happened to Emma. But Morgan checked with highway
patrol... They haven't seen her. There've been no re-
ports of anyone fitting her description. It's like she
vanished. I'm sorry, Case."

Casey clenched his hands into fists, and repeated
aloud the words that had been echoing in his head all
morning. "She'll turn up."

"I hope so, but...something else happened last
night." Sawyer propped his hands on his hips and his
expression hardened. "Late last night, Ceily's diner
caught fire."

Slowly, Casey sank back against the rough wooden
post. "Ceily...?"

"She wasn't even there. It was way after hours,
during a break-in, apparently." Sawyer hesitated.
"Morgan's investigating the fire for arson."

"Arson? But that means..."

"Yeah. Someone might have tried to burn her
down."

On top of his worry for Emma, it was almost too
much to take in. Ceily was a friend to all of them.
Everyone in town adored her, and the diner was practically a landmark.

"It's damn strange," Sawyer continued, "but the

fire was reported with an anonymous call. Morgan doesn't know who, but when he got on the scene the fire was already out of control. Structurally, the diner is okay, but the inside is pretty much gutted. Whatever isn't burned has smoke damage.''

Casey felt numb. Things like arson just didn't happen in Buckhorn.

Of course, girls didn't accuse him of fathering a nonexistent baby very often either. ''Morgan's okay?''

''He's raspy from smoke inhalation, but he'll be all right. Ceily's stunned. I told her we'd all help, but it's still going to take a while before she'll be able to get the place all repaired and opened again.''

Barefoot, her long blond hair lifted by the breeze, Honey sidled up next to Sawyer. Automatically his father put his arm around her, kissed her temple and murmured, ''I just told him.''

Honey nodded. ''I'm so sorry, Casey. Morgan has his hands full with the investigation now.''

''Meaning he doesn't want to waste time looking for Emma?''

Honey didn't take offense at his tone. ''You know that's not it.'' She reached out to touch his shoulder. ''He's done what he can, but considering the note she left, there's no reason to consider any foul play.''

Sawyer rubbed the back of his neck in agitation. ''I know how you feel, Case. I'm not crazy about her being off on her own either. Hell, I've never seen such an emotionally fragile young woman. But Dell doesn't want to file her as a missing minor, so there's nothing more that Morgan can do. She'll come back when she's good and ready, and in the meantime, all we can do is wait.''

Honey patted Casey again. ''Maybe she'll contact you. Like Sawyer said, we'll wait—and hope.''

When Casey turned back to the meadow, both Sawyer and Honey retreated, leaving him alone with his worries. Yes, he thought, she'll contact me. She had to. They shared a special bond, not sexual, yet...still special.

He felt it. So surely she felt it too.

THE DAYS TICKED BY without word from Emma.

The fire at the diner had stolen all the news, and Emma's disappearance was pretty much skipped by most people. After all, she hadn't made any lasting friendships in the area. The boys had used her, the girls had envied her, and the schools had all but given up on her. Not many people missed her now.

In the next few weeks, the town gradually settled back down to normal, but an edgy nervousness remained because whoever had broken into Ceily's diner and started a fire was never found. Casey went through his days by rote, hurt, angry with himself as much as with Emma.

Three months later, he got a fat envelope filled with the money Emma had taken, and a few dollars more. In her brief note, Emma explained that the extra was for interest. There was no return address and she'd signed the note: *Thanks so much for everything. Emma Clark.*

Frustrated, Casey wondered if she always signed her first and last name because she thought he might forget her, just as the rest of the town had.

At least the return of the money proved she was alive and well. Casey tried to tell himself it was enough, that he'd only wanted her safe, that all he'd ever felt for her was sympathy with a little healthy lust thrown in.

But he'd be a complete fraud if he let himself believe it. The truth burned like acid, because nothing had ever hurt as much as knowing Emma had deliberately walked away from him.

He didn't ever want to hurt like that again.

Since she didn't want to return, didn't want to trust him, *didn't want him,* he couldn't help her. But he could get on with his life.

With nothing else to do, he went off to school as planned. And though he knew it hadn't been Emma's intention, she'd changed his life forever. He wanted her back, damn it, when he'd made a point of never having her in the first place.

Forget her? There wasn't a chance in hell that would ever happen.

CHAPTER TWO

Eight Years Later

THOUGH SHE COULDN'T SEE beyond the raised hood, she heard the very distant rumble of the approaching car and gave a sigh of relief. Damon, who had been about to set a flare on the narrow gravel road, walked back to her with the flare unlit. He stuck his head in the driver's-door window. "I'm going to flag this guy down and maybe he'll give us a hand."

Emma smiled at him. "The way this day is going? We'll be lucky if he doesn't speed on by and blow dust in our faces."

B.B. hung his head over her seat and nuzzled her ear. His doggy breath was hot and impatient. Likely, he wanted out of the car worse than she did. The winding gravel roads opened on both sides to endless stretches of overgrown brush that shielded anything from rabbits to snakes. B.B. heeded her call, so she wasn't really worried about him wandering off. But she also didn't want to take the chance that he'd get distracted with a critter on unfamiliar ground.

The day had already been endless with one hitch after another. What should have been a six- or seven-hour drive from Chicago to Buckhorn, had turned into eight and a half, and they hadn't even had a chance to stop for a sit-down meal. Even with the occasional breaks they'd taken and her quick stopover at the hospital, they were all beat. The dog wasn't used to being confined for so long, and neither was she.

Damon patted her hand. "Stay put until I see who it is. This late on a Saturday night, and in a strange town, I don't want to take any chances with you."

Emma rolled her eyes. "Damon, I grew up here, remember? This isn't a strange place. It's Buckhorn and believe me, it's so safe it borders on boring."

"You haven't been here in eight long years, doll. Time changes everything."

She scoffed at that ridiculous notion. "Not Buckhorn. Trust me."

In fact, Emma had been amazed at how little it had changed in the time she'd been away. On their way to the one and only motel Buckhorn had to offer, they'd driven through the town proper. Everything looked the same: pristine, friendly, old-fashioned.

The streets were swept clean, the sidewalks uncluttered. There were two small grocery stores at opposite ends of town, each with varying specialties. The same clothing store that had been there for over a hundred years still stood, but painted a new, brighter color. The hairdresser's building had new landscaping; the pharmacy had a new lighted sign.

Lit by stately lampposts, Emma had gazed down a narrow side street at the sheriff's station, situated across the street from a field of cows. Once a farmhouse, the ornate structure still boasted a wraparound porch, white columns in the front, and black shutters. Emma wondered if Morgan Hudson still reigned supreme. He'd be in his mid-forties by now, but Emma would be willing to bet he remained as large, strong and imposing as ever. Morgan wasn't the type of man ever to let himself go soft.

She also saw Gabe Kasper's handyman shop, now expanded into two buildings and looking very sophisticated. Apparently business was good for Gabe, not that she'd ever had any doubts. Women around Buckhorn broke things on purpose just to get Gabe to do repairs.

Then she'd seen Ceily's diner.

Her stomach knotted at the sight of the familiar building, quiet and closed down for the night but with new security lights on the outside. Everyone in town loved that quaint old diner, making it a favorite hangout.

Her heart gave a poignant twinge at the remembrance of it all.

"For once," Damon said with dramatic frustration, drawing her away from the memories, "will you just do as I say without arguing me into the ground?"

B.B. barked in agreement.

"You guys always gang up on me," Emma accused, then waved Damon off. "Your caution is unnecessary, but if it'll make you feel better, I'll just sit here like a good little helpless woman. Maybe I'll even twiddle my thumbs."

"Your sarcasm is showing, doll." He glanced at the dog. "B.B., see that she stays put."

The dog hung his head over her shoulder, mournful at the enormity of the task.

The approaching car finally maneuvered through all the twists and turns of the stretching road, and drew near. Arms raised, Damon rounded the hood to signal for assistance. It must be a nice vehicle, Emma thought, hearing the nearly melodic purr of the powerful engine. She'd learned a lot about cars while living with the Devaughns.

Unfortunately, she hadn't learned enough to be able to change a water pump without a spare pump on hand.

At first, because of the angle of the road, the swerving headlights slanted partially in through her window, blinding her. When the car stopped right in front of them, the open hood of her Mustang kept her from being able to see the occupants. In a town the size of Buckhorn, the odds weren't too bad that she might recognize their rescuers. Though few people had really befriended her, she'd grown up with them and could still recall many of them clearly.

Beside her, B.B.'s head lifted and he rumbled a low warning growl at the strangers. Emma reached over her shoulder to put her hand on his scruff, calming him, letting him know that everything was okay.

The purring engine turned off, leaving only the night sounds of insects. "Well, hello."

With amusement in his tone, Damon replied, "Good evening."

Emma couldn't see, but she could hear just fine, and the feminine voice responding to Damon was definitely flirtatious. She sighed.

Sometimes Emma thought he was too good-looking for his own good. He wasn't overly tall, maybe an inch shy of six feet, but he had a lean, athletic build and warm, clear blue eyes and the most engaging grin she'd ever witnessed on a grown man.

Everywhere he went, women turned their heads to watch him.

"Can we give you a lift?"

"Actually," Damon's deep voice rumbled, "I'd just like to make a call to Triple A. Do you have a cell phone with you? My battery went dead an hour ago."

A car door opened, gravel crunched beneath someone's feet, and the next voice Emma heard almost stopped her heart. "Sorry, I don't carry one when I'm not working. The ringing is too bothersome. But we can take you into town to make the call."

Stunned, Emma pushed her car door open and slowly climbed out. Damon wouldn't leave her alone to go to town and make the call, especially once he realized that he'd just flagged down the only person in Buckhorn that she had serious reservations about seeing again.

B.B. jumped over the seat and climbed out behind her, sticking close to her side. The big German shepherd moved silently across the grass and gravel, his head lifted to scent the air for danger, his body alert.

Emma paused a moment in the deep shadows, sucking in fresh, dewy air and reminding herself that she was now an adult, not a lovesick schoolgirl with more bravado than brains. There was no reason to act silly. No reason to still feel embarrassed.

Casey was nothing to her now. He'd never really been anything to her except a friend—and an adolescent fantasy. After what she'd done to him, and after eight long years, friendship wasn't even an issue.

She had planned to see him, of course. Just not yet. Not when she looked so... Emma stopped that line of thought. It didn't matter that she wore comfortable jeans and a logo sweatshirt, or that her eyes were shadowed from too little sleep over the past few days.

Smoothing her hair behind her ears and straightening her shoulders, Emma slipped around the front of the Mustang and stepped into the light of the low beams. B.B. stationed himself at her side, well mannered but ready to defend.

Emma took one look at Casey and a strange sort of joy expanded inside her. He looked good. He looked the same, just…more so. With every second of every day, she'd missed him, but she didn't know if he would even remember her.

"Well, I thought I recognized that voice," Emma said, proud that only a slight waver sounded in her words. "Hello, Casey."

Damon twisted around to face her, and Casey's head jerked up in surprise. Emma held herself still while the woman with Casey scooted closer to him, blatantly staking a claim.

Caught between the headlights of both cars, they all stood there. The damp August-evening air drifted over and around them, stirring the leaves and the tension. Moths fluttered into the light and wispy fog hung near the ground, snaking around their feet. Emma heard the chirp of every cricket, the creaking of heavy branches, her own stilted breath.

His body rigid, his thoughts concealed, Casey stared toward Emma. In the darkness, his eyes appeared black as pitch, intensely direct. He explored her face in minute detail, taking his time while Emma did her best not to fidget.

The silence stretched out, painful and taut, until Emma didn't know if she could take it anymore.

Finally, he took a step forward. "Emma?"

Like a warm caress, his familiar deep voice slipped over and around her. He said her name as a question, filled with wonder, surprise, maybe even pleasure. At eighteen, he'd seemed so grown up, but now that he was grown, he could take her breath away.

Her smile felt silly, uncertain. She made an awkward gesture, and shrugged. "That'd be me."

"My God, I'd never have recognized you." He strode forward as if he might embrace her, and Emma automatically drew back. She didn't mean to do it, and she silently cursed herself for the knee-jerk reaction to seeing him again. His physical presence, once so comforting, now seemed as powerful, as dark and turbulent, as a storm. The changes were subtle, but she'd known him so well, been so fixated on him, that they were glaringly obvious to her.

At her retreat, Casey drew to a halt. His smile faltered then became cynical, matching the light in his eyes. He veered his gaze toward Damon, and Emma knew he'd drawn his own conclusions.

When he faced her again, his expression had turned icy. "I'm surprised to see you here, Em."

"My father…he's in the hospital." She hated herself for stammering, but when she'd thought Casey might touch her, her heart, her pulse, even her thoughts had sped up, leaving her a little jumbled. *No, no, no,* she silently swore, wanting to deny the truth. Surely, eight years was long enough. It *had* to be.

But right now, with Casey so close she could feel the beat of his energy and the strength of his presence, it felt as if less than eight days had passed. Long-buried emotions clamored to the surface, and Emma struggled to repress them again.

Oh, it wasn't that she still pined for Casey, or that she carried any fanciful illusions. The time away had been an eternity for her. She'd gone from being an immature, needy girl to a grown, independent woman. She'd learned so much, faced so many realities, and she now considered herself a person to be proud of.

But seeing him, being back in Buckhorn...well, some memories never died and her last ones with Casey were the type that haunted her dreams. She could still blush, remembering that awful night and what she'd put him and his family through. Like old garbage, her father had dumped her on Casey's doorstep—and he'd taken her in.

That wasn't the only thing that made her hot with embarrassment, though. The nights that preceded her eventful departure were worse. She'd thrown herself at Casey again and again, utilizing every female ploy to entice him—and had always been rebuffed. The strongest emotion he'd ever felt for her was pity.

And now he had no reason to feel even that.

"I'd heard your dad was sick. Will he be all right?"

It didn't surprise her that he knew. There were few secrets in Buckhorn, so of course he'd heard.

Renewed worry prodded her, sounding in her tone. "He was asleep when I stopped at the hospital earlier, and I didn't want to disturb him. He needs his rest. But the nurse assures me that he's doing better. They have him out of intensive care, so I guess that's a good sign. I just...I wish I could have talked with him.''

''What happened?''

She swallowed hard, still disbelieving how quickly things had changed. The call from her mother had rattled her and she hadn't quite gotten a grip on her emotions yet. She hadn't seen her father in so long, but she'd always known he was there, as cantankerous and hardworking as ever. But now... Emma stared up at Casey and felt the connection of a past lifetime. ''He had a stroke.''

''Damn, Em. I'm so sorry to hear that.''

She nodded.

Casey shifted closer, scrutinizing her as if he couldn't quite believe his eyes. His expression was so probing, she felt stripped bare and strangely raw.

When Casey moved forward, so did the very pretty redhead with him. She plastered herself to his side in a show of possessiveness. ''You two have met?''

Casey glanced at her, then draped his arm over her shoulders with negligent regard. There didn't seem to be any real level of intimacy between them.

But then what did Emma know about real intimacy?

''Emma and I practically grew up together.'' Casey watched her as he said it, his eyes narrowed, taunting. ''We were close, real close I thought, but she's been away from town now for...''

''Eight years,'' Emma supplied, unwilling to hear him say any more. Close? The only closeness had been in her head and in her dreams. Dredging up her manners, Emma held out her hand and prayed the darkness would hide her slight trembling. ''I'm

Emma Clark, and this is my friend, Damon Devaughn.''

With a look of suspicion, the redhead released Casey to shake hands politely with both Emma and Damon. "Kristin Swarth."

"It's delightful to meet you," Damon murmured, and Kristin's frown lifted to be replaced by a coy smile. Damon had charisma in spades and the ladies always soaked it up.

Though Damon had no problem warming up to Kristin, he didn't treat Casey with the same courtesy. The second she'd first said Casey's name, Damon had gone rigid and he hadn't relaxed again.

Now, at the introduction, Casey eyed Damon anew, then drew the woman a little closer. "Kristin and I work together."

It wasn't easy, but Emma managed another smile. "I hope we're not interrupting your plans?"

"Not really." Casey gave her a lazy look. "I was just about to take Kristin home."

At the word *home,* B.B. let out a friendly *woof,* and Emma laughed. "I'm sorry, I almost forgot. This is my pal, B.B."

With a wide grin, Casey hunkered down in front of the big dog. "Hello, B.B."

Using noticeable caution, the dog sauntered forward, did some sniffing, and then licked Casey's hand. Emma had almost forgotten how good Casey's family was with animals, Casey included. His Uncle Jordan was even a vet, but they all loved animals and were never without a menagerie of pets.

"Where'd you come up with the name B.B.?"

Emma chuckled, her tension easing with the topic.

B.B. was her best friend, her comrade in arms when
necessary, her confidant. They'd comforted each other
when there was no one else, and now it often seemed
B.B. could read her mind. "Big Boy," she explained,
and B.B. barked in agreement.

"He's a gorgeous dog." Casey stroked along
B.B.'s muscled back, then patted his ribs. "How old
is he?"

Damon answered for her, his gaze speculative as
he watched man and dog bonding. "We're not sure,
but probably about nine or so. He was young when
Emma got him, more a ball of fur with nothing big
about him, other than his appetite."

Emma quickly elbowed Damon, hard. A history of
how she'd gotten the dog was the last thing she
wanted discussed. She didn't mean for Casey to wit-
ness that prod, but when she glanced down at him,
their gazes clashed and held. He didn't say anything,
and that was a relief. When she got Damon alone,
she'd choke him.

As Casey scratched the dog's head and rubbed his
ears, Emma absorbed the sight of him. It seemed impossible, but eight years had only made him better—
taller, stronger, more handsome. As a teen, he'd been
an unqualified stud. As a grown man—wowza.

The gentle evening breeze ruffled his dark-blond
hair, and his brown eyes caught and held the moonlight. He wore dark slacks and a dress shirt that fit
his wide shoulders perfectly. Emma forced her gaze
away. It was beyond dumb for her to be ogling him.

The car behind him was, amazingly enough, also a
Mustang, but surely a much newer, ritzier model.

Emma nodded at the car, trying to see it clearly in the shadows of the night. "Black or blue or green?"

Keeping his hand on B.B.'s head, Casey straightened. "What?"

"Your car."

He swiveled his head around and looked at the car as if he'd never seen it before. "Black."

"Mine is red and in desperate need of a water pump. If you're heading into town, do you think you could direct someone this way? Or is there even road service in the area yet?"

Casey shook his head. "Hell no. If you call Triple A it'll take them at least a couple of hours to get out here to you."

Emma groaned. She was dead on her feet and anxious to get settled. All she wanted to do was shower, eat and sleep, in that order. She'd already stopped at the hospital on the way into town. Damon had kept an eye on B.B., letting him walk about on the grounds while she'd spoken briefly with the nurses before visiting her father.

He'd looked so old and frail, and hadn't registered her visit. She'd wanted to touch him, to reassure herself that he was alive, stable. But she'd held back. Since the doctor was due to see him again in the early morning, she planned to be there so she could get a full update on his prognosis.

Casey moved closer to her again. "The garage is closed for the night, too. That hasn't changed. We still roll up the sidewalks by nine. But I can give you both a ride into town if you want."

Emma looked at Damon. He lounged back against

the car and smiled his sexiest smile. "We'll be staying at the Cross Roads Motel. Is that too far off?"

Casey cocked one eyebrow and gave Emma an assessing look. "You're not staying with your mother?"

"No." Just the thought of seeing her mother again, of being back in the house where her life had been so miserable, made Emma's stomach churn. Because Casey couldn't possibly understand her reserve, she scrambled for reasons to present to him, but her wits had gone begging. It didn't help that Damon was deliberately provoking Casey, suggesting an intimate relationship that didn't exist. "The house is small, and my mother... Well, I, ah, thought it'd be better if..."

Before she could say any more, Damon was there. "We've been driving for hours," he interjected smoothly, "and we're both exhausted. Just let us grab a few things and we can stop holding you up."

Casey frowned. "You're not holding me up."

"*I* need to be going," Kristin said, clearly miffed by the turn of events and the way everyone ignored her. Her tone turned snide and her eyes narrowed on B.B. "But I have my cat in the car and she doesn't like strangers. She especially doesn't like dogs. Casey, you know she'll have a fit if we try to put another animal in there with her. Besides, there's not room for everyone."

Casey turned to Emma with a shrug. "I'm afraid she's right. Kristin treated me to dinner because I agreed to help her move."

Laying a hand on his chest, Kristin turned her face up to his. "You know that wasn't my only reason."

Casey countered her suggestiveness with an inattentive hug. "We've got the last load in the car now. The floor and the back seat are already packed."

Damon brought Emma a little closer, and no one could have missed the protectiveness of his gesture. Emma refrained from rolling her eyes, but it wasn't easy. She was the last woman on earth in need of protection, but Damon refused to believe that.

"No problem." The baring of Damon's teeth in no way resembled a smile. And if Emma didn't miss her guess, he was relieved to send Casey away. She only wished she felt the same. "Perhaps you could call us a cab, then?"

"No cabs in Buckhorn. Sorry." Reflecting Damon's mood, Casey looked anything but sorry by that fact. "And you know, if you don't get to the Cross Roads soon, you'll get locked out."

"Locked out?"

"Yep." Casey transferred his gaze to Emma—and his eyes glittered with a strange satisfaction. "Emma, you remember Mrs. Reider? She refuses to get out of bed to check people in after midnight." He lifted his wrist to see the illuminated dial on his watch. "That gives you less than fifteen minutes to make it there."

The beginning of a headache throbbed in Emma's temples. She rubbed her forehead, trying to decide what to do. "It was difficult enough convincing her that B.B. wouldn't be a problem."

Casey lifted an eyebrow. "I'm surprised you *could* convince her. She's not big on pets."

"Paying a double rate did the trick. And I just know she'll still charge us if we don't make it there on time. Her cancellation policy is no better than her check-in policy."

Casey's eyes twinkled in amusement. "She's the only motel in town. She can afford to be difficult."

"Damn." Damon started to pace, which truly showed his annoyance, since Damon normally remained cool in any situation.

Casey stopped him with a simple question. "Can you drive stick?"

Somewhat affronted, Damon said, "Of course."

"Great." Casey pulled a set of keys from his pocket and tossed them to Damon, who caught them against his chest. "Why don't you take Kristin on home? The Cross Roads Motel is on the way. You can stop and check in, get your room keys, and then after you get Kristin unloaded, you can come back for us."

Damon idly rattled the keys in his palm, looking between Casey and Emma. "Us?"

"I'll stay here with Emma and B.B."

Emma nearly strangled on her own startled breath. Seeing Casey so unexpectedly had unnerved her enough. No way did she want to be alone with him. Not yet. "I can drive a stick."

B.B. looked at her anxiously and took an active stance. His muscles quivered as if he might leap after her if she tried to leave.

"Right." Damon sent her a look. "And you really think he'll stay alone with me on an empty street while you ride off with a stranger? He'll have a fit. Hell, he'd probably chase the car all the way into town. It'd be different if we were at the motel and you left, but out here…"

"Okay, okay." Damon was right. B.B. was so defensive of her, she often wondered if he hadn't been a guard dog in another life.

"Besides," Damon added, further prodding her, "the room is held on my credit card." He stared at Emma hard, undecided, then abruptly shook his head. "Hell no. Let's forget this. It's already late, so what's a few more hours? We can wait for Triple A and then find a motel back on the highway to stay in for the night."

Emma gave that idea quick but serious thought, and knew the only reasonable thing to do was to stop acting like a desperate ninny. She couldn't imagine finding another motel that would allow her to bring B.B. inside. Besides, Damon had driven most of the hours, and despite his suggestion, he looked exhausted. B.B. wasn't in much better shape.

She'd stopped being selfish long ago.

"It's all right, Damon." She gave him a smile to reassure him. "I'm beat and so are you. You go on, and B.B. and I'll wait here."

Kristin crossed her arms and struck a petulant pose. "Don't I get a vote on this?"

Casey spared her a glance. "Not this time." Then he added, "And, honey, don't pout." He walked her to the car, his large hand open on the small of her back, urging her along while he spoke quietly in her ear.

Damon used that moment to pull Emma aside. He practically shoved her behind the open driver's door and then bent close. "Dear God," he muttered, holding his head. "I can understand why he became your adolescent hero, Emma. He's testosterone on legs."

Emma couldn't help but laugh at Damon's look of

distaste. He wasn't into the whole machismo display. Damon was far too refined for that, a man straight out of *GQ*. He also knew exactly how to lighten her mood. Not that he was wrong, of course. If anything, Casey was more ruggedly masculine now than he'd ever been.

Emma decided to tease him right back. "I hate to break it to you, Damon, but he's obviously into women."

Refusing to take the bait, Damon glanced over at Kristin with critical disdain. "*I'm* into women. He's obviously into twits. There *is* a difference."

Casey and Kristin were still in quiet conversation, their bodies outlined by the reaching glow of the car lights. "You really think so?"

"That she's a twit? Absolutely."

"No, I didn't mean that." She swatted at him and stifled a laugh. "I mean, do you think they're a couple?"

"Worried?"

Damon knew better. She wouldn't be in Buckhorn long enough to get worried about Casey and whom he might or might not be involved with. Probably his girlfriends were too many to count, anyway. Until he'd turned sixteen, Casey had been raised in an all-male household. Sawyer and his three brothers had been the most eligible, respected and adored bachelors in Buckhorn. One by one they'd married off, starting with Casey's father. But Casey had inherited a lot of their appeal and long before Emma had left town, the females had been chasing him. "Only curious. I haven't seen him in so long."

Damon's look plainly said *yeah, right.* "I think he

wants to be into her, if you need true accuracy. Whether or not he likes her—who knows?'' Then he added with more seriousness, ''You know to most men, liking and wanting have nothing in common.''

That was Damon's staunchest requirement. He had to genuinely like and respect a woman to decide to sleep with her. Intelligence sat high on his list, as did motivation and kindness. The second a woman got gossipy or catty, he walked away. Unlike many of the men she'd known through the years, Damon wasn't ruled by his libido. Emma respected him for that, even while she knew he'd be a tough man to please.

Again Emma chuckled, but her humor was cut short as Casey called, ''You ready to go?''

Damon ignored him as he cupped Emma's face, forcing her to look him in the eyes. ''Will you be okay?''

''Yes, of course.''

''Too fast, doll. That was nothing more than an automatic answer.''

''But true nonetheless.''

He waggled her head. ''Just be on guard, okay? I don't want to see you hurt.''

''I'm not made of glass,'' she chided.

''No, it's sugar I think.'' He lifted her hand to his mouth, nipped her knuckles and said, ''Yep, sugar.''

Emma was well used to that teasing response— he'd been saying it to her since she was seventeen years old, when they'd first met. She'd been backward, afraid, alone. And he'd treated her like a well-loved kid sister.

Laughing, she turned toward the other car, and

caught the censure on Casey's face. He didn't say a
word, but then he didn't have to. She knew exactly
what he thought. And none of it was nice.

Worse, none of it was accurate.

CHAPTER THREE

EMMA STOOD in front of her car, watching Damon and Kristin drive away. With their departure, the previously calm evening air suddenly felt charged. She was aware of things she hadn't noticed before, like the warm, subtle scent of Casey's cologne, the nearly tactile touch of his watchfulness. The pulsing rhythm of her own heartbeat resounded everywhere, in her chest, her ears, low in her belly.

B.B. shifted beside her, restless and uncertain with this turn of events and her renewed tension.

Though he didn't make a sound, she knew Casey was now closer behind her. As if he'd touched her, she shivered in reaction, and continued to stare after the car.

"So how've you been, Em?" His voice was low and intimate, a rough whisper of sound somewhere above her right ear.

The twin taillights of the other car faded away, swallowed up by distance and fog, the inky blackness of the night. Left with nothing to stare at, Emma drew a deep breath, took two steps away and turned to him with a bland smile. "Good. And yourself?"

"Good." He visually caressed her face, slowly, thoroughly, as if he'd never seen her before. As if maybe he'd...missed her.

Emma moved to the side of the car, taking herself out of the harsh beams of the headlights. The dog followed and she leaned down to give him a reassuring pat. When she straightened, Casey was even closer than before and he made no attempt to move away. She felt vaguely hunted.

"You look so different, Em."

She wasn't about to back away a second time. Faking a calm that eluded her, she shrugged. "Eight years different."

"It's not your age," he murmured, once again looking her over in that scrutinizing way of his. "Your hair is different."

Emma started to reply, but the words hung in her throat as Casey reached out and caught a shoulder-length tress, rubbing it between fingers and thumb.

Both breathless and a little indignant, she tossed her head so that her hair fell behind her shoulders. That didn't deter Casey. He simply drew it forward again, making her frown. He was bolder than she remembered…. No, that wasn't true. He'd always been bold—with the girls he'd wanted.

He just hadn't ever wanted her.

"I don't bleach it anymore." Despite being annoyed, awareness trembled in her belly, sang through her veins. "This is my real color."

His long fingers tunneled in close to her scalp, warm and gentle, then lifted outward, letting the silky strands drift back into place. "I can't see it that well here in the shadows."

Her breath came too fast. "Light brown."

"I never really understood why you lightened it." He stroked her hair again, totally absorbed in what he did, unmindful or uncaring of her discomfort. "Or why you wore so much makeup."

She refused to apologize for or explain about her past. That was one of the things Damon had taught her—to forget about what she couldn't change and only look forward. "I thought it looked good at the time, but then, I was only seventeen and not overly astute."

Casey stood silent for only a minute. "Why don't we sit in the car? The air is pretty damp tonight."

Being that she was already far too aware of him, she didn't consider that a good idea. But the dog had heard him and, not wanting to be left out, quickly went through the open driver's door and performed an agile leap into the back seat.

Emma gave a mental shrug and scooted inside, leaving Casey to go to the passenger side. The consummate gentleman, he closed her door first before walking around the hood of the car. When he slid into his seat, she had only a moment to appreciate the sharp angles and planes of his face fully lit by the interior light. He closed his door too, and the light clicked off with a sort of symbolic finality that made her senses come alive.

Casey twisted sideways in his seat and spoke in a low vibrating murmur. "Better turn off the headlights, Em, or you'll have a dead battery to go with the busted water pump."

Though Emma knew he was right, she hated to be in utter darkness with him. Her awareness of him as a man defied reason.

He hadn't touched her, but God, she felt as if he had. All over.

"There's a flashlight in the glove box."

Casey opened the small door, moved a few papers aside and pulled out the black-handled utility light. He didn't hand it to her, didn't turn it on, but instead held it in his lap. She turned off the headlights and inky blackness settled in around them. Emma wondered if he could hear the wild pounding of her heart.

Her reactions irritated her as much as they distressed her. No other man had ever affected her this way. She'd had plenty of relationships since she'd grown up, and she'd assumed her tepid reactions had been mostly due to maturing, to wising up, to learning what was best for her. She'd accepted that sex was pleasurable but not vital. It eased an ache, provided comfort, added to the closeness, and nothing more.

Yet, sitting in a dark car next to Casey Hudson, she felt the biting greed of lust in a way that hadn't touched her since…since the last time she'd been this near him.

"So what have you been doing with yourself?" he asked, and Emma started in surprise.

"What?"

"It's been a long time." His voice held the same easy cadence she remembered from long ago, but there was an edge to it now. An edge to him. "You disappeared without a trace, so I'm just wondering what you've been up to."

Emma didn't want to get into this now. He wouldn't understand and she wasn't up to explaining. In truth, it wasn't any of his business what she did or had done while she'd been away from Buckhorn. But telling him so would have been too ballsy, even for her, and would have made her sound defensive.

Keeping her answer vague, she shrugged. "Working, like most people I guess."

She braced herself for the questions that would follow, and wondered at the hesitation she felt in explaining her job to him. Damn it, she loved her job and was proud of herself for doing it so well.

But Casey took her off guard by skipping her occupation and going straight to a more difficult topic.

"You and Damon involved?"

Anger flashed through Emma, pushing some of the sexual awareness aside. Regardless of their pasts, she didn't deserve an inquisition.

"Are you and Kristin?" Her voice sounded sharper than she'd intended, but Casey just laughed.

"No." His white teeth gleamed in the darkness. "As I said, she's a co-worker, a friend. No more than that."

Emma shook her head. Men could be so dense. "So you say. My guess is that she wants to be considerably more."

Casey touched her cheek, a casual gesture that felt hotly intimate and made her breath catch. "Yeah, well, I can be stubborn when I want to be."

She almost replied *I remember,* but caught herself in time. His honesty provoked her own. "Damon and I are friends."

"Uh-huh."

She didn't care if he believed her or not. *She didn't.* She turned away to stare out the window, letting Casey know without words that he could think what he wanted.

"If you were homely," Casey teased, "then I could maybe believe it. But Em?" He waited just

long enough to make her antsy. "You're far from
homely."

She tried to ignore him. The field to her left
sounded with a thousand insects: the buzz of mos-
quitoes, the singing of crickets. Like stars in the sky,
fireflies twinkled on and off.

She hadn't forgotten that Buckhorn was beautiful
in the summer, but somehow the clarity of it had been
blunted. The colors, the smells, the texture of the air
and the lush grass and the velvet sky...

Casey stroked one finger over her cheek, down to
her throat, then her shoulder. "Hell, if anything,
you're more attractive than ever, and you were plenty
attractive at seventeen."

Her heart punched painfully against her rib cage.
How had the conversation gotten out of hand so
quickly? Her laugh sounded more believable this
time. "I'm guessing you must have lowered your
standards."

Casey stared at her, not comprehending.

Emma rolled her eyes. "I've been in the car all
day, Case. I'm dressed in what can only be called my
comfortable clothes—and that's if I'm being generous. No makeup, my hair's windblown..."

"You look sexy as hell to me."

The way he growled that pronouncement robbed
Emma of clear thought. She searched her brain for
something to say, some way to derail him. "How
long will it take Damon to get back, do you think?"

Casey didn't take the hint. He didn't stop touching
her either. He smoothed her hair behind her ear and
curled his fingers around her head. "Men only pretend to be friends with women to get one thing."

Goaded, Emma shifted around to face him. His hand dropped, but his gaze, glittering in the darkness, remained steady.

Even the gearshift between them didn't hinder Casey's movements. He got so close that Emma inhaled the warmth of his masculine smell on every breath.

"Is that right?" Her voice shook, her hands trembled. "Then I guess we're enemies, because there's never been a single thing you wanted from me."

Beneath the fall of her hair, Casey's hand curved around her neck in a gentle restraint that felt far too unbreakable. Trying to be inconspicuous, she pressed into the car door. It didn't help.

With near-tactile intensity, his gaze stroked her face, then rested on her mouth.

"True." There was a heavy, thrumming beat of silence, and Casey whispered, "Until now."

KNOWING HE PUSHED HER, knowing it was unfair, Casey tried to pull back. But damn it, he wanted her. Seeing her again…it hit him like a ton of bricks, throwing him off balance, making him defensive and fractious and keenly alert. Emma had influenced his life when he hadn't thought that possible. Forgetting her hadn't been easy.

In fact, he'd never managed it.

Just the opposite.

At twenty-seven, his solid position within his step-grandfather's company should have been enhanced with a wife on his arm and a couple of kids underfoot, just as he'd always intended. Instead, no woman had ever quite measured up.

The bitch of it was, he had no idea what they

needed to measure up to. He didn't even know what he was looking for.

Until moments ago, when he saw Emma standing there.

As always, her eyes had been huge and soft, and all his senses had quickened with recognition. He hadn't experienced that rush of pure, white-hot intensity since... *No,* he wouldn't do that, wouldn't give her credit she didn't deserve. She'd run out on him and he wasn't quite ready to forgive her for that. But he was more than ready to take what he'd often regretted missing so many years ago.

Her small hands lifted to press against his chest, burning him, heightening the ache. "Casey..."

The way she said his name was familiar. Did she want him to stop or, like him, was she anxious to feel the flash fire of their unique chemistry? Her appearance, her attitude, were different. But her natural sensuality hadn't waned at all. Instead, it had aged and ripened and gotten better, richer. No woman had ever affected him like Emma did, and now, with no effort at all, she'd gotten him hot.

She wasn't a lonely, insecure child anymore.

She wasn't afraid, wasn't mistreated.

He had no reason to hold back, no reason to still feel protective. *Damn it.*

Without thought, Casey let his fingers stroke the nape of her neck. Just as it always had, her softness drew him, the remembered texture of her skin, her hair and her scent... God, he loved her scent. Heady and warm, it mingled with the damp fog and the gentle evening breeze.

He felt alive. He felt challenged.

"Emma?"

Her thick lashes lifted.

"Are you married?"

She shook her head, causing the silky weight of her hair to glide over his arm.

"Engaged?"

"No." She pulled her head back a little and Casey kissed her throat, nuzzling her fragrant skin, breathing her in. A sound of near desperation slipped past her open lips. "Are you...?"

"Hell no. There's no one." He didn't want to talk about that though. "You feel good, Em. You smell even better."

"Casey."

If she kept saying his name like that, he'd lose it. "You know, since you and Damon aren't involved..." If she had no commitments to anyone, then why not? It didn't matter that he rushed things. They were both grown now, both adults, so Emma could damn well make a rational decision now, rather than one based on fear and insecurity.

"Damon and I are friends." A measure of steel laced her declaration.

Had she misunderstood his suggestion?

Casey drew back so he could see her face. Her heavy lashes half covered her eyes as she watched him warily. She remained guarded, but she didn't push him away. He tried a different tack. "You're staying at the Cross Roads tonight."

"Yes."

Adulthood had provided new dimension to her features. Her cheekbones were more noticeable, her mouth wider, fuller, her jaw firm. She was lovely—

and he had to have her. "You'll be sleeping alone?" Which would make it easy for him to join her.

Her gaze flickered away, and his stomach knotted even before she spoke. "That's none of your business, Casey."

Frustration unfurled in his guts, making his tone raw with sarcasm. "Sounds like a *no* to me."

Chin lifted, she faced him squarely and confirmed his suspicions. "No. I won't sleep alone."

Very slowly, doing his best to rein in his seldom-seen temper, Casey released her and moved back to his own seat. The sexual turbulence remained, gnawing at him, testing him, but now other, darker emotions gripped him too. He didn't want to study them too closely. "I see."

He could feel her turmoil. And he could taste her interest, damn her. It was there, shimmering between them. Yet, she'd be with Damon, her *friend.*

Once long ago, Casey had been her friend. Probably her best friend, if not the only one. He'd told her then that he didn't share. That much hadn't changed. He wanted her, but on his terms.

And that's how he'd have her.

Emma slowly straightened in her seat and stared straight ahead. "I seriously doubt that you see anything."

The dog stuck his head over the seat and whined. Emma shifted enough to pat him, then buried her face in his scruff. "It's okay, B.B."

Casey sat in brooding silence for several moments, watching as she comforted the big dog. Slashes of moonlight silhouetted her body and the slow movements of her stroking hands through thick fur. She ignored him as if he didn't exist, not once looking at him. It didn't matter.

Despite any protest Devaughn might make, Casey knew he'd eventually have her.

By her own admission, she wasn't married, wasn't engaged, so no one, Damon included, had any real claim on her. That left Casey free to do as he pleased. And it would please him a hell of a lot to take care of unfinished business so he could get her out of his system and get on with his life. It felt as if he'd been on hold for eight years. Now, finally, he'd discover what he'd missed so many years ago. Finally, he'd appease the ache.

Because he knew he'd lost ground by letting her see his anger, Casey changed his tack. "I got the money you sent."

Startled, she released the dog. "I'm sorry I took it in the first place. It was wrong."

"You know I'd have given it to you if you'd asked." She nodded without recognizing the outright lie. Hell, if Emma had asked him for money, he'd have known her plans and rather than leave her alone that night, he'd have kept close to her. He'd have stayed with her and everything would have turned out different.

He wouldn't have lost her for so long.

Remembering that night still made Casey tense. So many times over the years, he'd replayed it in his head, thinking of things he should have done, should have said. He'd given up on ever seeing her again.

Now she'd returned, and he'd done nothing but paw her. He wanted to tell her that he'd missed her, that she'd left a void in his life. But, damn it, she'd walked out on him without a backward glance. It still pissed him off.

"Where did you go when you left, Em?"

More silence. She turned her head to stare out the window.

Not bothering to hide his exasperation, Casey said, "C'mon, Emma. Hell, it's been damn near a decade. Does it really matter if you tell me?" He couldn't soften his tone, couldn't soften his reaction to her. Emma had always had the ability to make him feel things he didn't want to feel, to feel things he hadn't felt since she'd left him.

He could see her resistance, her reticence. She didn't trust him, never really had, and that bothered him most of all. "You came to me once, Emma. Why can't you talk to me now?"

"People change over time, Casey."

"Me or you?"

"In eight years? I'd say both." Turning from the window, she looked at him and sighed. "I don't even know you anymore."

In so many ways she knew him better than anyone ever had. But he was glad she didn't realize it. "So where you went is a big secret, huh?" He rubbed his upper lip as he considered her. "Must be something scandalous, right? Let me think. Wait, I know. Did you become a spy?"

She rolled her eyes, looking so much like the old teasing girl he used to know.

"No? Well, let's see. Did you join up with a circus or get sent to prison?"

"No, no, and no."

"Then what?" Unable to help himself, he stretched

out his arm and cupped her shoulder. Her nearness made it impossible for him *not* to touch her. The ancient, baggy sweatshirt she wore all but hid her breasts. But Casey knew their softness, their plump weight. How they felt in his palms.

Oh yeah, he remembered that too well.

Emma lifted her face and met his gaze. "There's no reason to rehash old news."

"It's not old for me." He recalled the many nights he'd lain awake worrying about her, imagining every awful scenario that could happen to a girl all alone. It had made him sick with fear—and blind with rage. "I offered you help, Emma, and rather than take it you left me a goddamn note that didn't tell me a thing. You ran out on me. You stole money from me." *You ripped out my heart.*

She bit her lip, her face awash in guilt. "I'm sorry."

Damn it, he didn't want her apology. He thought to take back the words, but instead he drew a deep breath and continued, hoping to cajole her, reassure her. "I worried about you, Emma, especially when I found out you didn't have a relative in Ohio. I worried and I thought about you and wished like hell I'd done something different. I screwed up that night, and I know it."

Her eyes were wide and dark, filled with incredulity. "But...that's nonsense."

"I don't think so. You came to me, and I let you down."

"No." She leaned forward and her cool fingers caressed his jaw. His muscles clenched with her first tentative touch. "Don't ever think that, Casey. You

did more than enough. You helped me more than anyone else ever could have.''

"Right.''

"Casey…'' She hesitated, then she whispered,
"You were the best thing that ever happened to me.
You always made me happy, even after I'd gone
away.''

Robbed of breath by her words, Casey closed his
hand over hers and kept her palm flat against his jaw.
It was such a simple touch, and it meant so much to
him. "But I don't deserve an accounting? Or do I
have to go on wondering what happened to you?''

She tugged her hand free and let it drop to the
gearshift. Their gazes were locked together, neither of
them able or willing to look away. The dog laid his
head on the back of the seat between them, watching
closely. He gave a whine of curiosity.

B.B. probably felt Emma's distress, Casey thought,
because he sure as hell felt it. He regretted that he'd
upset her, but he needed to know where she'd gone
and how she'd gotten by. He *had* to know.

"All right.'' Her whispered words barely reached
him, then she cleared her throat and spoke with new
strength. "But it's a boring story.''

"Let me be the judge of that.''

With a sigh, she dropped back into her seat and
folded her hands in her lap. Her hair fell forward to
hide her face. Casey wanted to smooth it back so he
could better see her, but he didn't want to take a
chance on interrupting her confession.

"For the first two weeks I lived in a park. There
were plenty of woods so it was easy to hide when
they shut the gates. There were outdoor rest rooms

and stuff there, places for me to clean up and get a drink and…'' She rolled her shoulders. ''I had everything I needed. In a way, it was fun, like an adventure.''

''Jesus, Em. You don't mean…''

''Yeah.'' She dredged up a smile that didn't do a damn thing to convince him. ''I slept on the ground, using my backpack for a pillow. You know, it reminded me of all those nights we used to stay out late on the lake. You remember how we could hear the leaves and see all the stars and the air was so cool and crisp? We'd get mosquito bites, but it was worth it. Well, it was like that. A little scary at times, but also sort of soothing and peaceful. It'd be so quiet I'd stare up at the sky and think about everyone back in Buckhorn.'' Her gaze darted away, and she added on a whisper, ''I'd think about you.''

Pained, his heart aching, Casey closed his eyes. Emma didn't know how her words devastated him, because she wasn't looking at him.

''That's where I found B.B. He was still a puppy, a warm, energetic ball of fur, and when we saw each other, he was so…happy to be with me.'' She laced her fingers together, waited. ''Someone had abandoned him.''

Just as her father had abandoned her?

''I picked ticks off him and used my comb to get snarls out of his fur and he played with me and kept me company.''

This time her smile was genuine, a small, sweet smile, as she talked about the dog. Casey wanted to crowd her close and put his arms around her and protect her forever. The urge was so strong, he sounded gruff as he asked, "Why did you stay in a park, Emma?"

"There was nowhere else to stay. I used the money I had—and your money—to pay for my bus fare to Chicago, and for food. After I got there, I couldn't get a job because I couldn't give a place of residence, and I couldn't get a place of residence without a job reference. I was afraid if I went to any of the shelters, they'd contact my family and…send me back home."

Casey scrubbed at his face. Emma was twenty-five now, but he saw her as she'd been when she left— young, bruised, scared and lonely. What she'd gone through was worse than he'd suspected, worse than he'd ever imagined. He'd held on to the belief that she knew someone, that she'd had someone to take care of her. But she'd been all alone. Vulnerable. And it hurt to know that.

"I'm not sure what would have eventually happened. But then one day B.B. got really sick. He'd eaten something bad and he was dehydrated, weak. He could barely walk. I was so afraid that I'd lose him, I chanced going to the vet clinic that I'd seen not far from the park. That's where I met Parker Devaughn and his son, Damon."

She turned to B.B. and hugged him close. Several seconds passed, and Casey knew she was weighing her words. "It took almost a week before B.B. was healthy again. I hung out there, staying by his side as much as they'd let me."

The images flooding his mind were too agonizing to bear. "What happened?"

"They…figured out my situation when I couldn't pay the bill and offered to let me work it off instead."

"They realized that you were homeless?" Casey wanted to hear all the details about where she'd slept, how she'd stayed safe. When the dog was sick, she'd been alone more than ever.

But one thought kept overriding all others. How bad had it been for her in Buckhorn that she'd rather sleep alone in a park with no one for company except an abandoned dog? What the hell had happened to make her run away?

Emma gave a small nod. "I couldn't leave B.B. and they wouldn't let me have him without explaining. I was afraid they'd turn me in and send me back home. But when I told them everything, they surprised me."

"Everything?"

She glanced at him, then away. Skipping his question, she said, "They took me in and they've treated me like family ever since. Parker even helped me to get my G.E.D. and to find a job I love. Life now is...great."

She'd left out everything painful, either to spare him or because she couldn't bear to talk about it. Casey didn't know which, and neither was acceptable. He suddenly wanted her to be his friend again, that young girl with the enormous soft eyes always filled with invitation. The girl who always came to him with open admiration and her heart on her sleeve. The girl who'd wanted him—and only him.

His decisions, his feelings for her back then, had seemed so simple and straightforward. He'd liked controlling things, only letting her so close, giving her only as much as he wanted and holding back everything else.

Or so he'd thought.

But somehow Emma had crawled under his skin and into his head, his heart. He hadn't known until she was gone that she'd taken more than he'd ever meant to give her. He hadn't known until she was gone, and a big piece of him was missing. Being apart from her while becoming a man hadn't changed how he felt. It had only complicated it.

Disturbed by his reaction to her, he teased her by tugging on a lock of her hair. "That story is so full of holes I could use it for a sieve."

"No, I've told you everything that's important."

"Em…"

"Thanks to Parker and Damon, I did fine," she insisted. She smiled a little, and her eyes glinted with humor. "In fact, I might owe them even more than I owe you."

Annoyance fought with tenderness, making his voice gruff. "You don't owe me a damn thing and you know it."

"I knew you probably felt that way." She shook her head, still smiling in that small, tantalizing way that made him want to lick her mouth. "That's one of the things that always made you so special, Casey."

Hearing her say such a thing took some of the edge off his urgency. He liked thinking that he'd been special to her, because she'd certainly been special to him. He just hadn't known it until it was too late.

Acting on impulse, he took her hand. "Have breakfast with me tomorrow. We can catch up on old times and you can fill me in on the pieces you're leaving out right now."

She gave a shrug of apology. "I can't. I'm going to the hospital first thing."

He'd almost forgotten about her father and felt like an ass because of it. It surprised him that she'd return to see the man who'd run her off, but he supposed time could heal those wounds. And Dell wasn't in the best of health. "We can make it dinner."

She closed her eyes on a sigh of weariness. "I don't think so, Casey."

Her rejection struck him like a blow. "I'm special," he asked, "but not special enough to share a meal with?"

She swiveled her head toward him. "I'm sorry—"

In an instant, his temper snapped. "Will you quit saying that!"

She flipped her hair back and her eyes flashed. "Don't yell at me."

"Then quit apologizing." And in a mumble, "You always did apologize too much."

B.B. let out a low warning growl, breaking the flow of anger. Emma turned to the big dog and rubbed his muzzle. In a calmer tone, she said, "I can't make any plans because I don't know what my schedule will be, or how much free time I'll have."

And she wasn't sleeping alone.

Casey cursed softly, but he couldn't blame Devaughn. If he had Emma warming his bed, no way would he let her out with another man.

He wouldn't give up, but he would slow it down. He'd been her friend once, maybe her only friend in Buckhorn. He'd build on that. He'd give her time to breathe, to get used to him again.

Until Emma got the water pump fixed, she'd need transportation to the hospital. He'd be happy to oblige, to give her a helping hand.

One thing was certain, before she took off this time he'd have all his questions answered. He'd be damned if he'd let her sneak out on him a second time.

CHAPTER FOUR

As IF FROM A DISTANCE, Emma heard the knock on the thin motel-room door. She forced her head from the flat, overstarched pillow and glanced at the glowing face of the clock. It was barely six-thirty and her body remained limp with the heaviness of sleep. She'd only been in bed five hours.

After Damon had finally returned and they'd transferred everything from her car to Casey's and gotten to the Cross Roads Motel, it had been well past one o'clock. She hadn't unpacked, had only pulled off her shoes, jeans, bra and sweatshirt, and dropped into the bed in a tee and panties. She'd been so exhausted, both in body and spirit, that thoughts of food or a shower disintegrated beneath tiredness.

Why would anyone be calling on her this early?

B.B. snuffled around and let out a warning *woof,* but Emma patted him and he resettled with a modicum of grumbling and growling. Stretched on his side, he took up more than his fair share of the bed. "It's okay, boy. I'll be right back."

Probably Mrs. Reider, she thought, ready with a complaint of some kind, though Emma couldn't imagine what it might be. They'd kept very quiet coming in last night and hadn't disturbed anyone as far as she knew.

B.B. was atop the covers, so Emma grabbed the bedspread that had gotten pushed to the bottom of the bed. She halfheartedly wrapped it around herself and let it drag on the floor.

Without turning on a light, she padded barefoot to the door, turned the cheap lock, and swung it open. The room had been dark with the heavy drapes drawn, but now she had to lift a hand to shield her eyes against the red glow of a rising sun. She blinked twice before her bleary eyes could focus.

And there stood Casey.

His powerful body lounged against the door frame, silhouetted by a golden halo. In the daylight, he looked more devastatingly handsome than ever. Confusion washed over Emma and she stared, starting at Casey's feet and working her way up.

Laced-up, scuffed brown boots showed beneath well-worn jeans that rode low on his lean hips and were faded white in stress spots, like his knees, the pocket where he kept his keys. His fly.

Emma blinked at that, then shook her head and continued upward. With the casual clothing, he'd forgone a belt. In fact, two belt loops were missing from the ancient jeans.

In deference to the heat, he wore a sleeveless, battered white cotton shirt that left his muscular arms and tanned shoulders on display. Mirrored sunglasses shielded his eyes, and his mouth curled in a lopsided, wicked grin. "Morning, Emma."

Her tongue stuck to the roof of her mouth, making speech difficult. "What are you doing here?"

Lifting one hand, which caused all kinds of interesting muscles to flex in his arm, he showed her the smallest of her suitcases. "You forgot this in the trunk of my car. I thought you might need it today."

"Oh." She looked around, not sure what to do next. She did need the case, seeing that it held her toiletries and makeup. But she could hardly invite him in when she wasn't dressed. Loosening her hold on the bedspread, she reached for the case. "Thank you..."

Casey removed the decision from her. Lifting the case out of reach, he stepped inside just in time to see B.B. bound off the bed and lunge forward with a growl. When he recognized Casey, he slowed and the growl turned into a tail-wagging hello. Casey greeted the dog while eyeing the bed he'd vacated. Being a double, it provided just enough room for one woman—and her pet.

He quirked an eyebrow at Emma as realization dawned. She hadn't slept alone, so he couldn't accuse her of lying. But she hadn't slept with a man either, which had been his assumption.

Casey grinned and reached down to pat the dog. "You've sure got the cushy life, don't you, B.B.?"

The dog jumped up, putting his paws on Casey's shoulders. Casey laughed. "Yeah, sleeping with a gorgeous woman would put any guy in a good mood."

Left standing in the open doorway, Emma hadn't quite gathered her wits yet. Too little sleep combined with Casey Hudson in the morning could rattle anyone. She certainly wasn't up to bantering with him. "He's always slept with me. It's one reason I bring him along everywhere I go."

"Gotcha." Casey looked around again, and his grin widened. "So. Where's Damon?"

He tried to sound innocent, but failed. Knowing the jig was up, Emma scowled at him. Would he now consider her fair game, since she wasn't involved? What would she say to dissuade him if he did?

Did she really want to dissuade him?

The connecting door opened and Damon stuck his dark head out. With only one eye opened, he demanded, "What the hell's going on?" Then he saw Casey, and that one eye widened. "Oh, it's you. I should have known."

In his boxers and nothing more, Damon pulled the door wider. Emma wasn't uncomfortable with his lack of dress. More often than not, Damon acted like her brother.

Casey took in the separate rooms with a look of deep satisfaction. "Morning, Devaughn."

"Yeah, whatever." Damon yawned, leaned in the doorway, and crossed his arms over his naked chest. His blue eyes were heavy, his jaw shadowed with stubble, and his silky black hair stuck out in funny disarray. "You country boys like to get up early, I take it?"

"Country boys?" Casey didn't sound amused by that description.

Undisturbed by Casey's pique, Damon lazily eyed him with both eyes this time, taking in the old snug jeans and the muscle shirt. "Brought it up another notch, I see."

Casey's scowl darkened. "What?"

Damon just shook his head and glanced at Emma. "Give me a minute to get dressed."

She didn't want to turn this into a social gathering, and besides, both men were bristling, which didn't bode well. "That's not necessary."

"No?"

"No." Emma saw Damon's surprise and rubbed her forehead. He looked as tired as she felt, so why didn't he just go on back to bed so she could deal with Casey in private? She moderated her tone. "It's fine, Damon. Get some more sleep."

He didn't budge. "You turned willing overnight?"

Her moderation shot to hell, Emma ground her teeth together. "Damon..."

"Was it the macho clothes that turned the trick?"

Casey shifted his stance but Emma growled, causing both B.B. and Damon to watch her warily.

Damon straightened in the doorway with dawning suspicion. "Have you had your coffee?"

Emma slowly looked up at him. A long rope of tangled hair hung over her bloodshot, puffy eyes. She wore only her T-shirt and a bedspread. Curling her lip, she asked, "Do I look to you like I've had coffee?"

"Shit." He turned to Casey with accusation. "So where is it?"

Casey blinked in incomprehension. "Where is what?"

As if speaking to an idiot, Damon enunciated each word. "The coffee?"

Casey shrugged, but offered helpfully, "They keep a pot brewing in the lobby."

"Right. In the lobby. And here I had the impression you knew something about women." Shaking his head at Casey in a pitying way, Damon turned to

Emma. "Just hang on, doll. I'll run down and snag you a cup."

On a normal day Emma would have thanked him and dropped back into bed. But this wasn't a normal day. Today, Casey stood in her temporary bedroom looking and smelling too sexy for a sane woman's health and she wasn't properly dressed. "It's okay. B.B. needs to go out too, so I might as well get the coffee myself." And then she wouldn't be left closed up in the motel room with Casey.

Apparently stunned, Damon blinked at her. "Are you sure?"

"I'm sure I'm going to smack you if you don't stop pushing me."

"All right, all right." Damon held up both hands, which should have been comical given that he wore only print boxers. "Hey, what do I know about a woman's needs? They're ever shifting and changing, right? One day coffee is a necessity before she can open her eyes. The next, no problem, she'll get it herself."

Emma turned away and stomped to the dresser to snatch up her jeans. Ignoring both men, she trailed into the bathroom and shut the door. She didn't exactly slam it, but her irritation definitely showed.

She heard Casey whistle low. "Wow. Is she always like that in the morning?"

"Be warned—*yes.*"

Casey chuckled, but Damon, clearly disgruntled, said, "I wouldn't if I was you. What you just saw is nothing compared to how grouchy she'll get if she doesn't get a cup of coffee real soon."

"I'll keep that in mind."

"You do that."

Emma brushed her teeth while praying that Damon would now go back to bed. He did, but not without a parting shot.

"I usually fetch her a cup before I wake her up, especially when she hasn't had enough sleep. But since you did the deed this morning, and at such an ungodly hour at that, you can deal with the consequences all alone."

She heard Damon's door close, then heard Casey mutter to B.B., "You won't let her hurt me, will you, buddy?"

B.B. whined.

Emma exited the bathroom. She slipped her feet into her sneakers, latched B.B.'s leash to his collar and stepped around Casey to head out the door. Obedient whenever it suited him, B.B. followed, and, without a word, Casey fell into step behind him. She'd only gone down three steps, her destination the lobby where fresh coffee waited, when she heard Casey begin humming some tune that she didn't recognize.

He knew she slept without a man. Emma wondered what he intended to do with that knowledge, because she knew Casey too well to mistake him now. He was up to something, and she dreaded the coming battle.

It was herself she'd have to fight, of course. She'd never been able to resist Casey, not then, and not now. Damn.

BEFORE SHE COULD HEAD for the lobby, Casey caught Emma's arm. "Take B.B. to the bushes, then park yourself at the picnic table. I'll get the coffee."

She looked ready to argue, so Casey reasoned with her. "You can't take the dog inside, and he's starting to look desperate. Really, fetching you a cup of coffee won't tax me. I'll even get one for myself. Okay?"

She glanced at the dog, who did indeed appear urgent, then nodded. "All right. Lots of sugar and a smidgen of cream."

"Got it." Casey sauntered away with a smile on his face. He'd spent the night thinking about Emma, and being sexually frustrated as a result. He couldn't say what he'd expected this morning when he'd knocked on her door, but the picture she'd presented had taken him by surprise.

Soft. That was the word that most often came to mind when he thought of Emma. Soft eyes, soft heart, soft breasts and hips and thighs…

This morning, still sleepy and wrapped in a bedspread, she'd been so soft she'd damn near melted his heart on the spot, along with all the plans he'd so meticulously devised throughout the long night. He'd taken one look at her and wanted to lead her right back to bed.

It had been doubly hard to give up that idea once he knew Damon had a separate room.

Seeing her sleek, silky hair tangled around her shoulders, her cheeks flushed, her eyes a little dazed had made him think of a woman's expression right before she came. Emma's very kissable mouth had been slightly puffy, and her lips had parted in surprise when she saw him at the door, adding to the fantasy.

Her legs…well, Emma had always had a killer ass and gorgeous legs. That hadn't changed. As a perpetually horny teen, resisting her had been his biggest struggle. As an adult, it wasn't much easier. In fact, he had no intention of resisting her now.

Unfortunately, she'd pulled on jeans rather than the ultrashort shorts he remembered in their youth, and her legs were now well hidden. But she hadn't bothered with a bra yet. With each step she took, her breasts moved gently beneath the cotton of her T-shirt, and the faintest outline of her nipples showed through.

Casey's muscles tightened in anticipation of seeing her again and he snapped lids on three disposable cups of coffee then plucked up several packets of sugar, two stirrers and some little tubs of creamer. He stuffed them in his pockets. Balancing the hot cups between his hands, he shouldered the door open and started back to Emma.

In limp exhaustion, she rested at one of the aged wooden picnic tables that had always served as part of Mrs. Reider's small lot. Guests used the tables often, but this early in the day no one else intruded. Casey didn't make a sound as he approached, and Emma remained unaware of him.

She'd kicked off her shoes, and her legs were stretched out in front of her with her bare toes wiggling. Sunlight through elm leaves, shifting and changing with the careless breeze, dappled her upturned face.

The air this time of morning remained heavy with dew, rich with scents of the earth and trees. Emma sighed and her expression bespoke a peacefulness that made Casey smile from the inside out. He liked seeing Emma at peace. When she'd been younger, so often what he'd seen in her eyes was uncertainty, loneliness, even fear.

She spoke a moment to B.B., who sprawled out in the lush grass at her feet, then she reached up and lifted her hair off her nape. Casey stalled in appreciation of her feminine gesture. Even from her early teens, Emma had displayed an innate sensuality that drove every guy around her wild. She stretched her arms high, and her hair drifted free to resettle over her shoulders.

Damn. He absolutely could not get a boner in Mrs. Reider's motel lot.

Neither could he allow Emma to affect him this strongly. He had to remember that despite her appeal and everything he'd once felt—still felt—she'd walked out on him and hadn't bothered to get in touch in eight long years. And she hadn't come back for him now. If her father wasn't so sick, she wouldn't be here.

"Here's your coffee." His emotions in check, Casey took the last few remaining steps to her and set the cups on the tabletop. "I hope you haven't chewed off any tree bark or anything." He scattered the sugar packets and creamer beside the cups.

Eyes scrunched up because of the sun, Emma turned to him with a frown. "Damon exaggerated. I'm not that bad."

"If you say so." He smiled at her. "But remember, I witnessed you firsthand. For a minute there I expected to see smoke come out of your ears."

She looked ready to growl again, but restrained herself. "I hadn't had much sleep."

"I'm sorry I woke you."

"You don't look sorry."

Casey shrugged and continued to smile.

Emma considered him a long moment, then took the coffee and quickly doctored it to her specifications. The second she tipped the cup to her mouth, she moaned in bliss. "Oh God, I needed that." She took another long drink. "Perfect. Thank you."

Casey sipped his own coffee, prepared much like hers. "Not a morning person, huh?"

She shook her head. "I'm barely civil in the morning. I've always been more a night owl."

He remembered that—and a whole lot more.

She didn't say anything else, made no effort toward casual conversation, which annoyed him. She sat with him, drank the coffee he'd brought to her, but kept him shut out.

To regain her attention, he touched the back of her hand with one fingertip. "I still think waking up with you would be fun."

Surprised by that comment, Emma froze for a good five seconds. Abruptly, she drained the rest of her cup and stood. She didn't look at him. "Thanks again...for everything." She started to step away.

Casey moved so fast, she gasped. In less than a heartbeat he'd reached over the table and snatched her narrow wrists, shackling them in his hands. He stared into her mesmerizing, antagonistic brown eyes until the air around them fairly crackled.

"Don't go." Two simple words, but his heart pounded as he waited.

She looked undecided.

"I brought you another cup." Casey stroked the

insides of her wrists with his thumbs, kept his tone easy, persuasive. "Sit with me, Emma. Talk to me."

He ignored the rise of her breasts as she slowly inhaled. Her hesitation was palpable, forcing him to think of more arguments, other stratagems, until she said, "Why?"

Sensing that she'd just relented, Casey relaxed. "Sit down and I'll tell you why."

With enough grumbling to wake the squirrels, she dropped into the seat. This time she slid her legs under the table and faced him with both elbows propped on the tabletop to hold her chin. "I'm waiting."

Casey took in her belligerent expression and swallowed his amusement. Not once in all the time he'd known her had Emma ever shown him disgruntlement. She'd shown him adolescent lust, feminine need, a few flirting smiles and occasionally her vulnerability.

It didn't make any sense, but he felt as if he'd just gained three giant steps forward. "Yeah. You know, I think I'll feel more secure if you drink the other cup of coffee first." He prepared it as he spoke, and handed it to her with a flourish.

She slanted him a look through her thick lashes. "With the way you've acted so far, you're probably right." She accepted the coffee and sipped. "You've been deliberately provoking."

Casey waited until she swallowed before he spoke. "There's still something between us, Emma."

She promptly choked, then glared at him before searching in vain for a napkin. Casey offered her his clean hankie. "You okay?"

She brushed away his concern. "Something, huh?"

Her voice was still raspy as she wheezed for air. "Well, I can tell you exactly what that *something* is."

Casey tilted back. "That right?"

"Sure." She finally regained her breath. "I'm not dead. I felt it too."

Her mood was so uncertain, he couldn't decide how to handle her. "You know, you're a lot more candid when you're crabby."

Without another word, she dropped her head to her folded arms. He didn't know if she was laughing, but he was certain she wasn't crying.

Casey wanted to touch her, wanted to feel the warmth of her skin. Her light-brown hair lay fanned out around her, spilling onto the table. The sun had kissed it near her temples, along her forehead, framing her face with natural golden streaks. Her hair looked heavy and soft and shiny. The length of her spine was graceful, feminine. Her wrists, crisscrossed under her head, were narrow, delicate.

Everything about her turned him on. At the first hint of her scent, the natural perfume of warm woman fresh from her bed, he got excited. Around her, he felt things more acutely than he had for years.

Making an abrupt decision, he stroked one large hand over her head, down to her nape. "I want you, Emma."

Her silent laughter morphed into a groan.

Casey waited, content to smooth her hair and rub her shoulder. Content just to touch her in this innocent way. For now.

When she lifted her head, she was smiling and her eyes twinkled with teasing devilment.

Dazzled, Casey let his hand drop to the table. He

couldn't pull his gaze away from her. "You are so pretty when you smile."

That made her laugh again. "Casey Hudson, you're as shameless as your uncles ever were, and God knows they were nigh infamous for their ways with women."

"Until they married, maybe." Her infectious smile soon had him grinning too. "Now they've taken to family life with as much gusto as they relished bachelorhood. I have a passel of nieces and nephews to prove it."

"Yeah, well, they were bachelors long enough for you to pick up their habits, I see. I've barely been in town a single night."

"But it feels like old times, doesn't it?" To him, it was as if she'd never gone away, they'd fallen into such an easy familiarity.

"Maybe, but it's still only one night, and already you're hitting on me."

"Tell me you don't want me."

Her smile disappeared, replaced with chagrin. "I wish I could."

His heart swelled and thumped. "Then…"

"No." The shake of her head seemed all too final. "Based on our pasts, I can understand why you think I'd just jump into bed with you. We both know I tried hard enough to get you there before I left. And I won't claim I've been a nun since leaving."

That made him wince. The thought of her with other men shouldn't have mattered, but it did. It always had.

"I'm only going to be in town for a short while

and having a brief fling for old time's sake isn't on the agenda.''

"Why not?" Though he didn't like what he wanted called a fling, he'd take what he could get for now. He wanted her that much.

She wrinkled her nose at him. "C'mon, Case. We're both older and wiser and more mature."

"Which only means we can damn well take advantage of the chemistry." He tipped his head, studying her. "The second I recognized you, Emma, I felt it. Again." Hell, it had nearly knocked him on his ass.

She stared at him a moment, then turned to look out over the street. "You know, I'd forgotten how wonderful it was to be in Buckhorn in the morning. In my apartment in Chicago, I don't hear birds first thing or see black squirrels running up a tree. The air I breathe isn't so fresh it has almost the same kick as my coffee. I'd forgotten the scents and the sights."

As hard as he'd tried, he hadn't forgotten a damn thing. He felt nettled—until she spoke again.

"I'd almost forgotten your effect on me." Emma's smile was a little sad, her dark eyes a little wistful. She picked a fat clover blossom from the ground and twirled it between her fingers. "I kept your shirt, did you know that?"

Watching Emma enjoy her surroundings, hearing the catch in her voice stirred him as much as being stroked by another woman would have. Casey felt primed enough that he would happily take her deeper into the trees and skim off her jeans right now—if she'd been at all willing.

But she wasn't.

Her old vulnerability, which had kept his baser instincts at bay as a teenager, was now gone. But in its place was something just as compelling to his heart. He took her hand. "What shirt?"

"The one you gave me the night I left."

"The night you snuck away."

"Semantics." Her crooked smile charmed him. "It smelled of you, so even when you weren't with me, you were. Do you know what I mean?"

He nodded. "It was something familiar."

"It was you. I still have it, though after all this time the scent is gone."

The idea of her hugging his shirt to her body night after night burned him. "Spend the night with me," he offered in a low rasp, "and you can have my whole damn wardrobe."

Her mouth curled, but the humor didn't spread to her eyes. "If I spent the night with you, Casey, I'm afraid I wouldn't want to go."

Her honesty surprised him, and it must have showed. She squeezed his hand and then pulled away.

"I don't mean to put you on the spot, I really don't. I'm not asking you for anything, because I don't need anything. I got my life together and I'm happy with it. But you were always my ultimate fantasy, and I have a feeling that indulging a real-life fantasy wouldn't be a good idea."

He discounted all that fantasy nonsense to ask, "Why?" A little indulgence sounded like a hell of an idea to him.

"It'd complicate things, when I won't be around long enough to deal with anything complicated."

Most of what she said seemed too difficult to understand. Her fantasy? He didn't want to be anyone's fantasy, but he did want to be her reality. In bed.

Anything more than that...well, he doubted he could ever trust Emma again. He'd wanted to be her savior, her protector, and instead she'd walked. And hadn't contacted him even once through all the long, lonely days that had followed. He'd gone from worried sick to angry to bitter.

Now she was back and all the other emotions faded behind the sexual greed, because that at least was easy enough to understand. "You just got here and you're already talking about leaving. How long do you plan to stay?"

She shrugged. "Damon's on a self-assigned sabbatical. He's rethinking his life, so he's able to stay as long as I want."

"A sabbatical from what?" Damon Devaughn seemed like a very real complication. He was close to Emma, no two ways about that. How close—that's what Casey wanted to find out.

"He's an architect, but he's tired of commercial design...you know, putting up shopping centers and parking lots. He wants to go into residential design and do single-family housing instead, because it's more personal. The thing is, starting over will mean realigning his life along with a huge cut in pay. Not that he can't afford it, but he's thinking things through."

It surprised Casey that he and Damon might have something in common—discontent with their current careers. For months, Casey had been rethinking his future plans, and wondering if he'd made a mistake in being lured by his stepgrandfather into a position

of money and influence. The job provided a challenge
and drew a lot of respect, but because his office was
in Cincinnati, it also took him away from his home.
At first his big corner office had seemed impressive,
but he'd quickly realized that he didn't like sitting
behind a desk and answering to others, working for
strangers instead of neighbors and friends. Dealing
with computers and electronic programs was so im-
personal, it left Casey feeling empty.

Unlike Damon, he hadn't yet made up his mind to
do anything about it. He wanted a change, but insti-
gating it would stir things up a lot.

"What about you, Emma? How much time do you
have off work?" She hesitated so long, Casey's irritation resurfaced. "Is it such a big deal telling me one
little thing about your life?"

She pushed her hair off her forehead, thoughtful
for a moment before she smiled and shrugged. "I've
already spilled my guts, so what difference does it
make?"

Another cryptic comment that he couldn't understand. "It doesn't."

"All right." She made up her mind and nodded.
"I suppose I can stay as long as I like too. I have my
own business. It's small, but I like it that way, and
since I'm the boss, I don't have to answer to anyone.
But, unlike Damon, I can't afford to stay off indefinitely. How long I stay depends on how my father
does, but I'm thinking that if I want to have a business
to go back to, I shouldn't stay more than a few
weeks."

Her obvious enthusiasm added to his curiosity, and
he asked, "What kind of business is it?"

She chewed on her smile, then rolled her eyes. "I'm a massage therapist."

"A...?"

"Yeah, a massage therapist. And I'm good." She went on in a rush, as if to convince him. "My shop is called The Soothing Touch and I've got a really dedicated clientele. When I told them all I'd be gone for a while, they wished me well and told me they'd be waiting for me when I got back."

Casey stared. Not a single intelligent comment came to mind.

At his continued silence, Emma's smile faded and she gave him a defiant look. "I started by working in the Tremont Hotel fitness center, then branched out on my own. Now I work from my own shop throughout the week, but I also do house or office calls over the weekend and in the evening. And once a month I teach sensual-massage classes to couples."

The images that leaped to Casey's mind left him numb: Emma rubbing oil over a man's naked back, his thighs. Emma visiting some corporate asshole in his office. Emma *enjoying* her damn job.

Doing his best to keep the cynicism out of his tone, Casey repeated, "Office calls, huh?"

She nodded. "A lot of executives have high-stress jobs. They'll pay big bucks to have me come to the office and relax them during their lunch hour or before a big meeting."

He absolutely hated the way she put that.

"I have portable equipment that I use. It's not the same as coming to the shop, but I carry special music and oils with me. Sometimes, if it's allowed in the offices, I'll light candles too."

"Candles?"

"Mmm." She looked displeased with his continued, short questions. "You surround the client with soothing ambience. Incense or scented candles, soft music, low lights. I can make a body go boneless in a one-hour session."

Casey's eyebrows pulled down in a suspicious frown. "I just bet you can."

She frowned right back. "You can stop right there, Casey Hudson. I know assumptions run wild and believe me, I've heard every stupid joke there is, so don't bother. Massage therapist is not a euphemism for call girl, you know. I'm not ashamed of what I do. In fact, I'm proud that I do it so well."

This new facet to Emma's personality fascinated Casey. He liked the way she stood up to him, how she defended herself. And because he knew he had jumped to some hasty conclusions, he relaxed enough to tease. "And here I was going to ask what you charge."

Her nose lifted. "Thirty-five an hour at my shop, fifty if it's a house or office call."

Casey considered her, and then had to ask, "I bet most of your clients are men, right?"

"What do you **want** to bet?"

Keeping the grin off his face wasn't easy. "A kiss?"

"Doesn't matter because you lose. Most are women in their mid-forties, early fifties."

"Really?" That relieved him, until she continued.

"But like I said, some are execs—male and female—with seventy-hour-a-week jobs. And some are athletes with sports injuries that still bother them."

"Athletes?"

"I treated one of the Chicago Cubs for a while early in the season."

New jealousy flared. "What the hell for?"

"He was in a slump and so every time he went to bat, he got tense." She spoke candidly and knowledgeably, using her hands to emphasize. "Massage can help loosen contracted, shortened muscles and at the same time, stimulate flaccid muscles."

Casey grunted at that. "With you touching him, I find it hard to believe there was anything flaccid on the guy." Sure as hell wasn't anything flaccid on him, and he was just *thinking* about her touch, not experiencing it. But he would. Oh yeah, he most definitely would.

Rather than get angry, she got exasperated. "Now you're just being nasty."

"I want you," he reiterated, as if it explained everything. And to his mind, it did.

Her mouth fell open. "I can't believe how pushy you've gotten. You know, you're the only man ever to say such a thing to me."

Casey examined her face, from her sexy mouth and stubborn chin, up to her hair gently teased by the morning breeze. When he locked onto her dark bedroom eyes, she fidgeted in a way that had Casey's insides clenching. "Sorry, Em, but no way in hell can I believe that."

She smirked. "Hey, I've heard other, more crude come-ons. But not an outright statement like *I want you*."

Never in his life had Casey sat with a woman and had such a discussion. In the normal way of things, if he wanted to get intimate, he made a move and she either reciprocated or not. He didn't spell out his intent and give her a chance to rebuff him. This was unique, exhilarating—and so was Emma. "Well, I do. Want you, I mean. So why shouldn't I be honest about it?"

"Oh, by all means, be honest. Just know that it's not going anywhere."

He didn't like hearing that, and he sure wouldn't accept it, so he changed the subject. "When can I get a massage?"

Her eyes widened. "Never."

"Why not?"

"Because..." She got flustered, and a blush rose all the way to her eyebrows. "I just know you too well. I'd be uncomfortable."

With his eyes holding hers, his body warm with memories, he said, "You've touched me before, Em. Plenty of times, in fact."

"That was a long time ago."

"You don't like touching anymore?"

She groaned and covered her face. "It's not that."

So she did like touching? Anyone, or him specifically? It made Casey nuts wondering what she'd done and who she'd been with...and how much she might have enjoyed it. "Then what, Em?"

She dropped her hands. Her gaze landed first on his face, then dipped to his chest, shoulders. She looked away to the parking lot. "I'll, um, give it some thought, okay? That's all I'll promise for now."

"Yeah, you do that." In the meantime, Casey knew damn good and well that he'd think of little else.

CHAPTER FIVE

THE IDEA OF GETTING her hands on Casey's bare flesh left Emma jittery. She'd given too many massages to count, and she'd always been friendly, talkative, but detached. She could never be detached with Casey.

She decided it was past time to go. Standing, she slipped her feet back into her shoes and avoided his astute gaze. "The coffee's gone and I've got a full day ahead. I should get on my way."

Casey stood with her and to her extreme relief, he dropped the topic of a massage. "What's on the agenda?"

"I have to get the car fixed first, then I want to take Damon into town so he can explore while I make the drive to the hospital." Both Casey and B.B. fell into step behind her when she started back toward the room.

"Several questions come to mind."

The day was already warming, and Emma knew that by ten o'clock, it would be sticky with humidity and heat. "Yeah? Like?"

"How're you going to get your car fixed when you're here, the car is on the road, and the garage is in town?"

"I figured I'd call a tow truck." She stopped right outside her door. She didn't want Casey in her room again. "I can do the work myself, but it's not easy without my tools."

"No kidding? You really know how to work on cars?"

Her feminist core insulted, Emma glared at him. "Do you know how to change a water pump?"

"Sure. But that's because I helped Gabe work on our cars and trucks often enough. I learned, but I wouldn't say it's something I'd choose to do."

Casey's uncle, Gabe Kasper, was known as a handy-man extraordinaire. He could build, repair or remodel just about anything. It made sense that Casey would have learned alongside him. "I helped Damon and his father work on cars, and they helped me with my Mustang. I like it. Besides, I've done all the restoration myself, so I don't trust many other people to touch it."

The smile he gave her looked almost...proud. Emma shook her head to clear it, refusing to disillusion herself.

"You baby your car."

Emma's chin lifted. "She's a seventy Boss in cherry condition. I rebuilt the 429 engine. Front and rear took me four years. After all that, of course I baby her."

"Damn." Casey laughed, but his expression was warm, amused. "Massage therapist, mechanic and beautiful to boot. A woman to steal a man's heart." He touched her nose with a dose of playfulness. "It was so dark, I didn't see your car that well last night, so I didn't notice..." He stopped, touched her cheek and sighed. "Okay, truth is, it wasn't your car that held my attention."

Emma had no idea what to say to that, so she just watched him and waited.

"Of course, now that I know it's a classic Boss, I can understand why you'd want to oversee the work. One problem, though."

"What?"

"It's the weekend and the garage won't open till Monday."

Eyes closed, Emma dropped back against the door. "Damn. I forgot about that."

"Around here, almost all the trade businesses still close on the weekends. Only the grocery stores and restaurants stay open. Buckhorn never changes, Emma. No one really wants it to."

"I told Damon as much when we drove in." Now what could she do? Wait another day to see her father? She might not have any choice.

"Can I offer a solution?"

Emma opened one eye. "What?"

"I'll give Gabe a call. He's got a tow truck and he can replace your water pump—I promise you can trust him. He'll treat your car with kid gloves. While he does that, I'll drive you to the hospital."

"No."

Casey crowded closer, blocking the sun with his wide hard shoulders, lowering his head closer to hers. "Why not?"

With him invading her space, Emma found it difficult to speak, but more difficult to move away. "I might be at the hospital for a while. I don't want you to have to wait."

"I've nothing else planned for the day."

She widened her eyes in disbelief. "It's Saturday

and you have nothing to do?'' *No dates with beautiful women?*

"Nothing important.''

She found that very hard to swallow, knowing first-hand of Casey's popularity. "Then you should just relax, not spend your time hanging out in a hospital.''

"You can pay me back by going boating with me. Do you still remember how to ski?''

Longing swelled up inside her. She missed being on the lake, missed the peacefulness of the water, the joy of skiing, the fresh air and sunshine. As a kid, she'd often escaped to the water, staying there late until it was safe to go home again. Sometimes Casey would hang out with her and they'd listen to the frogs croaking and the splash of gentle waves on the shore.

She'd also met plenty of other boys on the lake, and none of them had been interested in the frogs. In those days, sex in a quiet cove had been as much of an escape for Emma as anything else. "I haven't skied since I left here.''

"No kidding? The Devaughns weren't much for water?''

"It's not that. I was just…busy.''

Casey looked very unconvinced. "It's like riding a bike—you never forget how. And I bet B.B. will love being in the boat too. I haven't met a dog yet who doesn't.''

"What about Damon?''

Casey lowered his lashes, hiding his expression. "I thought he wanted to explore the town a little.''

"He might, but I'm not going to abandon him on his first day in town.''

Rubbing the back of his neck, Casey muttered, "So

he'll come along—'' he narrowed his eyes at her ''—if you insist.''

It was so tempting to give in to him, on all counts. She had missed the exhilaration of boating, the wind in her hair, the sun on her face. And accepting Casey's assistance would save her from the hassle of finding another ride to the hospital. ''Gabe doesn't mind working on a Saturday?''

''He wouldn't schedule work, no. But this is different. He's always willing to help out. I doubt it'll take him that long.''

''Why would he want to help me out?''

Casey's voice gentled in reproach. ''You've forgotten how my family is if you have to ask that.''

She gave a short laugh. ''No one in her right mind would ever forget your family. I half wondered if Buckhorn would have sainted the bunch of them by now.''

Casey's unselfconscious smile made him more handsome than ever. ''We like to lend a helping hand. Most everyone in Buckhorn does.''

Emma didn't reply to that. She remembered all too well how most of the locals felt about her. She'd been shunned at best, a pariah at worst. But his family had been wonderful.

''Let me be helpful, Em.''

Oh, she could imagine that husky voice seducing any number of women. That is, if they needed to be seduced. She'd be willing to bet the women had been chasing Casey most diligently. ''It'll take me a little time to get ready. I haven't even showered yet.''

His gaze warmed, then moved over her with slow deliberation. ''Take your time. While you do that, I'll come in and give Gabe a call. We can grab a bite to eat on the way to the hospital. How's that sound?''

B.B. scratched at the door, indicating he'd had enough of idle conversation. He wasn't much of a morning creature either. ''All right.'' She opened the door and watched B.B. head straight for the bed. With one agile leap he hit the mattress, circled once, twice, then dropped with a doggy sigh, his nose tucked close to his tail.

As she entered, she realized just how small and crowded the room was. The second Casey stepped in and closed the door behind him, it became even smaller. Emma laced her fingers together. ''Promise me that if Gabe has other plans, you won't push him. I'm sure I could figure something else out.''

''Absolutely.''

She wasn't sure if she believed him or not. Resigned, she went to the connecting door and tapped on it, then stuck her head inside. Damon was on his stomach, his face turned toward her, snoring. Ignoring Casey for the moment, she crept in and touched Damon's bare shoulder.

Immediately his eyes opened, but otherwise he didn't move. ''Hey, doll,'' he said in a rumbling, still half-asleep voice.

''You awake enough to catch an explanation?''

''Depends.'' He stretched, then pushed up to his elbows. ''Is Romeo gone?''

From his hovering position in the doorway, Casey said, ''If you mean me, no.''

Damon dropped his head forward. ''Persistent, isn't he?''

Casey showed his teeth in a false smile. "Afraid so."

"All right. I'm awake." Damon pushed into a sitting position on the side of the bed and ran his hand through his hair. "What's up?"

"The garage is closed on weekends. Casey's uncle is a handyman and we're going to see if he'll fix the car while I go to the hospital."

"Wait." Damon held up a hand, got sidetracked by a huge yawn, then eyed her. "You're saying you'll let someone else touch your car?"

"I know Gabe, or at least his reputation with cars. He's good."

"Yeah, yeah. I remember the stories. All the holy men of Buckhorn—"

Emma felt like throttling him, especially when she heard Casey chuckle rather than take offense. Through her teeth, she said, "You can either sleep in—"

"Nope, I'm awake now."

"—join us—"

He laughed and spared a glance for Casey. "Does *he* get a vote on that one?"

"—or go exploring."

"So many options. Let's see." He slapped his knees. "I choose C. That is, unless you want me to go to the hospital with you." His voice dropped and he caught her hand. "How do you feel about seeing your dad? You okay?"

Emma glanced at Casey and found him listening intently. Though her stomach was in knots at the idea of facing her father after so many years, she mustered a smile to relieve both men of worry. "I'll be fine, really."

"It's been a long time, doll."

"Exactly. Past time I visited."

Damon didn't look convinced, but he knew her well enough to let it go. "What about B.B.?"

"He'll be happy to sleep until I get back. Then I'm going to take him boating with me."

"Boating?"

Without turning to face Casey, Emma flapped a hand toward him. "He, uh, he has a boat."

"Of course he does."

Casey spoke up, his tone dry. "We have several boats, actually. A speedboat for skiing, a pontoon, couple of fishing boats. The biggest recreational draw for Buckhorn is the three-hundred-and-five-acre water reservoir."

"A man-made lake?"

"Exactly. Around here, everyone considers a boat as important as a car."

Emma cleared her throat and tried to sound enthusiastic. "I thought you might like to go along, Damon."

"Not I, thank you. I can already hear the awkward squeaking of that third wheel."

By his very silence, Casey agreed, but Emma rushed to convince him otherwise. "You wouldn't be a third wheel! And I'd love to show you the lake, Damon. It's beautiful and so peaceful. You could see some of the vacation homes built along there."

"I remember everything you've told me about it." He yawned again, stood, and scratched his belly. "How about we go check it out after the car is fixed and you've had a chance to visit and get reacquainted? Maybe in a day or two?"

"Are you sure?"

"Most positive." Damon strolled to his open suitcase resting on the dresser. He pulled out chinos, a black polo shirt and clean boxers. "I'm heading to the shower. I'll be ready in half an hour."

The second the bathroom door closed, Casey walked over to Emma and took her arm. "Why don't you go ahead and get ready too while I call Gabe? You don't want to miss the doctor at the hospital."

The town's small hospital, Buckhorn Memorial, was efficient and well run, but it wasn't equipped for anything life or death. She'd been reassured when she found out her father was staying there, rather than at one of the larger neighboring hospitals in the next city. It told her that a full recovery was expected.

Still, the idea of seeing him left her nervous, anxious and wary. She'd spoken to him regularly over the years, but because of how they'd parted, the mutual ruse they'd pulled off, their conversations always felt superficial. Despite everything, despite how she'd left him—how he'd *helped* her to leave—Emma knew he loved her.

Just not enough.

"All right." Putting off going wouldn't make it easier. She'd made her decision and now she'd follow through. "I won't be long."

Casey watched her as she riffled through her suitcase to locate a sundress, panties and sandals. The dress, a fitted chambray sheath with embroidered scallop edging, was casual and cool enough for the summer sun, but also dressy enough for the hospital. It

always packed well, but the white cotton blouse she'd
brought along as a jacket was wrinkled. Hopefully the
steam from her shower would help. As she headed
for the bathroom, Casey stretched out on the bed with
B.B., propping his back on the headboard and reaching for the only phone, situated on the nightstand.

Emma's mouth went dry, not only because he was
in her bed, where she'd slept, and he looked right at
home there. But because B.B. rolled to his back and
waited for Casey to scratch his chest—and Casey did,
as if they'd been longtime friends. B.B. was always
polite unless provoked, but he didn't warm up to
strangers easily. Yet he already treated Casey like a
pal.

Emma sighed and went on into the bathroom before
she did something stupid, like join Casey on the bed.
She felt melancholy, and with good reason. Like her,
it seemed her dog had a fondness for Buckhorn's
golden son. Well, they'd both just have to get over
it, because once her business was finished in Buckhorn, Emma fully intended to return to her old life,
the life where she'd found contentment.

Her life—without Casey Hudson.

OF COURSE, Gabe agreed to help out, just as Casey
had known he would. He hadn't yet told his uncle
who he was helping, just a lady friend. Casey wondered if Gabe would recognize Emma. The others had
known her better. His father because of Emma's trip
to their house. His Uncle Morgan because, as sheriff,
he'd had occasion to check up on Emma for skipping
school and breaking curfew. And his Uncle Jordan
would probably recall her from the hospital, the night

Georgia's mother had taken ill and he and Emma had
dropped in to help out. Granted, Jordan had been
mightily distracted with Georgia and her two children.
Casey was convinced that Jordan had fallen in love
with Georgia that night. But he'd surely at least noticed Emma.

His youngest uncle, Gabe, had only met her a few
times, interspersed with all the other girls that Casey
had dated. Casey didn't want any of his relatives
looking at him with speculation, wondering about his
feelings. It was better that Gabe be the only one to
know about Emma. At least for now.

Still idly rubbing the dog's neck, Casey listened as
B.B.'s breathing drifted into a doggy snore. He
grinned. B.B. was a beautiful, well-groomed, healthy
animal, testament to the care Emma had given him.
He obviously had a regular sleeping spot in the bed,
too.

Lucky dog.

Casey wouldn't have minded a little of Emma's
care directed his way, yet she seemed determined to
keep their involvement platonic. He'd have her alone
this afternoon and he'd begin working on her.

Knowing Gabe would be there soon, Casey got up
to stroll the room, peeking out the window to the
parking lot every so often. As he paced, he noted
Emma's open suitcase, stuffed mostly with casual
clothes. He also saw her bra on the only chair in the
room, strung over the arm. He stopped to stare, impressed with her feminine choice.

He absolutely loved lingerie, the sexier the better.

The discarded bra, likely removed the night before,
appealed in a big way. Made of ice-blue transparent

lace, it looked sheer, but had an underwire. The reason she would require an underwire tormented his libido with visions of her full breasts free, or held only by his hands. Casey picked up the bra, rubbing the delicate material between his fingers.

"That surely has to be illegal."

Disgusted at being caught, Casey dropped the bra and turned to face Damon Devaughn. "What's that?"

"Molesting a woman's clothing." Devaughn lazily moved into the room, propped his hip on the dresser and crossed his ankles. He wore pressed tan chinos, a black designer polo and casual loafers. "Does Emma know that you have these kinky tendencies?"

Casey narrowed his eyes. Around Emma, Damon acted casual but proprietary, intimate yet not sexual. Casey couldn't quite figure him out. Then he decided *what the hell?* and just blurted out his biggest question. "Are you gay?"

Damon blinked at him and a smile twitched on his mouth. Somewhat demure, he said, "Why do you ask?"

Stumped as to how to reply, Casey scowled. "It seemed pertinent to the situation."

"Ah, let me guess. It's my fashion sense, isn't it?" He smoothed his hands over his shirt. "No? My neatly trimmed hair?"

When Casey didn't bother to reply, Damon's eyes narrowed. He crossed his arms over his chest, and Casey couldn't help but notice that muscles bulged. He didn't understand Devaughn, but he had to admit that the man was no wimp.

"Or," Damon asked, dragging out the word until

Casey wanted to throttle him, "is it because I like Emma, even though I'm not screwing her?"

Casey took an aggressive step forward before he could stop himself. He felt like smashing Damon and wasn't even sure why. No, that was a lie. He knew he disliked Damon because the man was close to Emma. "It was a simple question, Devaughn."

"No."

"No *what?*"

"No, I'm not gay." Damon shrugged. "A simple answer."

Striving for control, Casey drew a slow deep breath, then another. They both heard the shower stop, and the telltale sounds of Emma moving around in the bathroom. Naked.

Casey swallowed, distracted by images of her toweling off. Staring toward the bathroom door, he muttered, "I didn't mean to offend you, Devaughn. I have nothing against—"

"Yeah, yeah, whatever. No offense taken." Suddenly the bathroom door squeaked open and Damon, too, turned to stare.

Emma, her hair wrapped in a towel, stuck her head out. She looked startled to find that she already had both men's attention. She glanced first at Casey, then at Damon. "I need a blow-dryer. Who has a motel without blow-dryers in the bathroom?"

She sounded very disgruntled, then answered her own question. "Obviously Mrs. Reider, which I should have guessed, but I stupidly assumed that she'd gotten a little with the times over the past decade."

Damon laughed. "I'll get mine. Hang on."

Casey mouthed silently, *I'll get mine,* then realized Emma was watching him. He pasted on a leering smile. "You need any help?"

Eyes wide, Emma asked, "With what?"

"Drying off?"

"Uh, no." She looked toward the connecting door as if willing Damon to reappear. He did, curse him.

"Here you go. Don't electrocute yourself."

Emma snatched the dryer out of his hand, cast another quick look at Casey, and shut the door. Seconds later, a loud hum reverberated throughout the room, ensuring Damon and Casey some privacy.

Damon took immediate advantage. Steely-eyed, he advanced on Casey until he stood a mere foot in front of him. "I haven't had many occasions to issue these hairy-chested, testosterone-drowned warnings, but I hope you'll listen despite my inexperience in these things, because I'm dead serious."

Casey drew back and it took him a moment to figure out what the hell Damon had just said. When his meaning sunk in, Casey shook his head. Damon was about the oddest damn duck he'd ever run across. "Yeah, I'm listening, Devaughn. Wouldn't miss it, in fact."

"I love Emma like a sister—a younger sister whom I feel very protective of."

That suited Casey just fine. As long as Damon didn't lust after her, he could love her all he wanted. "I'm glad to hear it."

"You crushed her once."

Casey scowled. How much had Emma told him? *What* had she told him? "If that's true, it wasn't on purpose.'' Hell, Emma had run out on him, not the other way around.

"Yeah, well, you were a kid." Damon's voice dropped to a harsh whisper when the blow-dryer got turned off. "But you're not a kid anymore. Don't hurt her."

Nettled at being chastised, Casey turned away to the window. "I wasn't planning on it." No, he planned on making love to her until they were both exhausted.

Damon followed. "Bullshit. You're on the prowl and we all three know it."

"All three?"

"Emma isn't a stupid woman and she's well acquainted with come-ons. In case you've failed to notice, she's got this natural sexuality about her that turns normal men into wildebeests in heat."

Casey's hands curled into fists. Was it his imagination, or was Damon getting stranger by the moment? "I noticed."

Damon's expression lightened, and he even grinned. "It was a facetious statement, man. Believe me, I noticed you noticing."

"Is there a point to this, Devaughn?"

"Yeah. If you're half as honorable as Emma claimed, you'll leave her alone."

Half as honorable? He again wondered exactly what Emma might have said about him. "I can't do that."

Angered, Damon stepped toward him—and Emma came out of the bathroom. She looked…astounding.

Casey immediately forgot all about Damon and his half-baked warnings. Emma's hair, loose and soft and

feminine, bounced gently around her shoulders and
caught the reflection of every light. She wore only a
touch of makeup, which made her eyes even larger,
darker. But it was the gloss on her lips that really got
to Casey. Damn, he wanted to lick it off her mouth,
then taste her, only her. Her mouth drove him nuts it
was so sexy.

The chambray dress fit her and emphasized every
womanly curve without seeming too obvious. She
carried a blouse in one hand, her sandals in the other.
Without looking at him, she bent and slipped on one
sandal, then the other. Enthralled, both he and Damon
watched in silence until she was ready.

"Is Gabe here yet?"

Casey shook himself out of his stupor. He moved
the utilitarian curtain aside and looked out the window. "Just pulled in. I told him I'd watch for him,
so we should go on down."

She nodded and went to sit on the side of the bed
next to B.B. The big dog raised up in silent query.
"I'll be back soon, bud. You sleep."

The dog's tail smacked hard against the mattress in
agreement, and Casey could have sworn he grinned.
Then he resettled his head and went back to sleep.

"He understands you?"

"He knows a lot of phrases, and he's smarter than
most people I know." Emma picked up her purse.
"Besides, he's used to dozing the day away when I
work. He'll be fine."

Damon held the door open and they all went out
to the parking lot together. Gabe stood lounging
against the side of his tow truck in dark sunglasses,
a backward ball cap, ragged cutoffs and an unbut-

toned shirt that showed his tanned chest. All in all, typical weekend wear for Gabe.

Emma smiled when she saw him and said in an aside to Casey, "He hasn't changed a bit." Then Gabe's youngest daughter, five-year-old Briana, stepped out from behind him and Emma laughed. "Well now, that's new!"

Casey grinned. "We wondered if there'd be any girl babies born into the family since the dominant gene appears to be male. But Gabe surprised everyone, including his wife, by fathering not one, but three daughters. They're five, seven and nine years old. All with blond hair and blue eyes. This is Briana, the youngest."

With twinkling eyes, the little girl scooted to Casey and held up her arms, obliging Casey to lift her. He hefted her to his hip, kissed her golden head, and gave her a fierce hug. "Hey, squirt."

"She's beautiful," Emma said, and stroked Briana's little shoulder. Briana beamed at her for the compliment.

"All three of his daughters are."

Emma laughed again. "Actually, she looks like a small feminine version of Gabe."

"Exactly. Makes him nuts, too."

Damon stepped forward with an outstretched hand. "Damon Devaughn. Thank you for coming out on a weekend."

Gabe, always jovial, shrugged off the remark. "Not a problem. Casey said you have a Mustang Boss. Can't very well leave a sweet car like that on the side of the road, not even here in Buckhorn."

"It's not my car. It's Emma's."

"Emma?" His uncle didn't seem to remember her at all, until he went to shake her hand, which caused him to look at her more closely. "You look familiar." He glanced at Casey. "Have we been introduced before?"

Casey wanted to groan. He sent Gabe a look, but his uncle was distracted trying to recall where and when he'd met Emma.

"I'm from here originally," Emma said. "And really, Mr. Kasper, we do appreciate the help."

"Good God, girl, no one calls me mister. Gabe will do, if you don't want to make me feel old." Gabe stared at her a moment more while attempting to recall her. A smile appeared. "That's right, I remember now. You're that girl who…"

He drew up short on his verbal faux pas, and Casey hurried to fill in the awkward silence. "Emma's been away for eight years."

"S'that right?" Gabe lifted the cap from his head, scratched his right ear and then replaced his hat, all the while grinning. "Welcome home, Emma."

Scrupulously polite, Emma said, "I'm just here for a visit."

Gabe took his daughter from Casey. "Don't be silly. You don't *visit* home, because you can't ever really leave it." Before anyone could argue that point, Gabe turned to Damon. "You're coming with me, right?"

Damon pulled his concerned gaze from Emma. "Yes. I have the keys to the Mustang. I was hoping to explore the town while you repaired the car."

"Have you had breakfast?"

"Not yet."

"Then I'll drop you at Ceily's diner. You'll get the best ham and eggs in three counties."

Damon and Emma shared a look of mutual wariness. Not understanding, Casey took Emma's arm. "You remember Ceily, don't you, Em?"

She looked stricken only a moment, and in the next instant her face was blank of any expression. She pulled sunglasses from her purse and slipped them on. Casey noted that her hand shook and her tone was clipped when she finally said, "Yes. I remember her." Her smile appeared forced. "You'll enjoy the food, Damon."

Casey didn't know what had upset her, but he decided it was past time to get on the road. "Damon, we'll see you later." Much, much later. "Gabe, thanks again." He waved to Briana. "Be good to Damon, sweetie."

When Damon slid into the seat next to her, Briana beamed at him and said, "You smell good."

"Why, thank you," Damon said with a chuckle.

Gabe groaned. "This is the penance I pay for my misspent youth. Three flirting daughters will definitely be the death of me."

Emma smiled at the exchange as Casey led her to his car. Her moods changed quicker than the breeze, but eventually he'd understand her. Once they finished the visit to the hospital, he'd have her alone on the lake. He'd get some answers, make some headway—and reestablish old bonds.

He could hardly wait.

CHAPTER SIX

DAMON FELT as if he'd stepped into another world, or at least taken a step back in time. "We're not in Kansas anymore, Toto," he murmured to himself.

Gabe Kasper, a very friendly, laid-back fellow with the absolute worst fashion sense Damon had ever witnessed firsthand, had dropped him off in the middle of the town—if you could call such a small, old-fashioned gathering of buildings a town. But the architecture was impressive, ornate yet sturdy, able to withstand the passing of time.

Prior to letting him out of the truck, Gabe had pointed in the direction of the diner and admonished Damon to stay out of the sun.

True enough, he wasn't much for tanning, and a ball cap, especially one worn backward as Gabe preferred, was out of the question. While looking around, Damon noticed that nearly every person he saw was dressed in a similar fashion. It was like being at Palm Beach during spring break. He wondered how many people constituted the local denizens and how many were vacationers visiting the lake.

Women paraded up and down the sidewalks in shorts and bathing-suit tops. Adolescent boys were shirtless. Some children were barefoot. Every doorway spawned several loiterers and damned if there weren't two grizzled old men in coveralls playing checkers under the shade of the barbershop awning. It was like landing in Mayberry, but with color. Lots and lots of color.

Enormous, lush oak trees lined the side of the road and provided some shade to most of the storefronts. The sky was so blue it dazzled. Flowers grew from every nook and cranny, and birds of every size and song flitted about.

Damon drew a deep breath and felt his lungs expand with fresh, humid air. Jesus, he liked it. A lot.

He strolled along the sidewalk, soaking in the atmosphere and acclimating himself. A few minutes later, he smelled the luscious scents from the diner even before he saw it.

When they'd driven through the night before, Emma had pointed the place out, but other than noting the location, he'd paid little attention. He'd been too worried about Emma, watching her to see how she took her return to Buckhorn.

As an architect, he now studied the simple but unique lines of each structure. The diner was spacious, in the same design as the other buildings around it, but modern windows and roofing materials had been added, making it somewhat unique. He knew that eight years ago it had been gutted by fire, which probably accounted for the improvements. Damon shook his head. Emma had retold the story so many times that he knew it by heart.

He continued along, nodding to the people who gave him cautious looks until he reached the diner. Up close, the modern materials were even more noticeable. Still, the reconstruction was a quality job, nicely executed.

The walkway had been swept clean, the windows were spotless, and the ornate oak front door stood propped open by a large clay flowerpot filled to overflowing with purple, yellow and red flowers. The quiet buzz of conversation mingled with the sounds of dishes clacking, food sizzling on the grill and a jukebox playing.

Damon peered inside, making note of the tidy rows of booths and tables, the immaculate floor, the utilization of every available space. Apparently Ceily did an efficient job of running the diner, and in hiring good help. He wondered if he'd be able to meet her. Based on everything Emma had told him about her, he was curious. He'd already formed an image of her in his mind and he wondered if she'd look as he pictured her—work-worn, tired, frumpy. As he was glancing around, a waitress moved into his view, drawing his attention.

The second Damon's gaze landed on her, everything and everyone else faded into the background. Lord have mercy, they grew the girls healthy in Buckhorn. He leaned into the doorway to watch her, and felt intrigued.

Damon had always considered Emma to be a luscious woman, healthy and earthy and sensual. The woman now bent to a booth picking up dishes was just as luscious, maybe more so because, damn, he didn't view her in any familial way.

He did a visual sweep of her body, taking in every detail and noting the lack of a ring on her left hand, as well as the delicate bracelet circling her slim ankle.

He also noted that she appeared busy but happy, rushed but energized.

Tight, faded jean shorts made her rump look especially round—a deliberate effort on her part, no doubt. A red cotton crop top hugged her breasts and showed off her trim, lightly tanned midriff. A sturdy utility apron with only a few spots on it had been tied loosely around her hips, looking more like decoration than protection against stains. Sun-streaked, sandy-brown hair hung to the middle of her back, contained in a loose ponytail that added to the country-girl charm. She wore snowy-white canvas sneakers on her feet. Cute.

He'd known, admired and sexually enjoyed a lot of polished, sophisticated women. Not once had he ever gotten involved with a country bumpkin. The idea appealed to his sense of adventure and variety. Would she romp with him in the hay? Make him biscuits and gravy the morning after? He grinned to himself, wondering at the possibilities and feeling a tad whimsical.

Someone at the table behind her spoke, and she laughed as she turned—and caught Damon's speculative stare. As if the meeting of their eyes snared her physically, she went still. Her wide smile faded but her green eyes remained bright. Damon estimated her to be in her early thirties. Their gazes locked for a long moment before the customers regained her attention. She dismissed Damon with a quick, curious smile and got back to work.

Miss Ceily had done all right in hiring that one, Damon decided. Not only was she a conscientious worker, but she provided some very nice scenery.

Propelled forward by his own curiosity, Damon
stepped inside. He watched her a moment more to
judge which tables were hers then he seated himself.
And he waited. He didn't stare at her again; that
would have been too obvious. But his awareness of
her was so keen he always knew just where she was
within the diner. He listened to her as she visited with
the other customers, and decided her laugh was nice.
Her voice had the same pleasant country twang he'd
noticed the first time he'd met Emma.

Satisfaction oozed through him as he sensed her
approach. It'd be interesting to see if she suited him.
And if she did, well, this visit might turn out more
stimulating than he'd anticipated.

She set a glass of ice water in front of him. "Hi
there." Without blinking, she leaned her hip on the
edge of his booth and met his bold gaze.

Damon allowed a small smile. Checking for her
name, he glanced at her breasts, but she wore no name
tag, so he couldn't look as long—or as thoroughly—
as he'd have liked. Glancing back at her face, he kept
his gaze fixed, his voice low and heavy in a way that
he knew would indicate his interest. "Hello."

The second he spoke, her slim eyebrows lifted. "A
visitor, huh?"

Her easy, friendly familiarity pleased him. "Guilty.
My lack of accent gave me away?"

"That it did, but don't worry. You won't stand out
too much. This time of year we have a lot of vacationers around." She looked him over, then asked,
"You staying at the lake?"

"No." Damon continued to smile without offering

further explanations. He waited to see if she'd push him or back off.

She did neither. "I didn't think so. You don't look much like a fisherman."

Startled by that disclosure—and a little relieved, because, really, who would *want* to look like a fisherman?—he said, "No?"

Her smile quirked. "Too tidy."

"You have sloppy fishermen in the area, do you?"

"Not sloppy. Relaxed." She straightened away from the table. "Fishing requires a lot of patience and time spent in the weather. You don't look all that patient, and you don't look like you hang outdoors much."

Now *that* sounded vaguely like an insult, causing him to frown. So he didn't have a tan. Hadn't she heard that too much exposure to the sun wasn't healthy for you?

With a look of innocence, as if she hadn't just deliberately riled him, she tapped the menu. "You had a chance to decide what you want, yet?"

Oh, he knew exactly what he wanted. Damon pushed the plastic printed menu aside without interest. "What do you recommend?"

Her smile widened and her lashes lowered in a coy, rather effective manner. "That'd depend. Whatcha in the mood for?"

Damn, her flirting stirred him. It had been far too long since he'd had the relief of sex. "I somehow doubt it's listed on the menu."

"We're not that backward." She shifted, and deftly managed to draw his attention to her legs again. "Why don't you give us a try?"

"All right." He eyed her shapely hips, not lingeringly, but with enough intent that she couldn't miss it. "How about something...hearty."

Suddenly she laughed in delight, tipping her head back and showing a seductive length of throat. She had a husky laugh, and it turned him on. But then, at that particular moment, everything appeared to be turning him on.

"Hearty, huh?"

"That's right."

Smoothing a wisp of tawny hair behind her ear, she said, "All right. We have a sinful egg and ham casserole that'll stick to your ribs till dinnertime."

"Sinful, you say? Interesting. And who prepared it?"

She looked at him beneath her lashes. "Me."

"Ah." He tilted his head to study her. Her lashes were long and thick, her eyes smoky, with small crinkles at the corners that showed her to be a woman used to laughing, a woman who lived her life with enthusiasm. Her nose turned up slightly on the end, giving her an elfin appearance in direct contrast to her earthy sensuality. And her body...he'd love to see her naked. He was fair sick of skinny women on a perpetual diet, honed so tightly that nothing ever jiggled. With a long, leisurely ride, this woman would jiggle—her breasts, her behind...

Feeling the heat expand inside him, Damon stuck out his hand, anxious to touch her. "I'm Damon Devaughn, by the way. I'll be in the area for a little while."

"S'that so?" She took his hand, but didn't perform

the customary shake. Instead, she just held on to him, giving her own brazen show of interest. "I'm Ceily."

Surprise momentarily made him mute. Damn, he hadn't seen that coming. To be sure, he asked, "Ceily, as in the owner of the diner?"

"One and the same." She smiled down at their clasped hands, one eyebrow raised, but she didn't pull away from him. And Damon didn't release her. She had a firm hold, her hand slim, warm, a little rough from work.

For whatever reason, he'd expected Ceily to be older, more timeworn, tired. Emma's memories of her had been of a grown woman, yet Ceily must have had responsibility for the diner at an early age because by his count, she was still young.

Beyond his sexual interest, Damon felt… impressed.

Knowing who she was slanted things though, made them a tad more difficult, but not impossible. He decided to test her before he got any more involved. "I'm here with a friend."

Disappointment made her green eyes darken. "Female friend?"

"Yes." He released her hand and leaned back in his seat, watching for her reaction. "You might remember her. Emma Clark?"

A brief moment of confusion crossed her features, then she brightened. "No kidding? I remember Emma. She's Casey Hudson's age, right?"

Damon scowled. Why the hell would she mention Casey? "That's right. In fact, she's with Casey today, visiting her father in the hospital."

Ceily turned and hollered toward the kitchen.

"Hey, I need a casserole and—" She looked back at Damon. "What do you want to drink?"

"Do you have sweet tea?"

Nodding, she yelled, "And an iced tea."

A dark-haired man in a hair net poked his face into an opening visible behind the bar that led into the kitchen. "Be ready in a sec."

"Thanks." Without being invited, Ceily sat down in the booth opposite Damon. "So Casey's already hooked up with her, huh?" Dimples showed in her cheeks when she grinned. "Doesn't surprise me much. From what I remember, she always did like him. And he's just like his uncles, meaning he's not one to waste time."

"How…reassuring."

Ceily laughed, then crossed her arms on the table-top and leaned toward him. It was a toss-up what fascinated him more—her mouth or her cleavage. "You with her, or just friends?"

"Friends." She wasn't wearing any lipstick, but her naked mouth looked very appealing. Her bottom lip was plump, her upper lip well defined. "If it was more, I wouldn't be flirting with you."

That sexy mouth tilted up. "So you are flirting, huh?"

"Of course." He stared into her eyes without smiling. "And you're flirting back."

She shrugged. "Around here, that might mean something—and then again, it might mean nothing."

"Around here?"

"We're all real sociable and quick to tease."

"I see. So which is it this time?"

She pondered her reply before answering. "I

reckon it means I wouldn't mind showing you around the area, if you're interested.''

Uncertainty made her offer casual, yet Damon noted her anticipation, the way she held herself hopeful. Oh yes, the trip had become quite intriguing.

''My interest has already been established.'' His body hummed with that interest as he began considering what the night might bring. The irony of it amused him. Emma might not like it, but then there was no reason she had to know right off.

He reached across the table and took her hand again. ''So tell me, Ceily. What time do you get off work, and how late do you want to stay out?''

CASEY WATCHED EMMA grow increasingly subdued the farther they got from town. The ride to the hospital took her back along the way she'd come in, to the outskirts of the city proper. The twenty-minute trip had been mostly silent, yet not uncomfortable. From the drive-through, they'd picked up two bottles of orange juice and breakfast sandwiches to eat along the way. Emma had also downed another cup of coffee.

After gathering the sandwich wrappers and empty bottles together, Emma had spent the remainder of the ride looking around with a mixture of awe, recollection and melancholy. She'd missed Buckhorn, that much was plain.

So why had she waited so long to return?

Casey didn't mind her silence as she reacquainted herself with the area. But the closer they got to the hospital, the more she retreated until he could feel her agitation. Was she worried about seeing her father again?

Old habits were indeed hard to break, and Casey found himself wishing he could shield her from the unknown. Would her father be happy to see her again? Or would he treat her with the same callous disregard he'd shown so long ago?

For the rest of his life, Casey knew he'd remember the look on her bruised, tear-streaked face the night her father had jerked her forward, presenting her as a problem, ridding himself of her.

It still infuriated him, so how must it make *her* feel to face Dell again?

The roads here were smooth, open, with no need to shift from fifth gear. Though the temperature had reached eighty already, with high humidity, Emma had been all for skipping the air-conditioning in favor of leaving the convertible top down. Casey glanced toward her, watching her hair dance behind her, seeing the concentrated, determined expression on her face.

He tightened his hands on the steering wheel, fighting the urge to reach for her. "Hey."

She started, then glanced at him. "What?"

"You okay?"

"Sure, I'm fine." She clutched at her purse in her lap, giving away her unease. "Just thinking."

"About what?"

"I don't know. Everything. Nothing." She turned toward him, folding one leg onto the seat. She had to hold her hair out of her face with her hand. "Buckhorn hasn't changed at all."

Her position exposed more of her thigh—something Casey made immediate note of. As a teenager, she'd kept a golden tan. Now she looked fair, with only a faint kiss from the sun. He had to clear his throat. "Not much, no."

"Everything seems exactly the same, maybe aged a little more. But still…the same."

"That bothers you?"

She leaned back in her seat and stared up at the sky. "No." She spoke so low her voice almost got carried away on the wind. Casey strained to hear her. "It's just that I've changed so much, and yet I still feel like I don't belong here."

A vague panic took Casey by surprise. "This is your home." He sounded far too gruff, almost angry. "Of course you belong."

Silence hung between them, pressing down on him, until she swiveled her head toward him. "If you have anything you need to do today, you can just drop me at the hospital."

It bugged the hell out of him how she kept trying to shove him away. "I'll wait for you."

"Dad's probably not up to a long visit, but it still might be an hour."

"I'll wait."

She stared at him, so Casey gave her a smile to counter his insistent tone and then, because he *had* to touch her, he opened his hand over the gearshift in invitation. She hesitated only a moment before reaching across and lacing her fingers in his. Like old times.

Now, that felt right—Emma reaching for him, accepting him. The touch of her hand to his, palm to

palm, fingers intertwined, filled him with a sense of
well-being.

Two minutes later, he parked in the crowded visi-
tors' section of the hospital lot. Emma, now utterly
silent, flipped down her visor to quickly comb her hair
and reapply lip gloss. He'd seen the feminine routine
performed by numerous women. But this was Emma,
and she fascinated him.

He went around to her side of the car and held her
door open. "You look beautiful, Emma."

She sent him a look of tolerance. "I'll settle for
passable, thank you."

"Very passable, then." Casey took her arm as they
crossed the scorching lot. Damp heat lifted off the
pavement in waves. "Do you remember the last time
we were here together?"

Nodding, she said, "With your Uncle Jordan and
his wife. But that was before they'd gotten married."

"The night they met, actually. Georgia's mother,
Ruth, was sick, and Jordan had brought them, along
with Georgia's two kids, to the hospital." While driving to the hospital to lend a helping hand, Casey had
found Emma walking on the side of the road. As if
the picture had been painted on his brain, he recalled
exactly how she'd looked that night in ultrashort
shorts, a hot-pink halter, and her skin dewy from the
humidity as she'd sashayed down the roadway. *All
alone.*

He'd been worried about her, as usual, and had
insisted on giving her a ride. She'd climbed into his
car, then made him sweat even more with wanting
her.

Shaking his head, Casey wondered why the hell he

hadn't taken what she'd offered. If he had, maybe he wouldn't feel as he did now. And maybe he wouldn't have felt this way for most of his adult life.

Putting himself back on track, he continued with the family discussion. "Ruth still has some problems with her lungs, but now she's hooked up with Misty and Honey's dad, and he pampers her. She's doing pretty good."

"Do you mean your grandfather? Do you work for him now?"

"Stepgrandfather officially, but yeah. I've been working with him since I finished college. I'm the executive vice president of sales and marketing."

"Wow." Emma sounded genuinely impressed. "That sounds like an important position."

Self-conscious about the rapid and consistent promotions, Casey grumbled, "My grandfather has shoved me right up the ladder. He takes every opportunity to give me a bigger office, a better parking spot, more perks. It's his goal that I'll eventually run the company for him."

"What exactly is his company?"

"Electronics, computer hardware. You know, very high-tech, state-of-the-art stuff for businesses. Boring stuff." He laughed at himself. "Very boring."

"I see." Her look was filled with comprehension in a way exclusive to Emma. She understood him, which made long explanations unnecessary. "So you don't like your job, or is it your grandfather you don't like?"

He avoided giving her a direct answer by saying, "I like him fine. He's loosened up a lot, especially since he and Ruth married."

That disclosure diverted her. "Wow, everyone is getting married."

Casey stared ahead, strangely annoyed. "Nope, not everyone."

Emma did a double take, probably trying to judge his mood. When she saw his sour expression, she went a little quiet. "Like everyone else, Casey, you'll eventually find the right woman and swear love everlasting."

She didn't sound overly thrilled with that prospect, which pretty much mirrored his own feelings on the matter. Marriage? Just the thought of it left him tight and uncertain in a way he refused to accept. "We'll see."

Emma bit her lip, feeling the new tension just as he did. In an obvious effort to lighten the mood, she said, "Georgia had two really cute little kids, right?"

"Yeah, but they're not so little anymore. Lisa is fifteen and a real heartbreaker, though she doesn't know it, or else doesn't care." He glanced down at Emma, saw her pensive frown, and regretted adding to her uneasiness. She had her hands full with the coming confrontation. "Lisa's more into her studies than boys, and she's so smart she scares me."

Emma relaxed enough to grin at that. "As I recall, nothing scares you—especially a female."

That was far from the truth, but Casey just shook his head. "Adam's thirteen, a helluva football player and real interested in becoming a vet like Jordan. He's even got the soothing voice down pat. They're great kids."

She gave a wistful sigh. "You've got a lot of nieces and nephews now, don't you?"

He shrugged. To Emma, it probably seemed like a lot. She had only her mother and father, and had been estranged from them for a long time. "Jordan has those two; Morgan has Amber, now eleven, and Garrett who's nine. And Gabe has the three daughters." Casey grinned. "By the way, they not only look like Gabe, but they all take after him, too."

"Natural-born flirts, huh?"

"Yep. And it makes him crazy. Gabe's about the most doting father you'll ever meet, and he shakes whenever he talks about his girls growing old enough to date."

Emma snorted. "He's probably remembering his own unrestrained youth."

"Gabe was rather unrestrained, wasn't he? Not that any of the women complained."

"'Course not."

Casey admired the way her eyes glowed, her cheeks dimpled when she was amused. Hearing Emma laugh was a treat. "I have a little brother too, you know. Shohn, who's almost ten now. He's a hyper little pug, never still, and he knows no fear." Knowing he bragged and not caring, Casey added, "He learned to water-ski when he was only five. Now he's like a damn pro out there."

"Uh-huh. And who taught him to ski?"

Casey pushed the glass doors open and ushered her inside. "Me."

Air-conditioning rolled over them as they stepped into the hospital and headed for the elevator. Casey transferred his hand to the small of Emma's back, and just that simple touch stirred him. Her waist dipped in, taut and graceful, then flared out to her hips.

Standing next to her emphasized the differences in
their sizes. He told himself that was why he felt protective. Then. Now.

Always.

Naturally, he cared about her. They'd been friends
for a long time, and that, combined with the sexual
chemistry, heightened his awareness of her. It wasn't
anything more complicated than that.

But even he had to admit that talking with Emma
came pretty easy. He couldn't remember the last time
he'd shared stories about his family. When he was
with a woman, he remained polite, attentive, but everything felt very…surface. There wasn't room for
personal stuff. Yet with Emma, he'd just run down
his whole damn lineage—and enjoyed it too much.

He was disturbed with his own realizations on that,
when he heard someone say his name. He looked
down the hallway and saw Ms. Potter, the librarian,
being pushed in a wheelchair by a nurse, followed by
her daughter, Ann. Casey drew Emma to a halt. "Just
a second, okay?"

He went to Ms. Potter and bent to kiss her cheek,
which warmed her with a blush. "Getting out today,
huh?"

"Finally."

"You were only here two days," the nurse teased,
then added, "And you were a wonderful patient."

Ms. Potter fussed with the elaborate bouquet of
spring flowers in her lap. "Even so, these will look
much better on my desk than on the windowsill
here."

Casey gave her a mock frown. "Your desk? Now
don't tell me you're rushing right back to work."

"Monday morning, and it's none too soon. I can just imagine what a mess my books are in. No one ever puts them away properly."

Ann stepped up to the side of the wheelchair. Her brown eyes twinkled and her dark hair fell in a soft wave to her shoulders when she nodded down at her mother. "The flowers are gorgeous, Casey. Thanks for bringing them to her."

"My pleasure." He saw Ann look beyond him to Emma, so he drew her forward. "Ann, Ms. Potter, do you remember Emma Clark?"

Ms. Potter, always sharp as a tack, said, "I do. It was a rare thing for you to come to the library, young lady."

Embarrassed, Emma stammered, "I—I've never been much of a reader."

"You only need to find the right books for you. Come and see me next week and we'll get you set up."

Emma blushed. "Yes, ma'am."

Casey did his best not to laugh. Ms. Potter had a way of putting everyone on the spot, but always with good intentions. She genuinely cared about people and it showed.

Ann stared hard at Emma before her eyes widened with recognition. "Now I remember. You went to school with me, didn't you?"

"A long time ago, yes. I think we were in the same English class."

"That's right. Didn't you move away before your senior year?"

"Yes." To avoid going into details, Emma grinned

down at Ms. Potter. "That's a doozy of a cast you have on your leg. And very art deco, too."

Ms. Potter reached out and patted Casey's hand. "You can blame this rascal right here. I was all set to keep it snowy white, as is appropriate for a librarian and a widow my age. But Casey showed up with colored markers." She pointed to the awkward rendition of a flower vine twining around her ankle in bright colors of red and blue and yellow. "Before I could find something to smack him with, Casey had flowers drawn all over me. After that, everyone else had to take a turn."

The nurse shook her head. "She loved it. She wouldn't let me move those markers and she made sure everyone who came in left their signature behind."

"Tattletale," Ms. Potter muttered with a smile.

Emma bent to look more closely and laughed. Casey had signed his name to his artwork with a flourish. Others had added a sun and birds and even a rainbow. "It looks lovely."

"I think so—now that I'm used to it."

Laughing, Ann said, "Mom is insisting on going back to work, but she'll only be there part-time and with limited duties. Your dad is stopping in later today to see her, to make sure it'll be okay, and he'll keep tabs on her."

Casey shook his finger at Ms. Potter. "I know Dad won't want you overdoing it."

Ann said, "That's what I told her, which is why I got two student employees to promise to stay with her and follow her directions. They'll be doing most of the lifting and storing of books." Ann winked at

Casey. "Mom'll have the library back in order in no time."

"I'll be checking in on you with Dad," Casey warned, "so you better follow doctor's orders. That was a nasty break you had." He took Ann's hand. "If you need anything, let me know."

Ann pulled him toward her for a hug. "We'll be fine, but thank you. And, please, thank Morgan again for us. If he hadn't found her car that night..."

Casey explained to Emma, "Ms. Potter ran her car off the road, and because of the broken leg, she couldn't get out to flag anyone down. Morgan was doing his nightly check and noticed the skid marks in the road. He found her over the berm and halfway down the hill."

"If you're going to tell it, tell it right. The deer ran me off the road." Ms. Potter sniffed. "The silly thing jumped out right in front of me. Of course, he escaped without a scratch."

"Thank God for Morgan. I thought she was at bingo and wouldn't have worried until she didn't come home. She might have been there for hours if it hadn't been for him."

"It's his job," Casey commented.

Ann turned to Emma, and her dark eyes were sincere but cautious. "I should get Mom home. Emma, it was nice to see you again."

Casey slipped his arm around Emma as she said, "Thank you. You too."

"Have you moved back home?" Ann asked.

"No, just visiting my father."

"He's here at the hospital too," Casey explained. But because he didn't want Ms. Potter or Ann to ask

Emma too many questions, he gave their farewells. Ann had been as nice as always, but anyone could blunder onto uncomfortable ground. He kissed Ms. Potter on the cheek again, and drew Emma away.

They moved inside the elevator and Emma pressed the button for the fifth floor. "Is Ann married?"

She asked that casually, but she looked and sounded stiff. Casey wanted to hug her close, but he had no idea why. "Not yet, but she and Nate—you remember Morgan's deputy?—are getting real friendly, especially since this happened with her mom. On top of the broken leg, she had more scrapes and bruises than I can count. Nate was the one who went to get Ann while Morgan took Ms. Potter to the hospital."

"They seem nice."

"Ms. Potter's a sweetheart, and Ann's just like her."

"Pretty too."

Casey shrugged. Ann had dark hair and eyes, and a gentle smile. He supposed she was an attractive woman. What he noticed most about her though was that she didn't judge others. She had a generous heart, and he liked that about her. "She's thanked Morgan about a dozen times now. She and her mom are really close."

Emma actually winced. If he hadn't been watching her so closely, he wouldn't have seen it. Emma quickly tried to cover up her reaction. "As big and bulky as he is, Morgan can be really gentle. He's a perfect sheriff."

Casey wasn't fooled. "I think so."

"Your dad's the same way." She spoke fast, almost chattered. "I remember when most every female in Buckhorn mooned over him and your uncles. Even the girls my age used to eye them and fantasize."

Casey put his hands in his pockets and leaned against the elevator wall. "You too?"

She cast him a quick, flustered look. "No. Of course not."

"How come?"

"I had my sights set on a different target." Her attempt at humor fell flat, even though she lightly elbowed him. "I was embarrassingly obvious."

Something in her tone got to Casey. Nothing new in that. Emma had always touched him in ways no one else could. "You never embarrassed me, Em."

She appeared rattled by the seriousness he'd injected, and quickly turned her attention to the advancing floor numbers. Casey crowded closer to her and inhaled the subtle aroma of her hair and skin. It was the same as and yet different from what he remembered. Would she taste the same?

The elevator door hissed open and Emma all but leaped out. He had to take big steps to keep up with her headlong flight down the hallway toward her father's room. Her nervousness had returned in a crushing wave. He could feel it, but was helpless as to how to help her.

When she reached the right door, she gave Casey an uncertain look. "There's a waiting room at the end of the hall if you want to watch a little television or get some coffee." She pushed her hair behind her ear with a trembling hand.

He glanced down the hall. It was empty. Not that it mattered. In that particular moment, he had to hold her. He pulled Emma against his chest and gently enfolded her in his arms. She resisted him for a moment before giving up and relaxing into him.

God, it felt good, having her so close again. He lowered his mouth to her ear, felt her warmth and the silk of her hair against his jaw. "I'll be waiting if you need me."

She lifted her head to stare up at him, embarrassed, confused, a little flushed. "I'm fine, Casey. Really."

The softness of her cheek drew his hand. He wanted to stroke her all over, find all her soft spots. Her hot spots.

Taking her—and himself—by surprise, he bent and kissed her. Her lips parted on a gasp, an unconscious invitation that was hard to resist. But Casey kept the kiss light, contenting himself with one small stroke of his tongue just inside her bottom lip. He leaned back, hazy with need, not just lust but so many roiling emotions he nearly groaned.

Using just her fingertips, Emma touched her mouth, drew a breath, and then laughed shakily. "Well, okay then." Bemused, she shook her head, turned and opened her father's door to peer inside.

Casey watched as she entered the room. Damn it, he'd rattled her when all he'd meant to do was offer comfort.

He heard her whisper, "Dad?" with a lot of uncertainty and something more, some deep yearning that came from her soul. Then the door shut and he couldn't hear anything else.

Humming with frustration, Casey stalked into the waiting room. There was no one else there, yet empty foam cups were left everywhere and magazines had been scattered about. He occupied himself by picking up the garbage, rearranging the magazines and generally tidying things up.

It didn't help. Pent-up energy kept him pacing. All he really wanted to do was barge into that room with Emma to make sure her father didn't do or say anything to hurt her. Again.

He hated feeling this way—helpless, at loose ends. Emma was a grown woman now, independent, strong. She neither wanted nor needed his help. There was no reason for him to want to shield her, not anymore.

Moving around didn't help his mood, not when his imagination kept dredging up the sight of her bruised face eight years ago.

After about ten minutes, he gave up. Telling himself that he had every right to check on her, Casey strode across the hallway and silently opened the door to Dell Clark's room. The first bed, made up with stiff sheets and folded back at one corner, was empty. A separation curtain had been drawn next to it so that he couldn't see the second bed where Dell rested. But he could hear Emma softly speaking and he drew up short at the sound of her pleading voice.

Without a single speck of guilt, Casey took a muted step in and listened.

CHAPTER SEVEN

DELL'S VOICE sounded weak and somewhat slurred, from the stroke or the medication, Casey wasn't sure which. But he could understand him, and he heard his determination. "See yer mama."

"Dad." Weariness, and a vague acceptance, tinged Emma's soft denial, making Casey want to march to her side. "You know I can't do that. Besides, I doubt she even wants to see me. And if I did go, we'd just fight."

Casey realized that Emma hadn't yet seen her mother. She hadn't even been to her home, choosing instead to stay in a motel. He frowned with confusion and doubt.

"She'szer mother."

"Dad, please don't upset yourself. You need your rest."

Shaken by the desolation in Emma's words, Casey didn't dare even breathe. Their conversation didn't make sense to him. Why would Emma make a point of coming to see her father, the man who'd run her off, but not want to visit her mother?

"Damn it." Dell managed to curse clearly enough, but before he spoke further, he began wheezing and thrashing around. Casey heard the rustling of fast movement, heard Emma shushing him, soothing him.

"Calm down, Dad, please. You'll pull your IV out."

In his upset, his words became even more slurred, almost incomprehensible. "Hate this...damn arm..."

"The nurse says you'll get control of your arm again soon. It's just a temporary side effect of the stroke. You've already made so much progress—"

"*'Mnot a baby.*"

A moment of silence. "I know you're not. I'm sorry that I'm upsetting you. It's just that I want to help."

"Go 'way."

There was so much tension in the small room, Casey couldn't breathe. Then Emma whispered, "Maybe this was a bad idea, maybe I shouldn't have come home..."

Casey's heart skipped a beat, then dropped like a stone to the bottom of his stomach. If she hadn't come home, he wouldn't have ever gotten the chance to see her again.

Dell didn't relent, but a new weariness softened his words. "She neez you."

As Emma reseated herself in the creaky plastic chair, she brushed the curtain, causing it to rustle. "Dad, she doesn't even like me. She never has. When she called to tell me about you, she made it clear that nothing's changed. I've tried to help her, and it's only made things worse."

"Can't help 'erself," Dell insisted.

Even before she spoke, Casey could feel Emma's pain. It sounded in her words, weary and hoarse and bordering on desperate. "You have to stop making excuses for her—for her sake, as well as your own."

"Love 'er."

Sounding so sad, Emma murmured, "I know you
do." Then softly, she added, "More than anything."

"Emma..."

Images from the past whirled through Casey's
mind. Emma hurt. Emma wandering the streets at
night. Emma with no money for new clothes or
schoolbooks.

Emma needy for love.

He fisted his hands until his knuckles turned white.
I know you do, she'd said. *More than anything.*

Or anyone?

With sudden clarity, Casey knew that Emma wasn't
estranged from her father.

No, as he remembered it, Dell Clark had been genuinely worried when Emma had run off. He'd blus-
tered and grumped and cast blame, yet there'd been
no mistaking the fear and regret in his eyes.

But her mother...not once had she asked about
Emma, or shown any concern at all. Casey had all
but forgotten about the woman because folks scarcely
saw her anymore. She stayed hidden away, seldom
going out.

Now Emma was in town, but staying at a motel
rather than her home. And despite her father's pleas,
she resisted even a visit with her mother.

In rapid order, Casey rearranged the things he
knew, the things he'd always believed, and decided
he'd come to some very wrong assumptions. Just as
Emma had fled to his house for protection, perhaps
Dell had gone along with that plan for the same reason.

Because she needed a way out.

Jesus. He propped his hands on his hips and dropped his head forward, trying to decide what to do, what to believe.

The door swung open behind him, making him jump out of the way, and Dell's doctor entered, trailed by a nurse. Recognizing Casey from his association with Sawyer, the doctor bellowed a jovial greeting. "Casey! Well, this is a surprise."

In good humor, he thwacked Casey on the shoulder. There was nothing Casey could do now but take his hand. "Dr. Wagner. Good to see you again."

"But what are you doing here?" Concern replaced Dr. Wagner's smile. "The family's okay?"

Emma stepped around the curtain, rigid, appalled, her attention glued to Casey. Her big dark eyes were accusing, her mouth pinched.

Casey got his first look at Dell and realized that he looked like death. His face was white, his eyes red-rimmed and vague from medication, one more open than the other. His mouth was a grim line, drooping on one side, and his graying hair stuck out around an oxygen tube that hooked over his ears and ran across his cheeks to his nostrils. More tubes fed into his arm through an IV. Machinery hummed around him.

Aw hell. Casey watched Emma for a moment, hoping to make her understand that everything would be okay now, that it didn't matter what he'd heard or what had happened in the past. But she turned away from him.

"The family's fine," Casey said without looking away from her. "I'm here with Emma."

The doc apparently sensed the heavy unease in the

room and glanced from one person to the next. "I take it you two know each other then?"

"Yeah." Accepting that everything had changed—the past, his feelings, his motivations—Casey moved toward her. "Emma and I go way back." His attention shifted to Dell. Damn it, the man was too sick to deal with Casey's anger right now. He drew a breath and collected himself. "Hello, Mr. Clark."

Dell gripped the sheet with one gnarled hand while the other flailed before resting at his side. "Sneakin' 'round."

"Of course I wasn't." He reached Emma and looped his arm around her stiff shoulders. She didn't look at him and, if anything, her expression was more shuttered now that he touched her. "I just stepped in to check on Emma."

Emma ducked away from him. "Dr. Wagner, I'd like to speak to you privately."

"Yes, yes, of course." The good doctor looked stymied.

Casey nodded to him. "We'll wait outside until you finish your checkup with Dell."

"Use the waiting room. I'll come for you there."

Emma shoved the door open and strode out. She'd only made it three steps when Casey caught her. His long fingers wrapped around her upper arm in a secure yet gentle hold. "Oh no you don't."

She whirled on him, equal parts furious, indignant and, if Casey didn't miss his bet, afraid. *"You had no right."*

Still holding her with one hand, Casey brushed the backs of his knuckles over her cheek with the other. "Now there's where you're wrong, sweetheart. You gave me the right eight years ago when you came to me. And this time, it won't be so easy for you to run off. This time you're going to tell me the truth.'' He touched the corner of her mouth. ''You can count on it.''

EMMA STRUGGLED to get enough air into her starved lungs, but the panic set in quickly. Nothing had really changed, she knew that now. Her reaction to Casey, his protective instincts, her smothering fear...it was all still there. It had only taken one day back in Buckhorn to make it all resurface.

Just like his father and uncles, Casey had a soft spot for anyone in need. She hadn't wanted him to see her that way. Not this time. Not now. But given what he'd just overheard, she knew damn well he'd be doling out the pity again. God, she couldn't bear it.

She licked dry lips and cautiously tried to free her arm. He didn't let go.

''Why are you doing this, Casey?''

All his attention remained on her mouth, unnerving her further. ''Doing what?''

She rolled her shoulder to indicate his hold. ''This...overwhelming bombardment. You insist on coffee, insist on giving me a ride, insist you have to know everything even though it's none of your business. Why nose in where I don't want you?''

''Where is it you don't want me, sweetheart?''

Oh, that soft, coaxing voice. She couldn't let him do this to her. She'd come home because she had to, and all along she'd expected to see Casey again. This time, however, she'd wanted his respect. "What's between me and my father doesn't concern you."

Filled with conviction, Casey started to lead her into the waiting room.

"Casey!"

They both looked up to see the young nurse who'd accompanied the doctor into her father's room. She'd slipped out the door and she had her sights set on Casey. As she bore down on them with a proprietary air, Emma tried to retreat.

She heard Casey's annoyed sigh as he tugged her closer and draped his arm over her shoulders. Emma didn't know if he did it as a sign of support, or to make damn sure she couldn't slip away. Whatever his purpose, it didn't matter. She couldn't let it matter.

But being tucked that close to him shook her on every level. He was so hard, so tall and strong and masculine. Heat and a wonderful deep scent seemed a part of him, encompassing her and filling her up in places she'd forgotten were empty. With every pore of her being, she was aware of him. He was her living, breathing fantasy, and he kept touching her in that man/woman way, just as she used to dream of him doing.

Only the timing was all wrong now. Or she wasn't right for him—and never would be.

She had to get away.

The nurse halted in front of them, her smile bold, her posturing plain. Unlike Ann, who had been cordial, not by so much as a flicker of an eyelash did this woman acknowledge Emma. "Casey, I had such a nice time last weekend." She spoke with a heavy dose of suggestion. "I sort of expected you to call."

While Emma went stiff enough to crackle, Casey was loose and casual and relaxed, as if he didn't hold Emma prisoner at his side, forcing her through this awkward come-on.

"I've been busy." And then to Emma, "Lois and I were both at the same party last weekend."

Lois? Forgetting her own discomfort for a moment, Emma took in the bouncing brown hair and heavy hazel eyes. Recognition dawned. "Lois Banker?"

With an effort, Lois pulled her gaze from Casey. She lifted perfectly plucked eyebrows. "That's right. And you are…?"

Unbelievable, Emma thought in wonder. At least the maturity had shown on Ann. Her dark hair was shorter now, and there'd been a few laugh lines around her eyes. But Lois…she looked just as she had in high school. She was still pretty, perky, stacked.

She still had a thing for Casey.

Emma dredged up a smile even as she lifted her chin, preparing for the worst. "You don't remember me, but we went to school together." She held out a hand. "Emma Clark."

Lois scowled as she scrutinized Emma, and then slowly, with the jogging of her memory, her lip curled. "Emma Clark. Yes, I remember you." She shifted away from Emma's hand as if fearing contamination.

Emma found the petty attitude ridiculous, but not unexpected. Lois had never hid her dislike of her. But Casey pulled Emma a little closer and his fingers on her shoulder contracted, gently massaging her in a manner far too familiar. Of course, Lois made note of it, and her expression darkened even more.

Casey said, "Emma is back for a visit."

"A brief visit?"

You wish, Emma thought, and then was appalled at herself. Good God, she had no claim on Casey, and Lois certainly had no reason to be jealous of her. "Until my father is well."

Lois's eyes narrowed. "I hadn't made the connection." She glanced at Casey's hand on Emma. "Mr. Clark... He's the one who was drunk when he had a stroke, isn't he?"

Emma took the well-planned words like a punch on the chin. They dazed her. And they hurt.

"My father doesn't drink." Defensive and a little numb, Emma retreated. "Excuse me, please."

Casey released her as she pushed away. "Emma?"

On wobbly legs, Emma wandered into the waiting room and headed for a plastic padded seat, praying she wouldn't embarrass herself by tearing up.

Why would Lois say her father had been drinking? Emma knew for a fact that he never touched alcohol. Like her, he'd made other choices.

In order to find answers, would she have to go see her mother, after all? Memories fell over her in a suffocating wave.

Then Lois's voice reached her, offering a much-needed distraction.

"Casey, what in the world are you doing with that nasty girl?"

In response to the slur, Casey became terse. "Nasty girl, Lois? Just what the hell does that mean?"

"Oh come on, Case." Lois's laugh of disbelief

grated along Emma's nerves until she shivered. "She was the biggest slut around and everyone knows it. Besides, from what I've heard, you certainly had first-hand knowledge about—"

"Shut up."

Lois gasped, but otherwise remained silent. Emma squeezed her eyes shut. Firsthand knowledge? Is that what people thought, that Casey had given in to her relentless pursuit? What a laugh.

Then a worse theory occurred to Emma and she curled her arms around her stomach. Oh no. Surely no one had heard her outrageous claims of being pregnant. Her father wouldn't have told a soul, and Casey's family wasn't the type to gossip. Yet Lois had inferred something...

"You need to grow up, Lois, and learn some manners."

"*I* need to learn manners?" Her outrage was clear. "I'm not the one who slept with every guy in Buckhorn."

Casey snorted. "As I recall, not that many guys were asking."

"Casey!"

"See ya around, Lois."

The sound of Lois's angry, retreating footfalls couldn't be missed. Emma sighed, aware of Casey's approach but unsure what she should say to him. Already she'd caused him problems, but he didn't want to hear her apologies, he'd been plain about that.

She felt steadier now, but still swamped in confusion. Her father didn't drink—never had—and she knew in her heart he never would. What had Lois meant by her comment?

Emma expected Casey to seat himself. Instead, he crouched down beside her. "Em?"

Startled, Emma stared at him.

With concern darkening his brown eyes, he said, "Hey. You okay?"

Casey came from a long line of caregivers. As a doctor, his father tended everyone from infants to the elderly. Being the town sheriff, Morgan set out to protect the innocent, and Jordan was the perfect vet with a voice that soothed and a manner that reassured. Even Gabe, the resident handyman, made a point of lending a helping hand to anyone who needed it.

She understood Casey's nature, but did he think she was made of fluff? "Why wouldn't I be?"

"Lois is a bitch."

Emma couldn't help but chuckle at that. "No, she's just hung up on you. She saw your arm around me and misunderstood."

"She understood." He put his rough palm on her knee with his long fingers curling around her. She hadn't realized the back of her knee could be so sensitive until Casey's fingertips brushed there. "I'm sorry she said what she did."

Trying to ignore his touch, Emma put her hand over his. "It's not the first time, Casey. If you go around alienating your friends over me, you're going to find yourself pretty lonely."

He ignored her warning to ask, "She's called you names before?" As he spoke, he clasped both her knees and Emma had the flashing thought of him pushing her legs open and settling between them. The image had an instantaneous effect on her body: her breath hitched, her belly tingled, her flesh heated. She didn't have the time or concentration for this.

In a rush, she shoved to her feet and stepped away. "Of course she did. Most of the boys from here—men now, I suppose—wanted to get me in bed and most of the girls hated me because of it."

Very slowly, Casey came to his feet. "She's jealous."

How ridiculous. "Hardly. Everyone always knew that I wanted you, but that you always turned me down."

Casey looked pained. "I'm sorry, Em."

"What did she mean when she said you had first-hand knowledge about me?"

He hesitated.

"Casey?"

With a shrug in his tone, he said, "For a while, people thought you ran off because of me." His eyes narrowed. "No one knew about that night, how your father brought you to me. No one knew that I asked you to stay—but you left anyway."

Startled, Emma could have sworn she heard resentment in his tone. But that didn't make any sense. "I'm glad that's all it is."

Sounding almost lethal, Casey repeated, "You're glad?"

He couldn't understand. "I didn't want you insulted, but I don't care what she says about me—I never have."

Casey watched her with brooding intensity. "I don't believe that."

The day had been too tumultuous for her to hold on to her temper. "And I don't care if you don't believe it. I made my choices and I've lived with them.''

''Em...''

''I slept around. So what?'' Bitterness that had simmered for years suddenly boiled over. ''Just because I'm female it's a huge sin to enjoy sex, to enjoy being touched? How many females have you slept with, Casey?''

His jaw tightened.

''Ah. Should I take that blank expression to mean there are too many to count? What about Lois's reference to last weekend? Did you sleep with her then?''

''No.''

She found that hard to believe and let him know it with a look. ''But because you're male, that's just fine, right? Better than fine. What makes you a stud makes me a whore.''

''Stop it, Em.''

The furious rasp of his voice didn't register. ''No one's ever talked about all the guys who bed hop, the guys who came to me. But a woman...''

''*Stop it.*''

Emma went slack-jawed at his raised voice. Never in her life had she heard that particular tone from Casey. With her, he'd been cajoling, teasing, concerned, sometimes firmly insistent. Always gentle. But never outraged.

Of course, she'd known him only as a boy. Now he was a man.

She blinked at him, a little awed by the level of his anger. It showed in every taut, bunched line of his muscled body. His jaw was clenched, his hands curled into fists. Oh boy.

Emma pulled herself together. She hadn't intended to ever have this discussion with Casey, but since it had begun, she wished she'd chosen a better place than a hospital waiting room.

More in control of herself, and her voice lower now, Emma sighed. "Casey, I'm not ashamed of my past. At least, not that part of it." There were other things, things her family had done, things she'd covered up, the way she'd always pressured him, that still made her hot with regret. But not her sexuality. "I was young and healthy and I enjoyed sex. I still enjoy sex."

A low savage sound escaped him, similar to a snarl. He locked his hands behind his head and paced away.

His reaction stunned her. It almost looked as if he was restraining himself—and had a devil of a time doing so. "If you can't deal with that then you should head on home now. I'll find a ride back to the motel."

Casey turned and stalked to the waiting-room door. For one heart-stopping moment, Emma assumed he was going to storm out in a rage. He was leaving her and her heart hurt so badly she nearly doubled over with the crushing pain. She knew Casey would never love her, but she'd already started hoping that they could be friends.

Instead, he belatedly snapped the door shut to afford them some privacy. When he turned to face her, he still looked livid but he, too, had lowered his voice.

"I don't give a royal fuck how many boys you slept with, Emma."

Despite herself, his wording made her mouth fall open.

Very slowly, with intimidating deliberation, Casey stalked her. "But I do care that you were too young to be making those decisions."

Her chin lifted. "You're telling me you waited?"

"Apparently longer than you did." He pointed a finger at her. "And before you say it, before you assume that being in an all-male household gave me encouragement to screw any female who offered, you should know that I got a lot of lectures on responsibility. Dad, Morgan, Jordan—hell, even Gabe—they all endlessly harped on about ramifications. What might be meaningless sex to me could mean a whole lot more to a girl, especially if she got pregnant, or her folks found out. So, no, I didn't indiscriminately indulge in opportunities."

"And it bothers you that I didn't show that same restraint?" She kept her chin high, but the idea that he'd start judging her now hurt.

"What bothers me is that you did a hell of a lot of stuff because you were always lost and alone." His expression hardened, his jaw drew tight. "And I didn't do enough to help you."

"*No*—"

He gave her a warning look that made her swallow her automatic denial. "It's my turn, Emma, so you just be quiet and listen."

Emma snapped her mouth shut and began backing up as he kept advancing. Never had he looked so big, so imposing. So irritated with her.

She bumped into the wall and was annoyed with herself for retreating. She wasn't afraid of Casey. Out of all the things she'd ever felt for him, not once had fear ever been an issue.

Casey crowded into her, caging her in with his body. When she started to sidle away, he gripped her shoulders and held her firm. They stared at each other in silence until Emma gave up and held still.

"I care that you've been lying to me from the start."

"But..."

"I care that I let you get away."

Her eyes widened. *Let her get away?* Far as she knew, Casey hadn't wanted her to stay. Oh, he'd offered her help because Casey was the type of man who could do nothing else. But he'd made it clear many times that she didn't factor into his future. Well, this *was* his future, and just because she'd materialized didn't mean...

His hands kneaded her shoulders absently, while his gaze burned. "And you can bet your sweet ass I care that *I've* never had you." He leaned closer and his voice dropped to a guttural whisper. "I care about that a lot."

Her heart thundered, and her pulse went wild. Unable to maintain eye contact with him so close, Emma looked away. But Casey wasn't allowing that. He put a fist under her chin and brought her face back around, forcing her to meet his burning gaze. His eyes had narrowed with intent, starting a trembling deep inside her. "You quote double standards to me, but you wanna know what's really unfair?"

"No."

He pressed into her until she felt his hard flat abdomen against her belly. Oh God. Her whole body came alive, quivering with primal awareness.

"It's unfair for a gorgeous young woman to keep throwing herself at a guy until he can't sleep nights for wanting her too much. And then she runs off and no other woman will do because he has a taste for her—a goddamned hunger—yet, damn it, she's gone."

"Casey..." She gave the breathless complaint automatically. She couldn't allow herself to believe him. Always, he'd rejected her, wanting no more than friendship. Time apart couldn't have changed that.

His fingers tunneled into her hair, holding her head still. He lowered his forehead to hers and his eyes closed, his voice going rough and deep. "It's unfair because now that you're here again, all grown up and sexier than ever, you no longer want me."

She felt his warm breath on her lips, felt the heat of his frustration, his urgency, which sparked her own. Her body was melting into his, her nerve endings tingling and alive. Not want him? She was dying for him.

"I'm sorry, sweetheart," he murmured against her mouth, "but I don't intend to let you get away with it."

He said that so simply, sort of slipping it in there on her, it took a second for his statement to sink in. When his meaning dawned on her, Emma became alert with a start, only to have any thoughts of rejecting him quelled beneath a ravaging kiss. He didn't ease into the kiss. No, he took her mouth with ruthless domination.

Emma loved it.

All objections scattered, as insubstantial as a hot summer breeze. Aware of her surrender, Casey groaned low in his throat and tilted his head, fitting his mouth to hers more securely. He continued to hold her immobile, pressing her to the wall. She felt the muscled hardness, the vitality of his body against her breasts, her belly and thighs. She tried to squirm, to get closer, but his grip didn't allow it.

The kiss was an onslaught, never broken, always going deeper, taking and giving, and Emma forgot they were in a hospital with people milling around outside the room.

Casey didn't forget. Slowly, reluctantly, he pulled back. His thumbs brushed the corners of her swollen mouth. Emma fought to get her eyes open.

"I love your mouth, Em. So damn sexy." He nipped her bottom lip, licked her upper, took her mouth again. He sank his tongue in, soft and deep.

Emma groaned.

"I used to imagine your mouth on me," he whispered, "and it made me nuts."

Hearing him say it made her imagine it now. *"Yes."* She would love to taste Casey—everywhere. "Yes." She reached for him again.

Casey stepped them both away from the wall and urged her head to his shoulder, then wrapped his arms around her to hold her tight. He took several long, unsteady breaths, which allowed her to do the same. Emma was so shaken that if Casey hadn't supported her, she thought she might have melted into a puddle on the floor.

"I'm going to give you time, Emma."

She flattened her hands against the firm wall of his

chest, relishing the feel of him. Time? She didn't need time. At the moment, she didn't want time. Unless it was time enough to explore him, to kiss him everywhere, to feel him deep inside her. Oh God, she *would* melt.

"I'm going to wait so you won't feel rushed."

She couldn't stop shaking. "I won't."

He went still, cursed softly, then turned his face in and kissed her ear. "Shh. Not yet. First you're going to get comfortable with me again. Then we're going to talk, and I want the truth this time, Emma."

Her heart, which had only just begun to calm, kicked into a furious gallop again. "No…"

"And then." His tongue touched her earlobe, licked lightly inside to make her shiver. "*Then* I'm going to lay you down, strip you naked and sate myself on you." He groaned as if being tortured. "I've got nearly a decade of lust to make up for, sweetheart, so it's going to take me a really long time to get my fill. I hope you're up for it."

Emma shuddered. She had no idea what to do, what to say. But in that single moment, she made a decision. She wouldn't leave Buckhorn again without having Casey first.

If that made her feelings for him harder to deal with, so be it. She wasn't a weak woman with silly illusions. She knew from past experience that Casey wouldn't want her as a permanent fixture in his life. She knew she'd never fit into Buckhorn. She never had.

When she'd left, there'd been a lot of things she wanted. Security, respectability, a close family…and

Casey Hudson. But of all those things, it was only Casey who had kept her awake at night.

She had the security and respectability that came with a good job, an attitude adjustment, maturity. She had a family; not her own, but the Devaughns were very special to her and she loved them. She'd attained things of value, but she'd also learned that they weren't enough. She hadn't admitted to herself what was still missing in her life until Casey made it clear that he wanted her.

She'd never be close with her own family; seeing her father again had proven that. But she could have this—she could have her memories of Casey. With everything combined, she'd make that be enough for a lifetime.

She looked into his mellow golden eyes, glittering with excitement. His sharp cheekbones were flushed with arousal. For her. Emma whispered, "All right."

The heat in his eyes flared, but was quickly banked. "God, Emma." He took several deep breaths, leaned back and finally managed a smile. "The minutes are going to seem like hours until I can get you alone."

Emma nodded.

"Until then, let's talk about your dad—and what really happened the night he dropped you on my doorstep."

CHAPTER EIGHT

CASEY SAW the shuttered way Emma guarded herself. Well, too bad. Sometimes the truth proved painful but, damn it, he deserved that much.

He couldn't stop touching her, smoothing her warm cheek, relishing the feel of her. He could barely wait until she was naked so he could rub his hands, his face, over her whole body. He wanted to stroke her breasts, her belly. Between her thighs.

The second she'd agreed with him, he'd gotten semihard and he had a feeling he'd be that way until he got her alone. Heat snaked through him, adding to the sexual tension and making his voice gruff. "Come on, Em. You know you can tell me anything."

She closed her eyes tightly. "People don't just fall into old relationships that easily, Case."

"You and I do." Spending the day with her had reaffirmed that much. Emma looked different, and her attitudes were wiser, more confident. But the closeness between them existed as strong as ever. No other woman had ever touched him so easily. "Regardless of what you ever thought, Em, you've always had a special place in my heart."

"Casey." She sounded strained and covered her face with her hands.

He couldn't keep from kissing her again, but he

contented himself by pulling her hands away and brushing his mouth over her forehead. ''I care about you—I always have. In all the time you were gone, that hasn't changed.''

''No? You want to sleep with me now. That's sure not how I remember it.''

Something else that was different—her lippy comebacks. They amused him. ''I always wanted you and you know it.'' He leaned down to see her face. ''I think you enjoyed tormenting me, sending me home with a boner, knowing I'd be miserable all night long.'' The fact that he could tease even when he was this aroused said a lot about Emma and how relaxed he was in her company.

She denied his accusation with a quick shake of her head. ''You didn't have to be miserable. I would have taken care of you.''

Casey's moan turned into a laugh. ''You're still tormenting me. Now, enough with the distractions. What happened that night, Emma? Why were you so desperate to get out of Buckhorn?''

''You don't really want to know.''

''Of course I do.''

''Then you don't really *need* to know. Casey, I don't want to involve you. It wouldn't be fair.''

She looked truly set in her decision, and Casey knew she wouldn't tell him a thing. He was contemplating ways to get around her stubbornness, when the waiting-room door opened and Dr. Wagner stuck his head in. ''Am I interrupting?''

Casey stepped back from Emma. To keep her from ushering him out of the room, he said, ''Not at all. We're anxious to hear how Dell's doing.''

Emma made a sound, clearly aghast at his audacity in including himself. Casey pretended not to hear. She wanted to shut him out again, but he wasn't about to budge. She'd agreed to sleep with him, to accept him as a lover. She could damn well accept him as a friend and confidant too. Whatever Dr. Wagner had to tell her, he could share it with them both.

Lois, peeved and hostile, stepped in behind the doctor. The way she watched Emma was so malicious, it should have been illegal.

Casey had never paid that much attention to Lois before now. He'd thought her cute, a little silly. He'd been out with her once or twice, casual dates that didn't amount to much and definitely didn't go beyond a few kisses. But he hadn't known how catty she could be. Poor Emma, to have put up with her and the other women like her.

He had new insight into what Emma's teen years must have been like in Buckhorn, and it was decidedly worse than he'd thought.

"Let's sit down," Dr. Wagner suggested.

Emma went to a chair and Casey stood behind her, his hands on her shoulders, making it clear to the doctor and to Lois that he was there for her.

Many times in the past, he'd stood in front of her, trying to shield her. He knew now that she was stronger than he'd ever suspected. She had to be to have survived with her naturally generous nature still intact. Standing behind her, offering her support in what she chose to face, and respecting her strength to do it, seemed more appropriate.

The doctor pulled up his own chair facing Emma, and Lois sat beside him. Dr. Wagner pasted on his patented reassuring physician's smile. "Ms. Clark, your father is doing much better today. I see improvement not only in his mental capacity in identifying objects, but also in his mind/eye coordination." The doctor turned grave. "But, to be truthful, for a little while there I thought we might lose him."

"Lose him?" Emma stiffened in alarm. "But I thought…"

"You're seeing him now, with much improvement. For three days he had no clear recognition of most things. He knew what he was seeing, but he couldn't find the word in his memory to identify it."

Emma bit her bottom lip. "I came as soon as I was told, but I had to pack up and I didn't arrive in Buckhorn until late last night. I stopped here first. My father was asleep, so I just looked in on him." She twisted her hands together. "The nurse said he'd be okay."

"And she's correct. But I anticipate quite a bit of therapy not only to help him deal with what he's suffered and his diminished capacity—which should be only temporary—but to help rebuild his coordination. We'll get his meds regulated—blood thinner and blood pressure medicine to keep him from having another stroke."

For several minutes, the doctor explained the causes and effects of a stroke, and Emma listened in fretful silence.

"He'll need to be monitored for TIAs—or mini strokes."

Emma nodded. "The nurse said that he also fell?"

Dr. Wagner's eyebrows rose in surprise. "Your mother didn't tell you he fell off the porch steps when she called you? She said she found him unconscious, which is why she called the paramedics. And good thing too, as I've already said.''

Lois made a face. ''He'd been drinking, so his wife thought he'd just passed out.''

Scowling, Dr. Wagner twisted around to face the nurse. ''Incorrect, Ms. Banker. Alcohol had been spilled on him, but he had not consumed any noticeable amount.''

When he turned back to Emma, his expression gentled and he reached out to pat her hand. ''It's my guess that he was carrying a bottle of whisky when he had the stroke. It spilled all over him and, yes, we could smell it. I had thought to question his wife about it, but haven't seen her yet.''

Emma stammered, ''Mom d-doesn't get out much.''

Casey wanted to roll his eyes at her understatement. Her mother was a recluse. She was seldom seen around town, and apparently she hadn't even ventured out to visit her husband.

''I see.'' The doctor gave her a long look, then referred to his notes. ''Well, he did some further damage with his fall. We got the MRI back on his ankle, and luckily it isn't broken, though it is still severely swollen and I'm certain it's causing him some pain. Add to that the bruising on his ribs and shoulder…well, he took a very nasty spill. I'm relieved he didn't break his neck.''

Emma nodded. ''Me too.''

''You say you're from out of town. Will you be able to stay around to attend him, and if not, is your mother capable of the task?''

"I…" She glanced at Casey, who squeezed her shoulder, then back at the doctor. "What kind of care will he need?"

Appearing to be a little uncomfortable, Dr. Wagner explained, "I don't anticipate he'll go home for a while yet. But when he does, he'll need help with everyday tasks until he regains control of lost motor skills. He'll need transportation back and forth to the hospital for therapy. He may even need help feeding himself, dressing…at least for a while. As I said, his improvement so far is quite promising, but we can't make any guarantees."

"I understand." She waited only a moment before giving a firm nod. "I can be here as long as I'm needed."

Casey wondered if she could stay indefinitely. She'd made a life in Chicago…by all accounts, a happy life that suited her. But her roots were in Buckhorn. Whatever had driven her away the first time, he'd be here with her now, offering her support in whatever way she needed. Maybe it'd be enough.

Emma dropped back in her seat, and Casey noted the weariness in her face. She looked beautiful to him, so he hadn't at first noticed. But now that he did, he felt guilty. She'd been given worrisome news, spent several hours on the road yesterday with only a few hours' sleep to recoup, and then faced her father.

And he'd been bulldozing her straight into an affair. He suddenly felt like a bastard. No, he wouldn't change his mind. He couldn't. But he would treat her gently, give her plenty of time.

"I hope I've relieved your mind," Dr. Wagner said.

"You have. I'm sure I can handle things, as long as you tell me everything I need to know."

"Yes, of course. When he's ready to be discharged, we'll give you a list of his prescriptions, along with instructions on his general care. He'll have regular checkups and you can always reach someone here at the hospital or at my office if you have questions. Thanks to his injured ankle and ribs, he'll spend a good deal of time in bed, so you'll also need to rotate his position until he's back on his feet. He's going to be very sore for a while."

Wearing a half smile, Emma admitted, "I'm a massage therapist, so I know about sore muscles."

"A massage therapist?" Lois asked, looking down her nose.

"Excellent," Dr. Wagner said at almost the same time. "It's too bad you don't live here. I could have used your services last week after a day spent fishing." He chuckled as he rubbed the small of his back. "I'm getting too old to sit on the hard bench of a fishing boat for hours on end. I was stiff for two days. But the wife had no sympathy. None at all."

Emma laughed with him. "I'll be glad to help you out while I'm here. Just give me a call. The desk has my number."

Dr. Wagner brightened. "Careful now. I'll hold you to it."

"It'll be my pleasure. A thank-you for all the good care you're giving Dad."

Casey wasn't at all sure he liked the sound of that, and then he caught himself. Dr. Wagner was a grandpa, for crying out loud. A kind old man who'd known his father forever. Yet…Lois had the same damn thought, given her spiteful expression. She smiled, but it was a smile of malicious intent.

Casey wondered how much Emma would let him help. Considering what he'd learned, he knew it wouldn't be easy for her to be home with both her parents. Yet her father's health dictated that she do just that.

He wanted to do what was best for her, and if that meant helping her with Dell... He and her father were not on great terms—not since the night Dell accused him of getting Emma pregnant—but Emma would have cleared that up with her father by now. Dell would certainly have realized that he wasn't a grandfather, and Casey wasn't a father.

Not that he didn't want to be. Someday. With the right woman.

He looked at Emma again and felt a strange warmth spread through his chest. Emma was such a gentle, affectionate, sensitive woman, she'd make a wonderful mother.

And if she knew your thoughts, Casey told himself, *she'd probably head directly back to Chicago.* Hell, he scared himself, so he could only imagine how Emma would react.

"You'll be hearing from me." Dr. Wagner shook her hand, then clapped Casey on the shoulder. "I'm off to see the rest of my patients."

He went out, yet Lois lingered. She looked Emma up and down with a sullen sneer. "A massage therapist? Is that what they're calling it these days?"

Casey felt like strangling the little witch for her insinuation, yet Emma only smiled. "Far as I know, Lois, that's what they've always called it. You didn't know that? I'm surprised, since the field of massage therapy has become an integral part of health care, and you *are* a nurse, after all.''

Stung, Lois pursed her mouth. ''It sounds like a shady front to me. I remember you too well. I can just imagine what you do while *massaging* someone.''

Emma leaned toward her, taunting, egging her on. ''It is scandalous. Why, I light scented candles and play erotic, relaxing music. But I'm good, Lois, so good, that I get a lot of repeat customers.'' She held up her hands. ''I'm told I have magic fingers and that I can work the tension out of any muscle.''

Red-faced, Lois said, ''It's an excuse to get naked and get...rubbed.''

''You make that sound so dirty!'' Emma laughed. ''Actually, people with real physical ailments come to me. Strained muscles, stress, rehab after an injury...''

Lois sputtered in outrage. ''You should encourage people to see real professionals.''

''Oh? You mean like the massage therapists employed by the hospital? I noticed their offices downstairs. They're not quite as well equipped as I am, but they're still adequate.''

''They're accredited.''

''Me too.'' Emma fashioned a look of haughtiness. ''I'm certified with the AMTA and licensed by the city of Chicago. You know, you look so puckered up, you should really try a little massage. All that frowning ages a person and gives her wrinkles.''

''I do see a few frown lines, Lois,'' Casey managed to say with a straight face. It was strange, but seeing

Emma so confident, even cocky, turned him on. "Maybe the folks downstairs will give you an employee discount."

Clearly knowing she'd lost that round, Lois stalked out in a snit.

Unwilling to let Emma leave the same way, Casey caught her elbow. She'd put up a good front for Lois, but he could see that she was miffed over his interference with the doctor. "Do you want to visit with your father some more before we head off?"

She considered it, and finally nodded. "Maybe just to smooth things over before I leave."

Casey hated for her to face him alone again, but he already knew he wasn't welcome. "Hey." He touched her chin and resisted the urge to kiss her. "Don't let him get you down, okay? He's bound to be a little grouchy, all things considered."

"It's not that." She started out of the room. "There are some things my father and I will never agree on, that's all. But I don't want to argue with him here, not while he's hurt and sick."

This time Casey waited for her in the hall, but he could hear them speaking. The words were indistinct, but the tone was clear: Emma calmly insistent, Dell complaining, even whining. Casey winced for her. Under the circumstances, being Dell's caretaker wasn't going to be easy.

When she emerged ten minutes later, looking more agitated than ever, he slipped his arm around her waist. They walked down the hallway to the elevator in silence, but once inside, Casey pulled her into a hug. "Ms. Clark, I'm noticing a few frown lines on you, too."

A reluctant smile curled her lips, but her eyes remained dark with worry. "Is that right? Think I should stop for a massage?"

"What I think is that you should talk me through it. Maybe I have magic fingers too."

The smile turned into a grin. "I never doubted it for a second."

"But first, a day on the lake with the sun in your face will work wonders."

To his surprise, Emma sighed. "Oh, that does sound like heaven."

Aware of a slow, heated thrumming in his blood, Casey urged her off the elevator and through the lobby. Already he visualized her in a bikini, her skin warmed by the sun, dewy with the humidity... He had to swallow his groan to keep from alerting her to his intent. He'd have her alone in the boat, on the lake, with no way to escape. Touching her, kissing her, was a priority.

But first he intended to discover all her secrets. Something had happened to her, something bad enough to make her leave her home. Bad enough to make her leave him.

He wasn't letting her off the boat until he knew it all.

CHAPTER NINE

B.B.'s HOT BREATH pelted Casey's right ear as he drove. The dog, like Emma, enjoyed having the top down, his face in the wind.

Emma's long hair whipped out behind her and she constantly had to shove it from her face. In something akin to awe, she breathed, "It's so beautiful out here."

Glancing at her, Casey agreed. Now that they'd hit the back roads leading toward the lake, the foliage was thicker, greener, lush. Blue cornflowers mixed with black-eyed Susans all along the roadway. Cows bawled in sprawling pastures, goats chewed on tall weeds grown along crooked fence posts. Blue-black crows as fat as ducks spread their wings and cawed as the car went past.

The narrow roads forced Casey to slow his speed, but he didn't mind. Watching Emma reacquaint herself with her hometown made every second enjoyable. She waved to farmers in coveralls who tipped their straw hats to her and then lazily waved back. She strained to see tobacco huts and tomato stands and moss-covered ponds. She embraced the wind in her face and the sun in her eyes.

She laughed with the sheer joy of it all.

And Casey felt positively frenetic with lust. It

burned his stomach and tightened his throat and kept him uncomfortably edgy.

If, as he'd first assumed, he had only lust to deal with, he'd have already pulled over to the side of the road and taken Emma beneath a tree on the sweet grass. She claimed to be willing and there was plenty of privacy here once you got far enough from the road that no cars would notice you. Making love to Emma with the hot sun on his back and the birds overhead would be downright decadent, something straight out of his dreams.

But he was afraid what he felt for her was more than mere lust. He wasn't sure how much more and he wasn't sure how hard it'd be to convince her of it. Emma seemed hell-bent on remembering how he'd once rejected her, instead of giving them both a chance to get reacquainted as adults. Not that he blamed her. Looking at her now, he couldn't understand how he'd ever turned her down.

Emma was as earthy and sexual and appealing as a woman could be. And she was in her element here.

She belonged in Buckhorn. Did she belong with him?

They'd stopped at the motel where Emma had changed into her suit and a zippered terry-cloth cover-up. Snowy-white and sleeveless, it hung to midthigh, showing off the shapely length of her legs. She'd raised the zipper high enough to rest between her breasts. Casey could see the top of her beige, cro-cheted bathing-suit bra, which made him nuts wanting to know if it was a bikini or a one-piece.

She wore dark sunglasses and brown slip-on san-dals, and she had a large cotton satchel stuffed with a colorful beach towel, sunscreen, a bottle of water and her cell phone. She commented that she wanted the hospital to be able to reach her if they needed to.

Before they'd left the motel she'd also taken the time to call Damon on his phone, and discovered that the car was repaired and he was touring the area. Emma had promised him that she'd be back for dinner. Luckily, to Casey's way of thinking, Damon had explained that he had a date, so Emma should take her time visiting.

Emma hadn't seemed at all surprised or concerned with how fast Damon had gotten acquainted. Apparently he had a way with women, given the fond smile Emma wore while rolling her eyes.

Casey had no idea what Damon had planned, and he didn't much care. As long as Damon stayed busy, he couldn't interfere with Casey's pursuit of Emma.

He turned the car down the long driveway to his family's home. The property here was lined with a tidy split-rail fence to contain the few farm animals they kept. Their menagerie often varied, since some of his father's patients paid for medical services with livestock, which they in turn often donated to the needier local families.

At present, they had several horses, an enormous hog, a fat, ornery heifer and two timid lambs. They'd keep the horses, and Honey had grown partial to the lambs. But the hog and heifer had to go. They terrorized Honey every chance they got. Whenever Honey was around, the damn cow dredged up the most threatening look a big-eyed, black-spotted bovine could manage.

Casey adored Honey, and a day didn't go by that

he didn't appreciate her and all she gave to them, to his father. Because Sawyer's first marriage had been such a public fiasco, no one had ever expected him to remarry.

Casey had enjoyed being raised in an all-male household, but having Honey around had been even better. Softer. Over the years, she'd planted numerous flowers along the outside of the fence: enormous white peonies, tall irises and abundant daisies. Something was always in bloom, making the area colorful and fragrant.

Holding her hair from her face, Emma glanced around at the familiar stretch of land. "I thought we were going to the lake?"

"We are." He kept his gaze on the road and off the sight of her creamy skin. "But I want to stop at the house first. I need to change and grab the boat keys."

"You live at home?"

"In the apartment over the garage. I lived in Cincy for a while, just because I thought it'd be more convenient. But it didn't take me long to decide I prefer the forty-minute drive to and from work every day." Now, more than ever, Casey was glad he hadn't moved out of the area.

The sprawling log house came into view. Built on a rise and surrounded by mature trees and numerous outbuildings, it looked impressive indeed. In his younger days, Casey had lived there with his father and his uncles. Morgan now had a house farther up the hill, but not more than a ten-minute walk away. Jordan had moved into Georgia's house with her and the kids after they married, and Gabe bought a place in town with Elizabeth.

Morgan's newest official vehicle was in the yard. Because so many people in Buckhorn lived off the beaten path or in the hills, Morgan drove a rugged four-wheel-drive Bronco. Misty, his wife, had convinced him to trade from black to white last year. Actually, she'd wanted red, but Morgan had refused that. He said the sheriff's emblem painted on the side would clash.

Casey saw Emma take in the crowd in front of the house. With the dark glasses on, he couldn't see her eyes. But he watched the tilt of her head, the lack of a smile on her pretty mouth.

It appeared Morgan and Misty were dropping off the kids, Amber and Garrett. They stood on the steps, Morgan wearing his tan uniform and Misty in a casual dress. Sawyer and Honey were beneath the shade on the porch, drinking tall glasses of iced tea. Shohn was there, too, with Morgan's dog, Godzilla. All in all, they made an intimidating crowd of people.

When they saw Casey pull up and park beneath an oak tree, the kids raced to the car to greet him. The boys were shirtless and in sneakers; Amber wore a T-shirt and cutoffs and was barefoot.

B.B. twitched his ears, alert to the activity but not overly concerned. When he spotted the kids, his tail started thumping in earnest. Casey hadn't known they'd all be there. He waited, worried that Emma would be upset to be dropped into the middle of his overwhelming family.

Instead, she sat back in her seat with a sound of

wonder. "It's incredible, but they look almost the same."

Relieved, Casey reached over and smoothed a long lock of hair behind her ear. "Dad has gray at his temples now, but Honey says it makes him look distinguished."

"She's right. He's still so handsome it's almost unfair. And Shohn looks just like him. But, if anything, Morgan's gotten even bigger."

"Misty calls him a brick wall." Casey looked at his imposing uncle in time to see Morgan pat Misty on the rump. She swatted at him and he laughed.

Shaking his head, Casey said, "I swear, they still act like newlyweds."

"Yeah, and it's wonderful." Emma sighed. The kids had almost reached them. They were making a clatter, laughing and calling out. "You can see which kids are his. That shiny black hair, and just look at those blue eyes."

Emma opened her door, not waiting for Casey. B.B. jumped out beside her and whined in excitement, practically pleading to be released so he could play with Godzilla. The kids skidded to a halt in front of Emma and then stared.

Shohn squinted up at her. His dark hair was mussed and he had dirt on his knees. "Does your dog bite?"

"Only on bones." She grinned as she said it. "But not leg bones. Just steak bones."

Garrett held out a hand and B.B. licked it. "Can we play with him?"

The dog whined again with the most pitifully pleading expression, amusing the kids.

Because they had plenty of land for running, Casey

unhooked the dog's leash. "You guys go easy on him, okay? He doesn't know you yet."

Amber stroked his muzzle and giggled when his tail started furiously pounding the ground. "We'll watch him for ya, okay?"

Casey left it up to Emma.

"Honey won't mind having him loose?"

"'Course not." Luckily, Honey loved animals as much as they all did. Except for big cows and snarling hogs.

"All right." Emma scratched B.B.'s ear, then patted his side and released him by saying, "Go play."

B.B. bounded forward, leaping this way and that in his exuberance at seeing another dog. Godzilla went berserk with his own joy, which prompted the kids to do the same. Amber and Garrett ran off after the dogs, but Shohn hung back, still squinting. "You Casey's girlfriend?"

Casey started to reply, but Emma beat him to it. "I'm a friend and I'm a girl, so I guess you can call me a girlfriend."

"He's got a lot of girlfriends."

Emma's mouth curled. "I never doubted it for a second."

Shohn laughed, but in the next second Casey threw him over his shoulder and held him upside down. "Brat. Quit trying to scare her off or I'll have to hang you by your toes."

Casey pretended to drop him and Shohn roared with laughter. When Casey finally set him back on his feet, Shohn moved a safe distance away, posed to run, and gave a cocky smile. "If she turns you down, Case, I'll take her. She's real pretty."

Fighting a laugh, Casey feigned an attack and, like a flash, Shohn ran off to join the other kids. Casey looked at Emma and saw she wore an ear-to-ear grin, which prompted his own. So she liked kids, did she? A good thing, since there were quite a few in the family. "You're not going to turn me down, are you, sweetheart?"

Rather than answer, she said, "Gee, he reminds me of someone else I know. Now, who could it be?"

Every moment Casey spent with her canceled out the time they'd been apart. He pulled her into his side. "I was shy."

"Ha!"

"Shohn's only ten, but I swear he's girl crazy already. The little rat flirts with every female, regardless of her age. Makes Honey nuts. Dad just shakes his head." He gave Emma a squeeze. "And of course, my grandmother says he reminds her of Gabe."

Emma laughed. "Where is your grandmother?"

"She and Gabe's father, Brett, live in Florida, but they get up this way every couple of months to visit."

Because Casey was lingering in the yard, giving Emma a chance to brace herself for his family, Sawyer left the porch and headed toward them. It seemed he'd been seeing patients, given that he wore dark slacks and an open-necked button-down shirt with the sleeves rolled up. He smiled at Emma without recognition. "Hello."

He held out his hand and Emma took it. "Hello, Dr. Hudson. It's been a long time."

Cocking one eyebrow, Sawyer looked to Casey for an introduction. Casey stared at his father hard, trying to prepare him. "Dad, you remember Emma Clark."

The other eyebrow lifted to join the first. Sawyer still held her hand and now he enclosed it in both of his. If he'd been surprised, he quickly covered it up. ''Emma, of course I remember you. It has been a long time. How've you been?''

''Just great.'' B.B. charged up next to her, with Godzilla in hot pursuit. ''Casey said it was okay to let him run.''

Sawyer admired the dog for a moment, then nodded. ''He's fine, and obviously he doesn't mind the children.''

''B.B. loves kids. He's very careful with them.''

''He's a beautiful animal.'' Sawyer released Emma and gestured to the porch. ''We were just taking a break. Would you like something to drink?''

She glanced at Casey. ''We were going out on the boat…''

''There's time. I need to change anyway.''

She pushed her sunglasses to the top of her head and nodded. ''Then yes, thank you. I'd love to visit for a few minutes.''

Casey was amazed at her. He'd expected her to be uncomfortable, maybe embarrassed. Instead, she waved to Honey, strolled right up to the porch and began greeting everyone with a new confidence that was both surprising and appealing. Any awkwardness she'd felt as a youth was long gone.

Sawyer shot Casey a look filled with questions.

''She's in town to see her father.''

''The hell you say? After all this time? It's been…what? Over eight years.''

''Dell's had a stroke.''

"I heard." In a small town, news traveled fast. "He'll be okay?"

"Doc Wagner seemed to think so." They were still in the yard, out of earshot from the others. Casey rubbed the back of his neck, struggling with how much he wanted to say. But he'd always been able to talk to his dad and now more than ever he wanted to share his thoughts. "About when she left…"

Sawyer clasped Casey's shoulder. "I didn't think we'd ever see her again. I worried about that girl for a long time." He searched Casey's face. "I know you did too."

There was no denying that. Though he'd tried to hide it, his father knew him too well to be fooled. "You know…" He glanced up at Sawyer. "We all assumed the same things back then, with how Dell dropped her off here, and her bruised face, the way she was crying."

"But?"

"But seeing her with him today, I realized we assumed too much."

Sawyer gazed toward the porch where the women and Morgan gathered. "How's that?"

"I took her to the hospital today to visit him."

Again, Sawyer lifted his dark eyebrows. "When did she get to town?"

"Last night."

"And you're already chauffeuring her around?"

"It's not like that. We're…"

Sawyer waited.

"Hell, I don't know." He could just faintly hear Emma speaking on the porch, her tone friendly and natural. He watched her, saw the easy way she held herself, how she greeted Morgan and Misty. He shook his head. "I had a time of it, convincing her to let me hang around. She's different now, but how I feel about her is the same."

"How do you feel about her?"

Casey scowled. "I'm not sure, all right? I just... Seeing her again made me realize how much I'd missed her." He was starting to feel sixteen again, waiting for his father to give him another lecture on the importance of rubbers.

"Nothing wrong with that."

Casey shifted uncomfortably. "Her car broke down on the way into town last night. Gabe fixed it for her this morning, but she needed to visit her dad early so she could catch Dr. Wagner. I drove her, then waited around. And damn, listening to her with her father, well, things aren't as they always seemed."

"Honey is waving at us. Maybe you better catch me up later." They started toward the porch, but halfway there Sawyer asked, "Do you know what you're doing, Case?"

"Yeah." He frowned. "At least I think I do."

"Will Emma be moving back home?"

He shook his head. "She says not. She has her own business in Chicago, and some very close friends there."

"So she's only here for a spell?"

Not if he could help it. "I don't know."

"But you want her to stay?" Sawyer didn't wait for an answer. "Maybe we can help. As for her father, I'd planned to pay her folks a visit anyway, to see if there was any way I could help."

"I'll go with you when you do."

Morgan eyed them both when they finally started up the wooden porch steps. Because he'd spent some time hunting for Emma after she'd run away, Casey had no doubt he was bursting with questions. But Morgan would never deliberately make a woman uncomfortable.

Emma had already been seated in a rattan rocker across from Honey. She'd slipped her feet out of her sandals and had her toes curled against the sun-bleached boards of the porch.

Morgan said, "Why don't you take my boat. It hasn't been out in a while."

"All right." He peered at Emma, trying to read her expression. "Maybe I can talk Emma into skiing."

Emma held up her hands. "Oh no. I need to get used to the boat first before I try anything out of the boat."

Misty crossed her arms over the railing. "I finally learned how to ski, but I look pathetic when I do."

Morgan bit her ear. "You look sexy."

Rolling her eyes, Misty said, "Morgan is starting to drool, so I guess we better get going."

"A date with my wife," Morgan rumbled. "That doesn't happen very often."

Hands clasped together, forehead puckered, Emma came out of her seat. "Before you go, could I talk to you just a minute? I mean, all of you?"

Everyone stared. Casey held his breath.

Making a face, Emma said, "I'm sorry to hold you up, but since you're all here, I figured it'd be a good time to apologize." She sneaked a quick look at Casey. "And don't tell me it's not necessary, because it is to me."

"Damn it, Em..." He took a step up the porch stairs toward her.

Morgan laced his arms around Misty and pulled her back into his chest. "Well now, I suppose we've got a few minutes to spare."

Misty snorted. "And the curiosity is probably killing him."

"Casey's right." Honey leaned forward in her chair. "You don't owe us anything at all. But if you want to talk..."

With his hand on the back of Honey's chair, Sawyer said, "I'm curious too. Where'd you go the night you ran off?"

Casey glowered at his family. He thought about just flinging Emma over his shoulder, as he'd done to Shohn, and carrying her off. But that'd probably shoot any chance he had of getting on her good side. He could tell this was important to her, so he locked his jaw and waited.

Emma turned to Morgan first. "My father told me that you looked for me after I took off. I'm sorry that I put you to that trouble by not explaining better when I left, and I'm especially sorry that any of you worried about me. Kids do dumb things, and that night it didn't occur to me that any of you might worry."

Because no one had ever worried about her before? Casey didn't like that probability, but he knew it was likely true.

She turned to Sawyer next. "I never dreamed that you'd actually look for me."

"We just wanted to know for certain that you were okay."

Honey agreed with her husband. "You were awfully young to go off on your own."

"I know. And I appreciate your concern." Her cheeks dimpled with her smile. "It's why I came here that night, because I knew you'd be nice and that you'd understand. I'm sorry I took advantage of you."

"Enough apologies," Misty said. "Morgan likes to fret—it's why he's a sheriff—and Sawyer's no better. They're both mother hens. Obviously you and Casey have made up now, so all's well that ends well."

Casey took that as his cue to move to her side. Without confirming or denying Misty's statement, Emma said, "Thank you."

But Morgan wasn't ready to let it go. "So where'd you disappear to?"

Misty gave him a frown, which he ignored.

"Chicago. I met some very nice people who helped me figure out what I wanted to do. I finished up school and started my own business. Things have been great."

Bemused, Casey could only stare at her. If he hadn't heard the full story—or rather, a less condensed version—he would have believed her life to be a bed of roses. Damn, she was good at covering up. He'd have to remember that.

"What kind of business do you have?" Honey asked.

"Massage therapy. I have my own small studio."

"Ohmigod," Misty enthused. "I know women in town who drive weekly into Florence for a massage. They'll be all over you if they find out."

"Not that Misty needs to leave home for that sort of thing," Morgan stated, while rubbing her shoulders. Misty just smiled.

"Are you going to be in town long?" Honey asked.

"I'm not sure yet."

Casey caught her hand and laced his fingers with hers. He didn't want to hear about her leaving when she'd only just come home. "We have to get going."

"I thought you wanted to change."

"I will, but I figured we'd swing into the apartment on our way down to the lake." The house overlooked the lake, and from the back, it wasn't too far to walk to reach the shore. Casey's apartment above the garage was on the way, so he decided to just drag Emma along with him. The quicker he got her alone, the better.

"All right." Emma finished off her glass of tea. After slipping her sandals back on, she thanked Honey again.

"Will you be back in time for lunch?" Honey wanted to know.

If things worked out as he hoped, they'd spend the rest of the day together. "We'll grab something on the lake, but thanks." Casey hugged the women, said farewell to the men, and led Emma back to the car so she could get her satchel. They went around the side of the house to the garage apartment. Before Emma could call B.B., he fell into step beside her, along with all the kids. The dog almost looked to be laughing, he'd had such a good time.

"Where ya going?" Garrett asked.

Ruffling his hair, Emma said, "Casey is taking me boating."

Shohn perked up. "How about tubin' us, Case?"

Emma looked at Casey in question. She remembered tubing, Casey was sure. At one time or another, just about everyone on the lake had been bounced around on a fat black inner tube, tied with a ski rope and pulled behind the boat. It proved a bruising ride, one guaranteed to get water up your nose and make your body ache. Kids loved it, but most adults had more sense.

Likely Emma's questioning look meant it was up to him whether or not to include the kids.

He voted *not*. Casey wanted to grab Emma and run like hell. Instead, he told Shohn, "How about we save that for another day? Emma hasn't been home in a long time and I want to let her enjoy the ride, not scare her to death with your daredevil antics."

The boys looked downcast, making Casey feel guilty. Then Amber, the oldest of the bunch at a not-quite-mature eleven, elbowed them both. "You can go tubing anytime, dummy. Case has a date."

Shohn slanted a leering look at Casey and grinned like a possum, but Garrett shrugged. "So?"

"So he wants to kiss her. Don't ya, Case?" Shohn made smooching noises while pretending to hold a swooning female.

Emma surprised him yet again by snatching Shohn up close and kissing his cheek and neck until he screamed uncle. Everyone was laughing, Garrett pointing at Shohn, and B.B. jumping around in glee. Amber looked up at Casey, her dark-blue eyes twinkling with enjoyment. He hugged his niece, unable to stop smiling. Damn, having Emma around was nice.

Without even trying, she fit in—into Buckhorn, into his family. Into his heart.

Emma sat down on the bottom step leading up to the rooms over the garage. Casey smoothed his hand over her head. "I'll go change and be right back."

Panting, Shohn sprawled backward across her lap like a sacrifice, his arms spread out, his head almost touching the ground. "Take your time, brother. Take your time."

Emma laughed too hard to answer Casey, but Amber followed him up the steps and through the front door. She helped herself to a drink of water, then flounced onto his sofa while Casey went into the bedroom to change into his trunks.

"I like her," Amber announced, saying it loud so Casey would be sure to hear.

"Me too," Casey called out to her.

"You gonna keep this one?"

Inside his room, Casey chuckled. He remained endlessly amazed at how different his nieces were from the boys. The girls got together and planned, while the boys got together and scuffled. Occasionally the differences were less noticeable, like on holidays when they were all wild little monkeys, but overall the girls were more mature. "She has some say-so in that, you know."

"Daddy doesn't give Mom much say-so. He just picks her up and totes her wherever he wants her to go."

That picture brought about a laugh. Morgan did seem fond of hauling Misty around. 'Course, he'd seen his father toting Honey a time or two as well— whenever she'd fallen asleep on the couch, and several times when his dad had that certain look, which prompted Casey to give them immediate privacy. In Gabe's case, it was as often as not Elizabeth who was dragging Gabe off to bed. Jordan, however, was more subtle. He and Georgia connected with scorching looks that no one could misunderstand.

Casey finished changing into cutoff jeans, an un-buttoned, short-sleeve shirt and ratty sneakers. He snagged a beach towel and rejoined Amber. "Your mom lets Morgan get away with that because she likes it."

Amber sighed theatrically. "I know. Daddy says Mom has him wrapped around her little finger."

"Your mom and you both." Casey held his hand out for her and said, "Let's go before she runs off with Shohn instead."

"Yeah right." Amber slipped her small hand into his. "She's probably already in love with you. All the women act stupid around you."

Casey's heart jumped at that "L" word, but he said only, "You think Emma acts stupid?"

"No, silly. That's why I think you should keep her."

When they went back down the steps, they found Emma doing tricks with B.B. She threw a stick and he caught it in midair, then brought it back to her. She told him to roll over, to speak, to shake hands. The boys were suitably impressed with his every feat.

Without even thinking about it, Casey looped his arms around Emma from behind and kissed her ear. The kids all stared wide-eyed. "If you think her dog is neat, you should see her car."

That refocused the boys' attention.

"Is it as cool as your car?"

"What color is it?"

Teasing, Emma said, "It's better than his car."

Casey raised an eyebrow, but agreed. "Definitely. We both have Mustangs, but Emma's is a cherry-red classic. You know what that means?"

Garrett nodded. "It's old."

"But in great condition."

Frowning, Garrett said, "I'd rather have a new one."

"That's only because you haven't seen it yet," Emma assured him.

Casey gave her a squeeze. "How about we bring the car by here tomorrow and you rats can look it over?"

"Will you stay for dinner?" Amber asked, and even to Casey, who knew her private agenda, Amber looked like innocence personified.

Shohn aimed a thumb at his chest. "You could go out in the boat with us so I can show you how good I ski."

Emma stiffened with alarm, though why the idea of spending time with his family bothered her, he had no clue. She liked the kids, he could tell that much. And she'd been totally at ease even while apologizing and explaining to Morgan, Misty, Honey and his dad.

He let her push out of his hold and move a few steps away.

She turned to face him, saying, "I might already have plans..." But the words trailed off as she got a look at his naked chest. When a breeze blew by, parting the shirt a little more, Emma's mouth fell open, her eyes flared.

Satisfaction built within him.

Well now, that was nice. He was comfortable in his own skin, so casual around the lake he hadn't really thought about her seeing him when he yanked on the shirt. But Emma seemed to appreciate it. Once he got her on the boat, he'd lose the shirt and encourage her to lose the cover-up. He'd get her in the cove and hold her close, skin to skin...

Like perfect little strategists, the kids started begging Emma to return for dinner. Casey decided he would take them tubing—and soon. They deserved it.

He reached out and tugged on a lock of Emma's hair, then mimicked the kids. "Please?"

She swallowed, closed her mouth, and raised her eyes to his. "I'll try." Her smile was staged. "But I'll probably have to bring Damon along."

Casey groaned, grabbed his heart as if he'd been shot, and stumbled into Amber, who laughed while trying to hold him up.

"Who," she demanded around her smile, "is this Damon person?"

Casey straightened. He hugged Amber, then kissed her little turned-up nose. "He's no one important, sweetheart. Just Emma's friend. And if he comes to dinner with us, why then you can all show him how to catch tadpoles and crawdads on the shore, okay?"

Amber's small face brightened in understanding, and she gave Casey a conspiratorial wink. "Okay, Casey. That sounds like fun." She encompassed the boys in a look, and added, "It'll probably take him a long time to get the hang of it, but we'll be patient—even if it takes hours."

CHAPTER TEN

EMMA TRAILED her fingers in the cold water. She loved the sights, sounds and smells of being on the lake, but it all faded away with Casey so near. It wasn't easy keeping her gaze off him. In fact, it proved impossible.

But Lord have mercy, he looked good. He now wore only low-riding cutoffs and he was perched on the driver's seat at the back of the boat, steering one-handed while the wind blew his dark-blond hair and the sun reflected off his smooth, tanned shoulders and the firm expanse of his broad back. He had one muscular, hairy leg braced on the deck of the boat, the other in the seat. She let her eyes follow the line of his spine all the way to the waistband of those shorts…

She jerked her gaze away. Staring at Casey's muscled backside would not help her get it together. The air was hot, but it didn't compare to what she felt on the inside. Casey had matured in ways she hadn't counted on. His body had always been lean and strong, but now he had filled out and his strength was obvious in the flex of muscles in his upper arms, across his chest and shoulders. He wasn't a hulk like Morgan, just nicely defined and very macho.

He was hairier than she remembered too. Not too

much, but there was a sexy sprinkling of dark-brown hair on his chest that faded to a thin line toward his navel, then a silkier line still down his belly—and behind his fly.

Emma breathed too deeply, imagined too much, but she wanted to touch him, kiss him.

When they'd first gotten in the boat, B.B. had demanded all her attention. He'd tottered back and forth, looking out one side of the boat then the other, constantly whining. He didn't like the way the boat moved and kept him unsteady. But within ten minutes, he'd settled down and now he watched out the back, his body braced against the casing for the inboard motor. His tongue hung out the side of his mouth and his furry face held an expression of excitement.

Emma had been smiling over that when Casey casually pulled off his shirt and stowed it in the side of the boat. While she ogled him, he suggested she remove her cover-up. She'd declined, and had been trying not to stare at him, without much success, ever since.

The lake was crowded with boats everywhere, more so than she remembered it being in the past. At first Casey had driven at breakneck speed, cutting across the wakes of other boats, bouncing over choppy waves, causing the water to spray into the boat and making her laugh. He'd gradually slowed and moved closer to the shoreline so that now they glided through the water, watchful of skiers and swimmers and noisy Jet Skis.

A flashy cabin cruiser filled with sun worshipers zipped up alongside them. Lounged around the boat,

three men and three women waved, prompting Casey
to return the greeting. Emma saw his friendly smile,
the way his raised arm showed a tuft of dark hair
beneath, how his biceps bulged. She also saw how
the women coveted Casey with open admiration,
while the men leered at her. She didn't know if anyone recognized her, and she didn't stare back long
enough to recognize anyone herself, but before the
day was over, his friends would be talking. She hated
that, but had no idea how to avoid it. Whether it was
fair or not, she *did* have a reputation, and yet Casey
was determined to be seen with her.

Her thoughts scattered as he steered the boat into
a deep cove at the far end of the long lake, away from
the congestion. He didn't bother to speak over the
roar of the motor, but every so often she felt the intensity of his gaze settle on her. Little by little he
slowed until the motor only purred and the ride was
easy and smooth, just gliding through the water.

By the time they were out of sight from prying
eyes, she couldn't hold back any longer and moved
to the seat behind him.

Casey twisted his head toward her. He wore dark
reflective sunglasses, but she could tell by the set of
his mouth, the slight flare of his nostrils, that his mind
had centered on the very same thoughts.

Without saying a word, Emma knelt on the seat
and settled both palms on his bare shoulders, smoothing her hands down to his shoulder blades, then to
his sides in a deep, sensual massage. Hot. Taut. Silky-
smooth flesh over hard muscle.

Casey went still except for the expanding of his
chest and back with each deep breath he took. She

loved touching him, stroking him. "Emma..." he said, half in pleasure, half in warning. "Damn, you are good."

She leaned forward and pressed her open mouth to the spot where his shoulder melded into his neck. She breathed his heated scent while rubbing deeply at muscles, relaxing him and exciting him at the same time. "You're the most beautiful man I've ever seen."

He shuddered and reached back for her hand, then drew it forward to his mouth to kiss her knuckles. He held her that way, with one arm draped around his neck, her breasts flattened on his back. She put her cheek on his shoulder and hugged him. Strangely enough, she felt both content and turbulent.

"I want to show you something, okay?"

So overwhelmed with sensation, Emma could barely speak. She nodded.

He slowed the boat even more to drift into dark green, shallow water riddled with sunken tree limbs and covered with moss. This finger of the cove was narrow, barely big enough for a boat to turn around. Emma worried for the boat's prop, but figured Casey knew what he was doing.

That thought was confirmed when she spotted a skinny weathered dock with uneven boards at the very tip of the cove. It had old tires nailed to the side to protect the boat, with grommets for a tie-up. Casey brought the boat up alongside it, turned off the engine and secured it with the ease of long practice.

Enormous elms grew along all sides of the shore-line, with branches reaching far out across the water to form a canopy over the cove. She could hear the croak of frogs, the splash of carp, the chirp of katy-dids. The air smelled thick with all the greenery.

Casey brought her around next to him. Every line of his body was drawn tight. "You like it?"

"It's incredible."

"I bought it. There're two acres, and the little cabin up the hill." He didn't look away from her as he explained that. "More like a shack, really. But it's secluded and peaceful."

Emma slipped off her sunglasses to peer into the surrounding woods. Sure enough, halfway up the hill a small house was just barely visible through the thick trees and scrubby shrubs. Like the dock, it was constructed of weathered wooden planks and consisted mostly of a sloping screened-in front porch. A skinny dirt path led down to the dock.

She gazed up at the tall trees, blocking all but a few rays of sunshine, then she listened to the quiet. Her tone low in near reverence, she whispered, "It's almost magical."

B.B. whined, then leaped nimbly from the boat to the dock. He started sniffing, working his way to the shore.

Still staring at her, Casey asked, "Will he be okay?"

Emma nodded. "He won't take off. He just wants to explore the area."

"If he goes too far, he'll find a few cows on the adjoining farm. But that's it. For all intents and purposes, we're alone here."

He touched the zipper of her cover-up, right between her breasts, with one finger. His dark glasses

still in place, his voice a low murmur, he said, "Let's
lose this now, okay?"

Trembling from the inside out, Emma nodded.
"All right." Uncertainty made her feel clumsy. She
wasn't shy, really, but it had been a long time since
she'd experienced the freedom of the lake. Everyone
everywhere wore little more than a suit, some skimp-
ier than others. In comparison, hers was modest, con-
cealing as much as a regular bra and panties might.

But that wasn't the point. She knew Casey would
touch her, knew he wanted to have sex with her, and
the very idea of it had her near to moaning. She kept
her attention on Casey's chest, instead of his face, and
dragged the zipper all the way down. She stood in
front of him, while he sat in the driver's seat, his face
level with her breasts, his knees open around her legs.

With an absorption that shook her, Casey set his
sunglasses aside, reached out and caught the top of
the terry cloth and tugged it slowly down her arms.
Amber eyes took in the sight of her body as he
dropped the cover-up on the seat behind her.

Leaves rustled overhead. Water lapped at the shore.
A bird chirped. Neither of them spoke.

Casey wrapped his hands around the backs of her
thighs, making Emma quiver. He stroked her, sliding
his palms slowly and deliberately up over her hips to
her waist where his thumbs dipped in near her navel,
back and forth across her belly. He watched the
movement of his fingers, then leaned forward and
pressed an openmouthed kiss to the rise of one breast,
another in her cleavage, lower, on her ribs.

Shaking under the sensual onslaught, Emma braced
her hands against his shoulders. "Casey..."

"It seemed like you were gone forever, but now that you're back, it's like you never left." He licked her navel, took a gentle love bite of her belly. In a gravelly voice, he rasped, "This has been a long time coming."

Closing her eyes, Emma tunneled her fingers through his thick, warm hair. She stroked his nape, then pulled him closer. "Yes."

His hands moved back down her body to her bottom. He kneaded her, groaned, closed his mouth around her nipple through the bathing-suit bra. She felt the press of his hot tongue.

"Casey."

In the next instant, he stood and Emma found herself flush against him, his mouth on hers, his tongue sinking deep. He pressed his rigid erection into her belly, his breathing labored, his hands trembling as he touched her everywhere with a gentleness that bordered on awe.

He lifted his mouth and looked at her. The heat in his eyes stole her breath, then he kissed her again, easy, slow. Against her mouth, he said, "Emma, honey, as gorgeous as you are in that suit, all I can think about now is getting you out of it."

Emma looked around the area, which was deserted but still out in the open. "It...it's been a long time since I made out in a cove..."

"Don't." Casey's hands tightened on her and he squeezed his eyes shut. Three deep breaths later, he got control of himself. Despite his obvious turmoil, he cradled her close and spoke quietly near her ear. "I'm talking about making love, not making out. And I thought we'd go up to the cabin. It's clean, and no one ever comes here." He opened his mouth on her neck, pressed his tongue to her wildly thrumming pulse. He groaned again. "I need a long time, Emma. Hours. Days." Her heart thundered, and she heard him barely whisper, "A lifetime."

Her knees nearly buckled. But men often said things they didn't mean when they were aroused. She had to remember that so she didn't set herself up for disappointment.

Flattening her hands on Casey's chest, she levered him back, smiled and said with absolute certainty, "Yes."

B.B. FOLLOWED THEM up the hill and into the enclosed front porch. The dark screening kept bugs out and shaded the room, but let in the fresh air. With the small house buried in the dense woods, it was cool and smelled a little earthy.

The dog did a quick reconnaissance of the area, sniffing everything, pushing his nose into every corner. He decided it bored him, and went back out through the screen door into the yard. They watched him as he wandered down to the dock, found a heated spot beneath a ray of sun. He turned around, circled and dropped.

Emma smiled. "He's so lazy," she said, her voice sounding thick.

Suffering the most raging case of lust he'd ever known, Casey seated himself on the side of the twin-size bed. The white cotton sheets were rumpled and the pillows still bore the imprint of his head from his last retreat three days ago. Then, he'd been consid-

ering his life, his future, what he wanted to do.
There'd been many decisions to make.

Now all other concerns were pushed aside in his
need to have Emma. Again, he clasped her hips and
looked at her adorable belly, the way her bra lifted
her breasts, how the waistband of the bottoms
stretched across her hipbones. The bikini was nearly
the same color as her skin, but nowhere near as soft.

"I put the bed in here when I bought the place. It's
great for napping, and I like to come here and think."

As bold as ever, Emma straddled his lap, then settled onto him, groin to groin, belly to belly, breasts
to chest. Her eyes were heavy, her face flushed, her
lips parted. She touched his jaw with her fingertips
while staring at his mouth. "What do you think about,
Casey?"

You, he started to say, but caught himself. Damn,
she looked ready. But he wanted to go slow, to make
it last. He pushed his hands into her bottoms, cuddled
her firm cheeks and rested his face against her breasts.
"Work. Life. Hell, I dunno." He'd often thought
about her, wondering where she was and what she
was doing. "I just like kicking back here, getting
away from everyone."

Emma nuzzled against his ear. "Do you bring
women here for sex?"

He jerked back, offended and annoyed. "Only you,
Emma."

Her big brown eyes darkened, and turned velvet
with emotion.

Without even trying, she twisted him inside out.
"Kiss me, Em."

She did, and damn, she knew how to kiss. Her enthusiasm singed him and left him so primed it was a wonder he didn't slide her beneath him right now.

Patience, he reminded himself. He wanted more than one quick fuck. He wanted... Hell, he didn't know everything he wanted. But he wanted more. Of her. Of this.

Her bra ties slid free easily enough, yet the closeness of their bodies kept it in place. Casey clasped her shoulders and held her away from him. The cups dropped away from her breasts and Emma, while smiling at him, removed the top completely.

Beautiful. Casey held her steady as he leaned forward and closed his mouth around her left nipple. Her body flexed the tiniest bit in reaction and she made a sound between a groan and a purr.

He locked his arms around the small of her back to keep her from retreating as he feasted upon her. He took his time, loving the taste and texture of her, the small sounds she made. When her nipple was tightly beaded, he switched to her other breast.

At first, the gentle rocking of her body didn't register. When it did, Casey had to look at her. With her head tipped back, her lips parted, her fingers caught in his hair, she epitomized female abandon.

Using his teeth with devastating effect, he further taunted her nipple, until she whispered, "Casey, please..."

He shuddered in reaction. "I love hearing you say my name." He couldn't wait any longer. Lifting her to her feet, he quickly finished stripping her. She didn't say a word when he hooked his fingers in the waistband of her bottoms and skimmed them down her legs. She stepped out of the material, he set them aside, and they both went silent.

So often in his dreams, he'd imagined having Emma just like this.

She stood there with her belly pulled tight, her nipples wet from his mouth. His to take. Casey drew a heated breath—and knew he was falling hard all over again.

It should have bothered him. Emma had walked out on him once; she kept secrets from him still. She'd only been back in town for a day and had definite plans for taking off again. But, at the moment, none of that mattered.

Keeping his eyes on the neat triangle of pubic hair between her legs, he unsnapped his shorts and shoved them down, removing his boxers at the same time. He kicked them aside on the dusty porch floor. He knew Emma was staring at his erection. He locked his knees and let her look her fill, but it wasn't easy when his every muscle strained against the need to hold her again.

In a breathless whisper, she said, "I hope I'm not dreaming."

That made him smile and relieved some of his tension. "Come here, and I'll make sure you're awake." The words were barely out of his mouth and Emma was there, her small hands sliding up and over his chest to twine around his neck, her belly pressing into his groin, her mouth turned up for his. She showed no reserve, no hesitation. And the kiss she gave him left him shaking.

Hoping to slow her down, he lowered them both to the bed and moved to her side. The urge to climb on top of her and sink deep into her body was already strong. With her encouraging murmurs and touches, holding back was hell. But he'd been waiting for over eight years so what did a few more minutes matter?

And he had been waiting, he knew that now. The dissatisfaction he'd felt with every female since Emma now made sense. They'd been lacking simply because they weren't Emma. She was special in ways he hadn't realized.

Propping himself up on his elbow, Casey stared down at her.

She shifted, trying to bring him back to her, flesh to flesh. "Casey?"

"Shh." Fingers spread wide, he settled his hand on her belly and felt her muscles contract. "I love just looking at you, Emma."

Her velvety brown eyes, so hungry, so hot, held his as she caught his wrist and urged his hand lower, between her parted thighs. She started at the first touch of his fingers there, moaning softly, her breath hitching.

Watching her face, Casey gently opened her with his fingertips, stroked over her swollen vulva, her clitoris. She was wet, hot. His own heartbeat roared in his ears.

As he teased, her back arched off the mattress, making her breasts an offering. He dipped down to gently suck on her nipples at the same time he sank his middle finger deep. Her reaction was startling—and damn exciting. Inner muscles clenched tight around his finger, her body shivered, her legs stiffened.

"*Casey.*" So much pleading in one small word.

Hell yes, he loved hearing his name, especially the way she said it now, with all the same need he felt.

A rosy flush covered her body, warming her skin and intensifying her luscious scent. Casey took his time suckling her, fingering her, enjoying her. Perversely, the more frantic Emma became, the more she moaned and writhed and pleaded, the more determined he was to take his time, to leisurely make her crazy with lust. And to prove to her that she couldn't feel this with any man other than him.

She was so easy to read, not because her hands clenched fitfully in his hair and her broken moans were so explicit. Not because her hips rocked against his hand, faster, harder. But because he knew this one particular woman better than any other. It seemed he always had. And he knew he always would.

He felt her begin to tremble, felt the stillness that signaled the onset of her release, and he surged up from her breasts to take her mouth in a voracious, claiming kiss.

Goddammit, she was his. She'd always been his. She…

The clench of her nails on his shoulders shattered his thoughts and warned of her release. Heart ready to explode, he rode out the climax with her, kissing her face, murmuring to her, maintaining the steady press and stroke of his rough fingertips between her thighs until she finally pulled her mouth away to gulp frantically for air. She took her pleasure as naturally as a woman should—relishing it, giving in to it.

"Oh God," she groaned as she slumped back into the mattress, still breathing too hard, still shivering. Her eyes were slumberous, heated. Damp with tears.

He wanted more.

He needed it all.

Casey came to his knees to look over her temporarily sated body—temporary, because no way in hell was he done with her. He touched her everywhere, parting her legs wider, stroking her with both hands, catching her already sensitive nipples. He luxuriated in the feel of her warm, soft flesh in places that he'd once considered forbidden to him.

"You care about me, Emma. It's still there—whatever it is between us."

Her eyes were closed, her face turned slightly away. She nodded, sniffed, and more tears seeped out around her thick lashes.

Frowning, Casey trailed his fingers down her body, over her belly, through her pubic hair and between her lips. She was creamy wet now, swollen, throbbing. He watched her eyes open...and thrust three fingers into her hard.

She cried out softly, twisting on the sheets.

"Admit it, Em. Say it." He waited, but she stared at him with that lost expression that had the ability to rip him apart. His teeth clenched. "Tell me it's still there. *Tell me you care about me.*"

She swallowed hard and offered up a small, shaky smile. Looking more vulnerable than any woman ever should, she whispered, "Always, Casey." Her voice broke, and she laid one palm over his heart. "Always."

A tidal wave of feelings took his breath. He couldn't wait a second more. He snagged the condom from his shorts pocket and rolled it on in record time. Emma waited until he started to settle over her, then she rose up and pushed him to his back. Eyes still glistening with tears, that small secret smile still in place, she stared into his eyes. "It's my turn."

Casey groaned. That husky purr of hers would be the death of him. His muscles cramped when she wrapped both hands around his erection and stroked, slow, easy. Again and again.

He was still trying to get himself under control when she lifted herself over him, positioned him against her tender sex, and sank down so languidly he nearly lost it there and then.

"Emma..." His awareness of her was so heightened, he felt everything, every tiny movement and touch. Like the press of her smooth legs around his hips, and her buttocks on his thighs. The way her hands contracted on his chest and how her body squeezed him with each retreat, then softened around him as she sank down again.

Her breasts swayed, drawing his hands, then his mouth. Much as he enjoyed seeing her astride him, she was too far away. Craving the touch of her body to his, Casey sat up and pulled her closer so he could reach all of her, her slim back, the luscious flare of her hips and the firm resilience of her ass cheeks. He kissed her, keeping her mouth under his even as he felt his testicles tightening with his climax.

As she wrapped her legs completely around him, Emma never missed a beat, rising and falling, rising again. She didn't let him hold back, didn't give him a chance to regain control. When he came, she took his harsh groans into her mouth and gave back her own sweet sounds of release. Their bodies strained, clung, and then shuddered roughly. Her arms wrapped around his neck, Emma leaned into him.

Casey felt her heartbeat rioting against his jaw and he pressed a kiss to her breast. Emma's fingers stroked idly through his hair, petting him, hugging him tight every couple of seconds. The contentment lasted for long minutes. He felt at peace, whole in a way that had eluded him until now.

But with the edge taken off his hunger, Casey knew he had to tend to other things. He mentally braced himself, then carefully stretched out on the bed with Emma resting over his chest.

He was still inside her when he kissed her temple and said, "Now we talk."

"Mmm." She toyed with his chest hair, and Casey could hear the sleepiness in her voice, reminding him once again that she was short on rest, heavy on worries. "About what?"

Staring at the warped boards in the ceiling, Casey tightened his arms around her back so she couldn't run from him. "About you." He kept his tone calm, firm. "About what happened that night you came to my house."

She stiffened in alarm, but he couldn't relent. This was too important. She tried to struggle away from him but he stroked her, hoping to soothe her, to offer reassurance.

"Casey..."

He held her close to his heart. "I want to talk about your mother."

"No."

"Yes."

She lifted her face so he could see her disgruntled

frown. Casey smoothed her tangled hair back and studied her taut expression. He touched the corner of her mouth with his thumb, and said, "She's a drunk, isn't she, Emma?"

DAMON SMILED at the picture Ceily made in her sundress and sandals. Given the understated outfit, she should have looked innocent. Instead, she looked hot. Tantalizing. Like a wet dream.

He knew women well enough to know she'd spent extra time preparing for him. It showed in the carefully applied makeup, the subtle sexiness of her clothes.

She'd spent the last hour showing him around Buckhorn, not that there was that much to see other than the beautiful scenery. They'd had ice cream, and watching Ceily lick a cone was a special form of foreplay he wasn't likely to forget anytime soon. Damon was sure it had been deliberate. And it had worked.

He'd barely been able to take his gaze off her as they'd waved to a hundred of her "close friends" and browsed the one and only gift shop.

After showing him all the landmarks, she'd driven her small compact to the outskirts of town, parked near a pasture and gotten out. Carrying a small cooler of drinks and with a plaid blanket over his arm, Damon followed her. He had to be careful of cowpatties, a unique concern that.

He wasn't quite sure where Ceily was leading him, but he gladly followed. Walking behind her, taking in the sway of her lush hips, certainly wasn't a hardship.

The humid breeze ruffled her hair and played with

her skirt when she twisted to look at him over her shoulder. "There's a beautiful creek right down here."

The entire area looked splendid—the perfect place to build some small vacation cabins or retirement homes. "Is this your property?"

"No, it belongs to my grandpa."

He wondered if her grandpa would be willing to sell. "You've lived here your whole life?"

"Yep." She stopped in front of a crystal-clear creek filled with churning water. The sound alone could mesmerize, but with the wildflowers here and there, birds circling and Ceily close by, it was outright magnificent.

Damon spread the blanket and watched her settle onto it. Ceily wasn't an introverted or uncertain woman. She had a teasing, confident presence that aroused him.

He dropped next to her and slanted her a teasing look. "If I get too hot, do you intend to throw me into the creek?"

Utilizing considerable thought, she plucked a long blade of grass. "I thought we might both cool off when the sun sets."

Damon arched an eyebrow. "Skinny-dipping?"

Her mouth curled while she positioned the blade of grass between her thumbs. "I bet you're a virgin, huh?"

"Was it my uncommon restraint that led you to that conclusion?"

Laughing, she said, "I mean a virgin to skinny-dipping. Somehow I can't see you frolicking outdoors in the buff."

Damon rested back on one elbow. "I'm always up for new experiences, especially when they're initiated by a beautiful woman."

He jumped when she raised both hands to her mouth, the blade of grass somehow caught between, and gave an earsplitting whistle. When she looked at him for approval, he asked, "Is that how country girls whistle?"

Pushing her hair behind her ear, Ceily nodded. She didn't quite look at him when she idly tossed out, "Wanna see how country girls kiss?"

Feeling a curl of heat, Damon murmured, "That's a dumb question for such a smart girl."

She laughed and came down over his chest, knocking him flat. "I like you, Damon."

"Is that so?" He smiled, enjoying her silly banter. "Show me."

"All right." Her eyebrows lowered. "But I should warn you first that I don't sleep with a guy on the first date."

"Pity." Did she expect him to start complaining? He held his grin back with an effort, ready to disappoint her. He liked Ceily, and he appreciated her honesty. He held her hair away from her face and brushed his lips over her chin, her throat.

"You're not mad?"

"That you've been teasing me? No. I happen to be enjoying your efforts."

"Unbelievable."

Feeling smug, he grinned at her, knowing he had just surprised her. "So how many dates will it take me?"

She stared deep into his eyes, lowered her mouth to his and groaned. "Let's play it by ear."

The second her mouth touched his, Damon was lost. Damn, she was sweet, and yet she was also brazen. A delicious combination.

Slowly the kiss ended. Ceily licked her lips, sighed and rested her head on his chest. "Want me to teach you how to whistle like that?"

Damon was in the most powerful throes of lust he'd felt in years, and she wanted to teach him how to whistle. He laughed, liking the novelty of it, liking her more by the moment. "That's exactly what I was thinking about. Whistling. And with a blade of grass, no less."

She poked him in the ribs. "Liar."

He tightened his arms around her so she couldn't prod him again. "At the risk of sounding trite, what's a smart girl like you doing in Buckhorn?" Damon could easily picture her in the city, charming one and all.

She pushed up to see his face. "This is home. Where else would I be?"

The way she said it, he felt foolish for asking. Though he'd come with a distinct sense of contempt for the town that had ostracized Emma, Buckhorn had managed to charm him as well. The relaxed air, the openness, the sense of being where you belonged, fed something in his soul. The idea of settling here teased at him. "Your grandfather own a lot of land?"

Her sigh held a wealth of melancholy. "He does, but soon he'll have to sell a major portion of it, including this spot, which is one reason I brought you here. I don't know how much longer I'll get to enjoy it."

"Is he selling to developers?"

"He doesn't want to. But he needs the money, so..." She shrugged.

A variety of emotions clamored for attention. Damon hated that Ceily would lose something important to her, but at the same time his mind already churned with the possibilities. It would be an insult to the land to clutter it with shopping centers or parking lots, but a few cozy cabins spaced out along the creek...well, it'd be lovely. And lucrative.

He couldn't think about purchasing the land without thinking about Ceily as well. She was in her mid-thirties, single, which prompted another question. "Okay, so why isn't a warm, sexy woman like you married?"

Her cheeks dimpled with a smile. "I suppose I have high standards, and all the best men were taken."

"And those standards are...?"

"Mmm. Let's see." Somehow, her hand on his chest just happened to be over his left nipple. If she stroked him one more time, he was going to have to jump into the icy creek on his own volition. "He'd need to be caring, like Sawyer Hudson."

A dark cloud intruded on his contentment. "Case Hudson's father?"

"Yep. Sawyer is a local doctor and everyone in these parts loves him. He's almost perfect, but I'd want someone to be bold and vigilant too, like his brother, Morgan. He's the sheriff."

Damon saw a definite pattern beginning. "For crying out—"

"And gentle like his brother Jordan, handy like Gabe…"

"Enough." Damon rolled her beneath him. In a growl, he said, "I think you're teasing me again."

She laughed up at him, proving him right. "Maybe. But I've always been a *little* in love with each of them." Her gaze moved over his mouth and she added gently, "No one else ever quite measures up."

Damon's eyebrows lifted. "By God, that sounds like a challenge."

She looped her arms around his neck. "Does it?"

Damon had the feeling she knew exactly what she was doing. Never in his life had he felt the need to compete for a woman, and he wasn't about to start the barbaric ritual now. Despite those assurances to himself, he tangled his hand in her hair, tipped her mouth up to his and said, "I don't want to hear you say their names again."

"But—"

He kissed her, not just a kiss, but full-body contact, heartbeat to heartbeat, and long minutes later when he felt her thigh slide up along the outside of his, he lifted his head. Her lips were wet, her eyes smoky.

Satisfied, Damon pried himself away from her and stood. "Now," he said, while trying to subtly readjust himself, "about that dip in the creek…"

CHAPTER ELEVEN

EMMA GAVE UP TRYING to get away from Casey. Oh, if she flat out told him to release her, he would. But then he'd wonder at her overreaction, especially in light of what they'd just shared. She didn't want to give away more than necessary.

She settled back against him—a most comfortable place to be—and made her tone as unaffected as possible. Despite her wariness in discussing her problems with him, she felt mellow and sated and emotionally full.

She kissed his chest and asked, "Why do you want to know?"

"I want to know everything about you. When we were younger I was so busy trying to resist you, I never thought to ask some important questions." He patted her behind. "It took all my willpower and concentration to say no."

She smiled.

Casey relaxed his hold to stroke her back. "I always assumed that your dad mistreated you. Did you know that?"

A logical assumption, she supposed, but mostly untrue. "No, my dad never physically hurt me."

"Okay, not physically." He'd caught her small clarification and asked for one of his own. "But he did hurt you, didn't he, by not putting you first, as all parents should?"

Perhaps, Emma was thinking, she should tell him some of it. It would help to show the broad contrasts in their lives and make him understand why she couldn't stay in Buckhorn. It wouldn't be easy for him to understand because Casey had always known love, always had security. Could he even comprehend what her life had been like?

But she'd taken too long to answer him. He turned to his side so that Emma faced him. With a tenderness that felt *almost* like love, he tipped up her chin and kissed her nose. "Trust me, Em."

"I do. I was just trying to figure out how to say it, where to begin."

"Your mother is a drunk?"

"For as far back as I can remember. All our holidays and special occasions were tainted because she'd drink too much, and once she started, she'd keep drinking for days, and then need more days to recover." Somehow, telling Casey about her darkest secrets wasn't as bad as she'd anticipated. He held her, warm and strong, and it made it so much easier. "She got to where she didn't need a reason to drink. She'd just decide to and the times between episodes narrowed until she was drinking almost as often as not." Emma took comfort in the steady thumping of his heart and admitted, "She's not a nice drunk."

Casey's eyes were steady on her face, not giving her a chance to retreat emotionally or hold anything back. "She got violent?"

"Sometimes." That was so awful to admit, Emma immediately tried to explain. "Her judgment was off when she drank. She'd take everything wrong, no matter what you said or what you did. And she'd get furious.''

Casey muttered a low curse and gathered her closer.

''It's all right.'' Emma gave him one truth that she'd learned long ago. ''Being hit wasn't the worst part of it.''

''No?'' He drew a shuddering breath, and his voice sounded raw. ''What was the worst part?''

She shrugged. ''Being afraid. Not knowing when it would happen, not knowing what to expect or when. I hated walking on eggshells, always being so uncertain.''

She'd never talked about her mother with anyone, and now she found there were things about her mother's illness that she wanted to say. ''You know what? It was strange, but I got to where I could figure out when she'd drink just from the anticipation in her voice. Or her tone. Something about her mannerisms. I could even talk to her on the phone and I'd hear it and...I didn't want to go home.''

Breathing too hard, Casey kissed her temple, her ear. She felt his grim resolve to hear it all, so she continued.

''It might have been a week or a month. It might have been only a few days. But I knew if she started to drink, she'd get drunk.'' Emma sighed and turned onto her back to stare up at the roof. ''Those were the nights I'd stay out.''

''So she couldn't touch you?''

''That, and because she's so...ugly when she's

drunk. Mean and nasty and hateful. She made me feel
ugly, too.''

"Oh, Em." He squeezed her tight.

"By the morning, she'd be in a near stupor and
much easier to deal with. When she'd finally sober
up, she'd be sorry. Really, really sorry. And she'd be
sick for days.''

"Jesus." He gave a long, disgusted sigh.

She shrugged as if it didn't really matter—when
really it mattered too much. It always had. "Dad tried
to run interference—he really did. But he's always
worked two jobs and he…" Emma squeezed her eyes
shut. "He loves her. He'd tell her not to drink,
threaten to leave her. And once he even refused to
buy her any alcohol. But…that didn't stop her either." Emma hated remembering that night. It still
had the power to make her stomach pitch in fear.

She shrugged, shaking off the sensations of old.
"Dad loves her too much to ever really enforce any
consequences.''

"Hey." Casey's big hand opened on the side of
her face. "You deserve love too, you know.''

"I know." God, her voice sounded far too small.
She hated that, hated her pathetic childish weakness
when it came to this one topic. She'd grown strong
through the years, but it seemed she'd never outgrown
her childhood hurt. "That's why being with the Devaughns was so great. They do love me. Damon and
I are close. I had a…a normal life with them and it
was wonderful.''

Only they weren't her real family, just good people.
They'd felt sorry for her at first, but that pity had

turned to love. She knew it, felt it whenever she was around them. And she loved them in return.

"That's why Damon came with you?"

"He worries," she admitted. "I told him I'd be fine, but he didn't want me to be alone. He hadn't counted on you though." She turned her head toward him and had to smile. He was rumpled from their lovemaking, a little sweaty, his eyes still smoldering. And, for the moment, all hers.

"Damon knew about you, of course. I told him how I'd come to your house that night and he naturally had questions. I was prepared to see you again, Casey, but neither of us expected you to…"

Casey cupped her breast. "Reclaim you?"

"Casey Hudson, there's no way you can reclaim something you never had and never wanted in the first place."

His long fingers continued to caress her, shaping her breast in his palm, gently, easily, as if he now had the right. And she supposed he did.

"I was young too, Emma. I didn't know what I wanted until it was too late. I thought I had to stick to my grand plans and—"

"And I wasn't part of those plans. How could I be? I understand all that, Casey. And I'm so proud of you."

He wasn't looking at her, but rather at her breast. Now he leaned forward and briefly suckled her nipple, making her close her eyes on a moan. She was still sensitive from their recent lovemaking and just that easily her body softened for him again.

He released her only to blow a warm breath over her damp flesh. "I want a chance with you, Emma."

His eyes shifted to hers and the moment their gazes collided, she felt pinned in place. "I want you to give us a chance while you're here."

Oh God, that hurt, to even think of something permanent with Casey. She spoke the words aloud, not just for his benefit, but for her own so she didn't start reaching for things she couldn't have. "I have a life in Chicago."

Casey nodded. "I used to think I wanted a life in Cincinnati. But the more entrenched I've gotten there, the more I've realized that I hate the job with my grandfather, am sick of the damn commute and resent my time away from my home." He stared down at her with a thoughtful frown. "Haven't you ever felt that way?"

"No. There were things about Buckhorn that I missed." She tugged on his chest hair and teased, "You, of course. And the water, the air and the...freedom. But you have tons of friends here, and family who love you. I don't. You can't know what it's like to be the outsider, for your own mother to despise you and for your father to care more about her than anything else, including what she does to you. You can't—"

Casey sat up and swung his legs over the side of the bed. Startled, Emma visually traced the long line of his back down to his buttocks. Her throat felt thick.

He turned back to her as suddenly again, his expression devoid of emotion. "You know about my mother, Emma?"

She nodded. Most everyone in Buckhorn knew that Sawyer wasn't really Casey's father. Casey's mother got caught cheating and Sawyer started divorce proceedings. When she birthed Casey, she planned to adopt him out. Instead, Sawyer had been at the hospital with her because she had no one else, and once he held Casey, he'd immediately claimed him as his own. After some nasty gossip—spread mostly by Casey's mother—she took off. No one had heard from her since. But Sawyer, along with Morgan, Jordan and Gabe, had raised Casey, and there wasn't a soul who knew them who would question that Casey had been well loved.

"I looked her up once." His eyes lit with cynicism. "Bet you didn't know that."

"No." Emma, too, sat up and tugged the sheet over her lap.

"Not one of my better ideas. I don't know what I expected, but she wanted nothing to do with me. She was pretty damn plain about that." He rubbed a hand over his face. "I haven't told anyone else, not even Dad."

"I won't ever say a word." Stupid woman, Emma thought, then added out loud, "She doesn't deserve you, Casey."

His smile now was chagrined. "Like your parents don't deserve you? It's true. You're a beautiful person and pretty damn special. I hope you know that."

Such a lavish compliment made her blush.

"I wasn't looking for pity, though, any more than you were. I only told you because I wanted you to see that we do have some similarities."

Emma laughed. "Right."

"We both love Mustangs."

She gave him that one.

"And we both love the water." Casey bent and

kissed her throat. "And sex." He nuzzled her breast. "I'd say that's enough to build on."

"You're the only person I know who'd think so, which just goes to prove how extraordinary you are."

That had him raising his head and frowning. "I'm just me, Emma, prone to making lots of mistakes. Taking the job with my stepgrandfather was one of them, though now I'm not quite sure how the hell to get out of it."

"You don't think he'd understand?"

Casey grunted. "I don't know. He's made me the damn heir apparent, and while I hate the job, I'm rather fond of him. I don't want to disappoint him."

"What is it you want to do?"

"Something here. Something simple. Like you— which is another similarity—I want to have my own small business rather than help run a gigantic organization."

Prodding him, she said, "Like…?"

He laughed. "I don't know for sure, nosy. But I'm thinking maybe I'd try being an accountant and financial planner. I already have a BBA in accounting and an MBA in accounting and taxation. I could get a CFP certification…" He finally noticed the comical confusion on Emma's face and drew to a halt. "Sorry. A lot of mumbo jumbo, huh?"

She couldn't hold back her grin. "Since the closest I got to a college was driving past in my car, and the idea of crunching numbers makes my brain throb, yeah. But I take it you're already qualified?"

He laughed. "For the most part. And I *do* enjoy crunching numbers, especially if I can help people plan better. You know, a lot of folks around here are selling land and not getting what they should. Some of the older people are retiring without enough to live on." He shook his head. "As I said, I'm still thinking on it. And thinking right now, with you sitting there looking like that, isn't easy."

Emma grinned, and hiked the sheet a little higher. "Better?"

"Hey now, I didn't mean you should…"

Emma swatted at him when he reached for the sheet and they both laughed. "Okay," she said when he retreated again, albeit with a big grin, "so that's one mistake you've made. And not even really a mistake because it sounds to me like you've already got it figured out. You know what you want to do—you're just dragging your heels about doing it. I say go for it. What have you got to lose?"

"A great job? Financial security?"

She snorted. "You'll be an overnight success."

He stared at her intently, then suddenly sounding too serious again, he said, "You know your faith in me is downright scary. Always has been."

Her faith was well deserved, but he didn't look open to hearing that.

He put his hand on her thigh and squeezed. "I'm not perfect, honey, and I don't even want to be. I've made more mistakes than I can count." His hand slid higher, under the sheet and up to the inside of her thigh. "But losing you was the worst of the lot."

He kept saying things like that, confusing her so much.

"The night you left me—you and your mother had been fighting?"

"I didn't leave you." Good God, where did he get these notions? "I left Buckhorn."

Casey just waited.

Her calm now shot to hell, Emma said, "Yes." But then she shook her head, trying to pick and choose her words. "Not really fighting, but she was drunk and Dad couldn't reason with her and things just got out of control..." *Boy, was that an understatement.* "I didn't want to stay for that anymore. I decided it was past time to go."

"If your dad hadn't had the stroke, you wouldn't have come back." He made it a statement rather than a question.

"No." This was the hard part, where she had to be really careful. "I'd talked to them a few times, but nothing had changed. They knew how to reach me, and though Dad called every so often, like on my birthday and holidays, Mom only called four times, and two of those times she was drunk."

Casey lowered them both to lie on the mattress. His hands held her face still for the soft press of his mouth to her forehead, chin and cheeks. "Don't let them continue to influence your life."

"I don't!"

"When you avoid Buckhorn because of them?" Put that way, she had no more denials to offer. "You're here now, and who knows for how long? Your dad may need you for months, maybe longer. He might never fully recover. Is your mother capable of taking care of him, considering she has a drinking problem?"

Surely that wouldn't be the case. She hadn't even

had the opportunity to consider such an eventuality. Things were happening too fast...

"Give us a chance, Emma. That's all I'm asking. Quit shutting me out and let's see how it goes." He moved against her and added, "Do you think you can do that?"

From breasts to thighs, his hard, naked body covered her. She could feel his erection against her belly, his warm, fast breath. Pushing all probable consequences aside, she reached for him. "Yes."

THEY'D FALLEN ASLEEP. Exhausted, Emma slept like the dead and woke with Casey propped on an elbow beside her, smiling. B.B. was splayed over their legs.

"He snuck in about a half hour ago."

Emma stretched up to peer at the dog. As if he felt her awareness, he rolled to his back and looked at her upside down. Casey chuckled and reached down to scratch his throat.

"I can see this might turn tricky. Maybe I should get another cot and set it up at the other end of the porch."

"Wouldn't work," Emma informed him. "He'd still crawl up here. He's too used to sleeping with me."

"He got dirt and leaves in the bed, but at least he's dry. And he didn't complain at having me here."

"He likes you." Emma stroked Casey's shoulder. "I like you, too."

"Yeah?" His slow smile warmed her heart. "Well, I'll have to remember this combination, huh?"

"What combination?"

"Great sex and a little rest."

Laughing, Emma stretched and said, "The sex was incredible, and I did need the rest." She peeked at him. "But do you think you can add food in there somewhere?"

"Whatever it takes to keep you happy."

If this was a dream, Emma thought, she didn't want to wake up. Casey was so attentive, constantly touching her, kissing her. Sharing details of her mother's sickness hadn't been nearly as painful as she'd feared, because Casey had shared some of himself in return. And best of all, he had no complaints about her dog. Every other man she'd dated had resented B.B.'s interference—which had made them very dispensable. But not Casey. Rather than scold the dog, he'd made room for him and even given him affectionate pats. But then when had Casey ever been like other guys?

After they got dressed, she finally got a tour of the little run-down cabin. It needed some repairs, no doubt about that, but it was still quaint, boasting a stone fireplace currently blackened from use, a minuscule bathroom—which she made use of—and a tiny kitchenette that even had running water. Other than the bathroom being sectioned off, it was all one open room.

Casey showed her where he'd like to erect a gazebo, where he'd clear an area for a picnic table and perhaps a shelter. The charm of the cabin would definitely be the seclusion and the surrounding nature. Casey promised to bring her there often, and Emma already looked forward to the return.

A few minutes later, after Casey insisted on covering her in sunscreen with excruciating, and exciting, attention to detail, they took the boat out again in search of food. First, Casey pulled in to the boat dock with the intention of getting hot dogs and chips. He changed his mind when, seconds after they'd docked, Lois and Kristin, along with a contingent of friends, converged on him. They'd docked their own boat and had been in the process of restocking their drinks and snacks.

It wasn't unusual to run into people on the lake. As Casey had told Damon, people used their boats almost as much as their cars. But to see the two women together...well, that boggled Emma's mind. Her luck couldn't be that bad. She caught Casey's apologetic shrug, prompting her to ask, "They're friends?"

"Everyone knows everyone else around here, babe, you know that."

"But...they both want you!"

That made him laugh, and shake his head at her. "I told you I work with Kristin, and Lois is—or rather was—a friend."

Apparently, he was still annoyed with Lois for her sniping remarks at the hospital. Emma tried to ignore both women as they sent her baleful looks while moving in on Casey. It wasn't easy. They wore tiny bikinis, gorgeous tans, and they were all too ready to play touchy-feely with Casey.

Because of the men who'd accompanied Lois and Kristin, Emma was grateful that she'd put her cover-up back on. They were being nice enough about it, only barely looking, but judging by their curious attention, she assumed Lois had already clued them in to her identity.

Casually polite, Casey spoke with the women while

gassing up the boat. Two of the men, dressed only in snug trunks, walked around the dock to Emma's side. B.B. gave a low growl of warning, alerting Casey to their approach.

One of the young men knelt down, which brought him closer to eye level with Emma. He grinned at her with what looked to be real pleasure. "Emma, I'd heard you were back. It's good to see you again."

Her dark glasses shielded her eyes and gave her a false sense of privacy. "Thanks. I'm sorry...do I know you?"

Chagrin added color to his already tanned face. "You don't remember me?"

"Should I?"

He ribbed his friend and they both laughed. "Naw, I guess not. It was a long time ago."

His friend added, "And you have lost some hair."

They laughed, and the first man held out his hand. "Gary Wilham."

The name jogged her memory, causing Emma to look closer. True, he had a bit of a receding hairline, but he was still quite handsome. And still built like a linebacker... "I remember now. You played football for the school."

"That'd be me."

"Sorry about that. I'm not real good with faces anymore." She and Gary had had a short-lived... thing. She wouldn't call him a boyfriend, and they hadn't officially dated. But if he expected her to be embarrassed, he'd be disappointed.

He kept the handshake brief and merely polite, surprising her. "So." He gave her the once-over. "You look terrific. How've you been?"

Relaxing, Emma said, "Good. And yourself?"

"Real good. You in town for long?"

"A few weeks maybe." Or months. She just didn't know yet.

"That's great." He glanced at Casey, then back to her with casual interest. "Catching up with old friends?" At her nod, he said, "Perfect. We're all going waterskiing. Want to join us? It'll give you a chance to get reacquainted with everyone."

Emma barely had her mouth open to make her excuses when Casey started the boat's powerful motor, making conversation more difficult. The men backed up. Emma turned and saw that Casey, too, wore his glasses—and a very false smile.

"Sorry, Gary. We've already got plans. Maybe some other time?" And he put the boat in reverse before Gary could offer any alternatives.

A little stunned at their hasty retreat, Emma waved to the men bidding her a fast farewell. Once they were several yards out in the lake, she said, "That was rather abrupt."

"He was about to ask you out. As to that, if he finds out where you're staying, he'll probably call."

Suffering faint disappointment at Casey's attitude, Emma raised an eyebrow. "You mean he'll expect to jump back into...old times."

Though his glasses hid his eyes, there was no mistaking Casey's annoyance. "No, damn it. I meant he and every other guy who looks at you will notice what an attractive woman you are and hope to get closer. Reacquainting himself is just an excuse."

"Oh." Emma felt small for projecting her own thoughts onto him. "Sorry."

"As to that, I'd appreciate it if you'd quit putting words into my mouth, okay?"

To give him his due, she winced theatrically. "Okay, I'll try."

"And while we're on the subject, I'd like us to come to an understanding."

That he was heading back toward Morgan's dock didn't escape her notice. "Two questions. One, is our day at the lake over?"

He stared straight ahead. "You're starting to look a little pink, despite the sunscreen. I think you've had enough sun, but I thought we'd head back to the house to eat. If Honey doesn't have anything ready, then we'll grab a bite at Ceily's."

Just hearing Ceily's name made her stomach clench. She swallowed hard, prayed Honey had dinner going, and nodded. "Question two, what understanding?"

His mouth flattened before he huffed out a long breath. In rapid order, he slowed the boat and reached for her hand, then pulled her up and into his side. Still looking severe, he drew her close for a brief kiss. "I have to get back to work tomorrow, but I'll cut my hours short and be home by five all week. That'll give us most of the evening to be together."

Amazed at the plans he made, at the way he wanted to adjust his routine to suit her, Emma could only stare at him.

"I have no right to ask you this," he went on, "but I was hoping you'd spend all your free time with me—and only me."

"My free time?"

He glanced ahead as another boat going at breakneck speed came around the bend. "Yeah. I realize you'll need to be with your father a lot, and I'm willing to do that with you too, whenever I'm around. But I…damn it, Em, I don't want you going out with other guys." He'd sounded belligerent, but just as quickly went tender with a self-conscious laugh. "I swear, it'd make me nuts."

It would take her time to get used to Casey wanting her. "I'd like that."

"Making me nuts?"

She laughed. "No, spending more time with you. But you're right that I need to see my dad often. It's why I'm here, after all. And since it looks like I'll be here awhile, I might need to drive back home to get more clothes…"

"We'll get it all worked out."

We. She really liked the sound of that. But would Casey still feel the same when he found out the truth of why she'd left? He'd asked her to tell him the whole truth, but through lies of omission, she'd denied him that. He'd also asked her to trust him, yet how could she? She knew Casey, knew what a good person he was. He'd been very understanding so far, but he wouldn't be able to understand everything she'd done.

When she'd only planned to be in town for a week or so, she'd thought she might be able to avoid confronting past transgressions. If she needed to stay a month or more, the chances of being haunted by her past increased.

Yet what else could she do?

She'd start by simply enjoying what time she could have with him. And she'd face demons as they arose, not a second before. If it all fell apart in the end…well, it was no more than she'd ever expected.

Probably no more than she deserved.

In the meantime, she'd take what she could—and wait for it all to come crashing down.

CHAPTER TWELVE

BY THE TIME Casey walked her to the motel-room door, it was past midnight. Exhaustion pulled at him, but he hated for the day to end. It had been a unique pleasure, watching Emma interact with his family. She'd helped Honey with dinner, fallen naturally into the routine of serving the kids, and when Gabe showed up with Elizabeth, she'd spent over an hour discussing car motors with him.

Casey knew everyone was curious about her, but they'd also enjoyed her company. Emma was very easy to be with, in a hundred different ways. Maybe if he brought her around them more often, she'd realize what he already knew—that she fit into his life with ease.

Emma turned at the door to smile at him, and Casey had to kiss her again. And once he kissed her, he wanted so much more. Making love to her this afternoon had been deeply satisfying...but not nearly enough. He wanted her again, right now. If she hadn't looked so weary, he might have invited himself in.

He consoled himself with the fact that she'd agreed to see him every day. He had no doubt that at least part of their time together would be spent in bed.

After a full day in the sun and water, and after the rambunctious attention from all the kids, B.B. was tired as well. While Casey feasted on Emma's sweet mouth, the dog collapsed in a heap at their feet.

Though he told himself merely to kiss her goodnight, Casey couldn't resist taking a little more. He flattened his hands on the door at either side of her head, angled his hips in, and relished the feel of her soft, accommodating body flush against his. Emma clung to his neck, taking his tongue, giving him her own. They both groaned at about the same time.

"You're hard again," she whispered against his mouth with what sounded like awe.

"And you're so damn soft," he growled, rubbing his nose against her cheek, her throat, her chin.

She stared into his eyes, slowly licked her lips, then offered, "If you'd like to—"

The door opened behind her.

With a yelp, Emma, who'd been leaning on the door with Casey's full weight against her, lost her balance and fell inward. Because his hands had been flat on the door, Casey couldn't stop himself from falling in too. He tried to brace himself, but his feet got tangled over the dog.

Damon said, "What the hell!" just before the three of them landed hard on the floor in a welter of arms and legs. Damon cursed again, Emma gave an *umph* as she got squashed, and Casey quickly tried to lever himself off her. But B.B. had been jerked awake with a start and found it all great fun. He jumped on Casey's back and knocked him flat against Emma again.

Everyone froze.

Into the silence, Damon, who was on the bottom of the heap, murmured dryly, "Well. My first ménage à trois, but somehow I never figured I'd be on the bottom.''

Emma started snickering, while it was Casey's turn to curse.

"I'm being quite crushed," Damon added. "So, Emma, doll, if you wouldn't mind…?"

"I'm trying," she claimed around her giggles. She realized her legs were open to Casey, cradling him. "But Casey—"

Flustered, Casey again felt B.B.'s paws on his back, then a wet tongue—the dog's—drag over the back of his neck. "No, B.B., *down.*"

The dog retreated, but stayed close, bouncing here and there, ready to leap in again if anyone looked willing. Casey shoved himself into a sitting position then assisted Emma off of Damon.

Damon, the idiot, just lay there, his hairy legs sprawled out, wearing no more than his underwear. "I'm flattened."

Casey wouldn't mind flattening him. But Emma laughed and poked him in the abdomen. "Get up, you big faker. You're not hurt."

He did, but he groaned and groused in the process.

Casey eyed him. "Do you live in your damn drawers?"

"I was ready for bed, I'll have you know, because unlike the two of you, I returned at a respectable hour."

"Yeah?" Emma grinned. "And when was that?"

"About twenty minutes ago," he admitted with a smile. "And I expected to find you in bed."

"I just bet you did," Casey grumbled.

"But," Damon said, dragging out the word, "you

stayed out rather late. So I was listening for you and worrying, as any self-respecting, pseudo–big brother would. When I heard the muted noise at the door, but no one came in, I got curious—and found myself sexually compromised.''

Emma apparently thought the guy was hilarious, given how she laughed. That earned her a tender smile from Damon, leaving Casey to feel like a damn outsider. He didn't like it, not at all. But he supposed he'd have to work on tolerating Damon, given Emma seemed so fond of him.

And he had called himself a big brother to her.

It dawned on them all at once that they were seated on the floor. Almost as one they stood, both men assisting Emma.

"Your nose is pink." Damon flicked her cheek with a finger. "Too much time frolicking in the sun?"

"We were on the lake a good part of the day. And it was wonderful. I can't wait to show it to you."

"I look forward to it. I've already explored a bit of the countryside—and you're right, doll, it's spectacular.''

Emma brushed herself off, then allowed Casey to draw her into his side. Around Damon, more than anyone else, he felt the constant need to display possessiveness.

"So who gave you the tour, Devaughn?"

Damon went very still while clapping his gaze on Emma. He replied to Casey, but it was Emma who held all his attention. "A friend of yours, actually. Ceily Brown.''

Emma gave a tiny jerk. "You were with Ceily?"

He rubbed the back of his neck. "Yes. I met her

while having lunch. I thought she was a waitress and didn't realize she was the owner of the place until we'd already been flirting back and forth a bit and things were…in progress.''

Startled, Casey asked, ''Ceily was flirting with *you?*''

''So?''

Uncomfortable with the idea, Casey shrugged. ''So she doesn't…that is, she normally…''

''I know.'' Damon grinned. ''She's discriminating. She told me so.''

Emma suddenly turned to Casey. ''Well, I suppose we should call it a night.'' She attempted to usher him—inconspicuously—toward the door.

Casey refused to budge. ''What's wrong?''

''Nothing.'' Her smile didn't touch her eyes. ''It's just that it's way past my bedtime and it has been a busy day. I'm ready to drop.''

B.B. agreed with that and headed for the bed. Casey decided he'd pressed her enough for one day. He'd made enormous headway already. ''All right.'' He went to the door, but brought Emma with him.

Damon didn't move, he just crossed his arms and watched them. In his underwear. Casey really didn't like him much at all.

''I'll see you tomorrow when I get home. Will you have your cell phone on you so I can find you?''

''Yes. I should be done visiting the hospital by then, but I'll need to think about a run back home.''

Damon asked, ''We're leaving already?''

Casey scowled at him, but Emma said over her shoulder, ''I'll explain in a minute.'' Then to Casey, she said a firm, ''Good night.''

He smiled. Then he laughed. His timid little Emma
was long gone, and in her place was a woman more
exciting than he'd ever known. "Good night, sweetheart." He bent and kissed her, but kept it quick and
light with Damon looking on. "Sweet dreams."

EMMA SHUT THE DOOR behind Casey. She apparently
heard Damon approaching, because she pretended to
faint, falling back against him. "Oh Lord, what a
day," she said.

Damon caught her under her arms and laughed.
"Made your knees weak, did he?" Seeing her so
happy made him happy too. From the second he'd
gotten a good look at her, he could see she positively
glowed, and not just from too much sunshine. Casey
had a startling effect on her, and that told him all he
needed to know.

Groaning, Emma straightened, but went to the bed
to flop down. "It's too incredible." She stared at Damon in what he could only call wonder. "He wants
to see me."

Damon pretended to gasp as he followed her over
to the bed. "No! He wants to see a gorgeous, sexy
woman? How strange. What do you suppose is wrong
with that man?"

Fighting a smile, Emma smacked at him. "It's
more complicated than that, and well you know it.
And he doesn't just want to see me a little. For as
long as I'm here, he asked that we be exclusive."

"He's a possessive ape. I picked up on that right
off."

"He is *not* an ape."

Damon noted she didn't challenge the possessive part.

"And Damon, we might be here a lot longer than we'd first planned. Or at least, I'll be. That's what I meant about making a run home. I'll probably need more clothes. But there's no reason for you to stay."

Damon could think of several reasons to hang around, and first and foremost was his astounding reaction to a certain small-business proprietor. Then there was the stretch of land Ceily's grandfather was supposedly going to sell. And his own dissatisfaction with his life...

Emma spent several minutes explaining her father's condition to him, and Damon, as usual, did his best to be a good listener. He had such wonderful, caring parents himself, he couldn't imagine the emptiness she had to feel, knowing hers cared so little for her. Yet, she still suffered with her own sense of responsibility toward them. It was another mark of Emma's generous spirit, and one of the reasons she was so easy to love.

"What are you going to do?"

Propping her elbows on her knees, Emma buried her face in her hands. "I don't know," she wailed with only slightly exaggerated frustration. "I want to be with him. God, to be truthful, I still have feelings for him."

He'd assumed that much all along, of course, which was one reason he'd insisted on accompanying her on this trip. Emma didn't love easily, but when she spoke of Casey, the love she felt for him was more than apparent. "And how does he feel?"

She shook her head and straightened. "At first, it

was almost like he thought he'd been slighted…
because he hadn't gotten to…uh…''

"Make love to you?" Yeah, Damon could see that.
Hudson might consider her the one that got away.
He'd been controlling things, keeping Emma at arm's
length—right where he wanted her, not too close but
within reach. Then suddenly she wasn't around at all
and he'd likely floundered with mixed feelings. Far
as Damon was concerned, it served him right.

But the way Emma avoided his gaze when she nodded, Damon wondered if the sex issue had already
been seen to. It would explain her glow and the heat
he'd witnessed in Hudson's eyes. He almost grinned.
''I take it once isn't enough?''

She punched him in the arm. ''You know me too
well.''

''I was talking about him, actually but, yeah, I
know you too well. And there's no reason to blush.
If you're happy I'm happy.''

Absently, she began to stroke B.B., and the big dog
gleefully dozed off. Emma was good with her hands
and she loved touching. If you sat by her, you could
expect to get as many pets as the dog. She made a
perfect massage therapist—and she'd make an even
better lover.

''I know getting involved with him, even temporarily, is beyond stupid.'' She winced. ''When I leave,
it's going to make it so much harder. But I just can't
resist grabbing this opportunity.''

Watching her closely, Damon asked, ''So who says
it has to be temporary?''

She blinked at him, laughed a little nervously. ''Because it's just sex.''

"Did *he* say as much?"

With an uncertain look, she shook her head. "No."

Damon squeezed her knee. "Then I think you need to stop making assumptions and give the guy a chance. If he just wanted sex, seems to me his little co-worker Kristin was more than willing."

She thought about that, then nodded. "True."

"And you definitely need to shake off that dark cloud. You're in Buckhorn two days and already you're reverting to that silly girl I first met."

"I wasn't silly."

He grunted. "You had no clue who or what you were. You kept trying to fade into the background, to disappear completely, which was very silly because a woman like you is always noticed."

Her eyebrow lifted this time. "A woman like me?"

"Smart, sexy, warm and sincere. Men have built-in homing devices for women like you. You can't be in the vicinity without males perking up—and I don't just mean their attention." He bobbed his eyebrows so she wouldn't misunderstand. "You're around, and men know it."

That had her laughing. "You are so absurd sometimes."

"No more absurd than you. Forget the past, doll. Forget the girl you used to be and the boy you always thought he was. Just take it day by day and see what happens. If Casey Hudson possesses even half the sterling qualities you always attributed to him, I'll be shocked if he doesn't fall madly in love with you." In fact, Damon thought the poor guy was already halfway there. He looked at Emma as if he wanted to eat her up, and he didn't even try to hide it.

"Now—" Damon stood to stare down at her

"—it's time to hit the sack. I'm seeing Ceily again tomorrow."

"You are?"

"Indeed. She's a charming little minx, I'll say that for her."

"If you say that *to* her, she's liable to clobber you."

Damon grinned. "I can handle her, don't worry. But she suggested I be ready early, and I'm beginning to realize that, around here, that means crawling out of bed before the sun comes up."

Emma gave him a long look, no doubt wondering how involved he planned to get with Ceily. He could understand her surprise. Hell, he was still reeling himself. Of all the women in Buckhorn, she was probably the last woman he should be spending extra time with, all things considered.

But as usual, Emma didn't pry except to ask, "So you're going to be staying too?"

He sauntered toward his own room, but when he reached the doorway, he looked back at her with a smile. "The infamous Casey Hudson sees me as competition, despite my assurances to the contrary, and I'm finding that amuses me a lot. So, yes, doll, I'm staying. In fact, wild horses couldn't drag me away." Damon couldn't wait to see how the town's golden boy worked this one out.

In the meantime, he'd be working on buying some land—and seducing Miss Ceily. Things looked promising.

And here he'd feared Buckhorn, Kentucky, might be boring. It was anything but.

MORGAN STOOD at the grill, turning burgers, rolling wieners and brats, and seasoning pork ribs. As the official cook for the day, he'd opted for a wide variety to please all the family who'd turned out for the impromptu get-together. All around him, the kids were playing and the animals were running about. Up on the porch, he could hear the wives chatting and laughing. Life was good.

He glanced over to where Casey and Emma sat beneath a tall elm tree, practically glued together. It was just like old times, except that two of Gabe's fair-haired daughters were with them, watching as Emma taught them how to weave clover buds together for ankle bracelets. The girls loved them, and when Casey made a larger one and placed it on Emma's head like a tiara, they giggled.

Sawyer walked up to him. It was his day off so he wore jeans and a tan T-shirt. "Out of the ten days she's been in town, this is the fifth time Case has had her over for dinner."

Morgan raised an eyebrow. "I knew they were getting tight. But that's sounding pretty serious considering he doesn't usually bring his dates around that often."

"Hell, the days he hasn't brought her here, he's spent with her somewhere else. Everyone in town and on the lake has noticed, which I think might have been his intent. I've never seen him chase a woman like this."

Shrugging, Morgan said, "Usually they're chasing him." He expertly flipped a burger, then stepped back as flames shot upward from the grease. "Misty told me that the gossip among the young ladies is getting kinda nasty. With Emma around, they're all out of the running, and apparently they're not too happy about that.''

"What kind of gossip?"

"Oh, that Case feels sorry for her. That he's using her. That she's using him." He shrugged. "Typical catty stuff. Misty was fit to be tied when she got home.''

Sawyer smiled. "I take it she straightened them out?''

"That she did. But stop grinning, cuz your wife was right there with her and just as adamant about stopping rumors.''

"You're on fire," Sawyer told him, then waited while Morgan retrieved a slightly charred hot dog and moved it to another part of the grill. "You know Honey dotes on him. If Emma makes him happy, then she's all for it.''

"She does appear to keep him smiling.''

"True. And if she's around, he's by her. Or watching her. Or watching that no one else is watching her. It's bound to cause talk.''

Grinning, Morgan said, "Reminds me a bit of me back in my day.''

"Reminds me a bit of any guy in love.''

Nodding thoughtfully, Morgan said, "Yep. That's about it, I suppose.''

Jordan strolled up with three frosty colas, one already opened and half gone, the other two for his brothers. Gabe followed along behind him. "What has you two over here gossiping like old women?''

Shoeless and in a sleeveless shirt, Gabe leaned

against a tree. "We could see your frowns from the porch."

Accepting his drink and taking a healthy swig, Morgan nodded toward Casey. "Think he's in love with her?"

Gabe snorted. "That's what has you all puckered up? Well, let me set you straight—yes. He loves her."

Jordan used his wrist to wipe the sweat from his forehead. "Hear, hear."

Sawyer said, "Hmm."

"You like her, don't you?" Gabe glanced over toward Emma in time to see his youngest daughter climb into her lap and give her a hug. "Because I like her fine. She's a pretty little thing. And she's damn good with cars. Almost as good as me." He shook his head. "Gotta admire that."

"She's damn good at neck rubs too."

Gabe squinted his eyes. "Do tell."

Grinning, Sawyer said, "Morgan helped Howard dig out a tree stump. And by 'helped,' I mean he did it himself. He seems to forget he's an old man now."

"I'm in my prime, damn it." Then Morgan raised his nose. "Just ask Misty."

"Yeah, well, prime or not, he pulled more than a few muscles showing off. Emma happened to be here when he started complaining and within minutes she had him blissfully relaxed and half-asleep."

Gabe stared over toward Emma. "Wonder if I could get her to show me how to do that."

"She showed Misty."

"And Honey." The two brothers grinned at each other.

"Needing help with Elizabeth, are you?" Jordan taunted Gabe.

"Naw, but the woman is insatiable. I figured if I could get her to sleep a little more…"

After everyone stopped chuckling, Gabe said, "You're fretting for nothing. Because if I know women—and you know I do—Emma is as much stung as Casey is. It's almost embarrassing, the way she looks at him."

Jordan elbowed him. "Like anything could embarrass you."

"Hey, I'm an old married man, completely oblivious to lecherous looks." He grinned sinfully as he said it.

"We all like her," Morgan pointed out. "But isn't she here only temporarily?"

Sawyer nodded. "That's what concerns me the most. Yet she's the only female Casey has brought around the family this much."

"That oughta tell ya something, I suppose."

Morgan rolled his eyes at Gabe. "Yeah, it tells us that he loves his adoring uncles and values our approval."

"She has mine."

"Mine too."

Sawyer shifted, running a hand through his hair and sighing. "She left here because she didn't like it, or because she had some mighty big personal problems. Whichever, I'd hate to see Case hurt."

"He's smart. He knows what he's doing." Jordan clapped Sawyer on the shoulder. "Of course, a man's finer senses tend to warp a little when he's getting his heart drop-kicked by love."

Morgan nodded. "It's cruel the way a woman can lay you low."

Gabe said, "As long as she's laying me...." The others lifted their drinks in a salute.

Just then, Misty yelled from the porch, "You got the meat ready for me?"

Morgan smiled while the others quickly turned their backs to snicker. "Always, sweetheart, always." Then under his breath to his brothers, "She can't get enough."

Jordan raised his eyebrows. "Yeah, well, your wieners are on fire."

Morgan hurried to move things around on the grill. Gabe glanced up, saw that Elizabeth had joined Misty in setting out side dishes, and yelled, "You ladies getting...*hungry?*"

She smiled back with a look guaranteed to knock the wind out of him. "Ravenous."

Gabe clutched his heart. "Oh God, I asked for that, didn't I?"

Sawyer called to Honey, "Be right there, sweetie." And he blew her a kiss.

Jordan said, "I like Emma's friend, Damon."

"He loosened right up, didn't he? When I first met him, he was such a starched shirt. Nice enough fellow, but so...precise." Gabe said that as though it were a dirty word. "Put my teeth on edge. Never thought he'd be the type to hang around here this long."

"He's still starched, but it's just his way." Sawyer nudged his brothers as he saw Damon come around the corner of the house, led by Amber and looking far from starched at the moment. Judging by his bare wet feet and wind-tossed hair, Amber had taken him along the bank hunting crawfish and minnows again—a pastime Damon apparently enjoyed, much to everyone's surprise.

Amber had insisted on his first such adventure, but since then he'd gone along willingly and they'd fallen into a routine of sorts. Whenever Damon came to the house with Emma, Ceily usually accompanied them, and they'd go to the shore with Amber and any of the other kids who were in attendance that day.

Sawyer also noted that Damon had his pant legs rolled up, his shirt mostly unbuttoned, and Ceily tucked close at his side. "Ceily sure likes him."

"Likes him?" Gabe grunted. "She's totally besotted, always sashaying around in front of him, batting her eyelashes and whispering in his ear. And he enjoys it—you can tell that much."

"Good for her." Morgan pointed a metal spatula at Gabe. "'Bout time she found someone."

"Hey, I got no problem with her being happy," Gabe groused. "It's just that I always figured it'd be someone local. I hope like hell he doesn't break her heart, or worse, talk her into moving away."

"Moving away would be worse than a broken heart?"

Jordan scowled at Morgan, then asked Gabe, "Why would she move away?"

"I understand he's a well-respected architect back in Chicago." Sawyer shrugged. "Can't see him giving that up."

The men all looked up as a scuffle started between Garrett and Shohn, who were a little too close in age at nine and ten not to compete at every turn. Adam, only slightly more subdued at thirteen, stood to the side shaking his head until Honey raced into the yard and said quite loudly, "That's enough!"

The boys broke apart, grumbled a little and, with Honey prodding them along, headed to the porch.

Morgan shoved a platter of hamburgers at Jordan. "Here, carry this. We better feed the savages before they turn on each other."

Laughing, Jordan took the food. "I can remember Mom saying the same thing back in the old days."

Gabe snickered. "Yeah, but usually she was saying it about Morgan."

"Last time I talked to her, she said she'd be coming to town soon. Seems Casey spoke with her yesterday when she called. He mentioned Emma a few dozen times, and now she's more than a little curious."

Sawyer laughed at Jordan. "Nosy is a better description." The brothers all agreed with fond smiles. "I expect she'll be here before too long."

Their mother lived in Florida with Gabe's father, Brett. After losing her first husband and divorcing her second, she'd found true love. It made them all glad to see her so happy, and since she got to Kentucky at least six times a year, they didn't mind that Brett had talked her into retiring in Florida.

Later, after the food had been devoured and everyone, except the kids, was feeling a little more lethargic, Sawyer seated himself near Emma. She and Casey were on the porch swing, their hands entwined, talking quietly.

"So, Emma, I hear you've been busy."

Her brown eyes warmed with a gentle smile. "Dr.

Wagner has scheduled several massages, and so has Ms. Potter. They're both very nice.''

"I hear the wives have been in line as well.''

She laughed. "Morgan too. But I enjoy it.''

Sawyer nodded, having noticed that she was indeed a "toucher.'' If Emma was near someone, she touched—rubbing a shoulder, hugging the kids, stroking the animals. She was very sweet, very open and friendly, and Sawyer liked her, yet still he worried. "How's your dad doing? Any word on when he might get to come home?''

"They tell me it's still too early to know for sure.'' Her expression grew troubled. "He had shown so much improvement at first, but this past week there's been no real progress. If anything, he seems more sluggish. They're adjusting his medicine, trying different therapy, but...I just don't know.''

Casey kissed her knuckles. "I went with her last night, and she saw him again this morning. He's still talking, not real clear though.''

Emma looked away. "He was crying this morning.''

Damn. Sawyer glanced at his son and shared his look of concern. But he was a doctor, not just a father, not just a friend, so he put on his best professional face and tried to reassure her. "That's not uncommon with stroke victims. I'm sure the doctor explained it to you?''

She nodded. "Emotional lability, he called it. He said depression is common. I just wish there was some way I could help.''

"Hey.'' Casey put his arm around her. "You're

helping a lot. You're here with him. You've rear-ranged your life. I'd say that's plenty.''

"I'd say so too," Sawyer agreed.

She didn't look convinced. "He's lost so much weight.''

That wasn't uncommon either. Sawyer asked, "They still have him strictly on IVs?''

"Yes. They're not sure yet how well he can swallow. I forget what they called it…''

"Dysphagia.'' Sawyer knew one side of Dell's mouth was weak, so they likely had to be careful of the increased risk of choking. "Emma, it hasn't been that long. Try not to worry too much, okay? He's talking, and he recognizes you. That's pretty mirac-ulous and a good indicator right there.'' He patted her hand, but he didn't promise her that everything would be all right, because he really didn't know.

A loud beeping broke the quiet, which had Morgan and Damon both reaching for their cell phones, then coming up with frowns because it wasn't theirs. Honey pointed to Emma's purse. "I think it's yours, Emma.''

She came off the swing in a rush and fairly dived off the porch to reach the bag she'd left at the picnic table in the yard. Casey stood to watch her, Sawyer beside him. It was the first call that she'd gotten to Sawyer's knowledge and, naturally, it alarmed every-one.

After Emma said a tentative "Hello'' into the phone, her lips parted and she slowly sank onto the bench seat at the wooden table.

Casey bounded off the porch steps in one leap and was at her side before she could say, a bit shakily, "I see." He stood behind her and put his hands on her shoulders. Damon sat down beside her. Everyone waited, alert.

Avoiding all the curious gazes, Emma said, "I'm so sorry, Mrs. Reider. Yes, of course, I'll be right there." She closed her eyes. "Yes, I understand."

Mrs. Reider? Sawyer thought. He'd presumed it was the hospital, that her father had taken a turn for the worse. But instead...

Emma pushed the disconnect button on her small phone, tucked it back into her purse and stood. "I'm sorry to rush off, but I need to go." At the word *go,* B.B. hurried to her side.

"I'll take you," Casey said.

She looked horrified by that idea. "No—"

"I'll take you." He wasn't about to be dissuaded, and Sawyer understood why.

Emma looked to Damon, received his nod, and finally agreed. "All right. I suppose you might as well."

He might as well? What the hell did that mean? Sawyer wondered. And why did she look as if the rug had just been pulled out from under her?

Reaching for his shoes and socks, Damon said, "I'm coming too."

"But..." With everyone watching the poor girl, she gave up. "Fine. But I do need to hurry."

Honey worried her bottom lip. "Your father is okay?"

"Yes—that is, he hasn't had a change." She patted the dog, but her smile was a bit self-conscious. "That wasn't the hospital."

Ceily sidled up next to Damon and asked, "Then what's wrong?"

Emma hesitated a long moment before admitting, "It's my mother. She's at the motel where Damon and I are staying. She wants to see me."

Damon looked far too grim, leading everyone else to wonder why a visit from her mother mattered so much. "You ride with Casey," he told her. "I'll drive your car."

Since that was how they'd arrived, she merely nodded.

"Emma?" At Sawyer's query, she turned. For a young woman who'd been smiling moments before, she now looked far too world-weary. It didn't make sense, and filled Sawyer with compassion. "Let us know if there's any way we can help." And he thought to add, "With anything."

She stared at him a long minute before nodding. "Thank you. Dinner was wonderful. Everything was wonderful. I... Thank you."

And then Casey led her away. Sawyer watched until she and B.B. had gotten into his son's car before turning to his wife. Honey hugged his waist. "I'm worried about him, Sawyer."

Sawyer knew exactly how she felt, but he repeated his brothers' reassurances, saying, "He knows what he's doing."

Honey nodded. "I know. But does he know what *she's* doing?"

CHAPTER THIRTEEN

THE PAST WEEK and a half had been wonderful, but now it was over. All the secrets, all the pretending. She didn't know how or why her mother had sought her out, but she knew their reunion was bound to be difficult—just as her relationship with her mother had always been.

"I don't want you to come up with me."

Casey didn't bother to glance at her. "Why?" His hands were tight on the steering wheel, his expression dark.

What could she tell him? That she didn't want everything to end with such an unpleasant scene? "She's my mother and I'll deal with her."

"You think I would interfere?"

"No, but..." She drew a breath and gave him part of the truth. "It embarrasses me."

Casey pulled the Mustang into the gravel lot. He put it in Park, started to say something to Emma, but then stalled as his gaze lit on something. "I'd say it's too late to worry about that."

Emma followed his line of vision and saw her mother. She was half slumped at one of the picnic tables, holding her head with one hand, a lit cigarette with the other.

Emma's heart got caught in her throat. Regardless

of anything else, of the past and the hurt feelings and the dread, she was seeing her mother again for the first time in years. And she was choking on her hurt.

Her mother's brown hair, like Emma's only shorter, was caught back in a blunt ponytail. She wore dark jeans, a short-sleeved white blouse and sandals. Seeing her like that, she could have been anyone's mother. She could have been a regular mother.

She could have been a mother who cared.

Emma knew better though. Ignoring Casey, she opened her door and stepped out. Her mother noticed her then and stood. She swayed, unsteady on her feet, and had to prop herself with one hand on the tabletop.

Of course, she was drunk, just as Emma had expected.

"Where the hell have you been, young lady?"

The slurred words were flung at Emma without regard for the quietness of the lot or the spectators close at hand. Somewhere in the back of her awareness, Emma knew Damon and Ceily had arrived. She knew Casey was close behind her, leading the dog. She knew Mrs. Reider and a few guests watched from the motel-lobby door.

It's not me, Emma told herself. *What she does, who she is, doesn't project on me.* She knew it, had lived with that truism all these years past, but still her shame bit so deep she could barely see as she made her way to the picnic table.

Her voice sounded wooden as she said, "Mother."

"Don't you call me that," her mother sneered, and Emma saw that familiar ugliness in her brown eyes, in the dark shadows beneath, in the pasty sheen of her skin and the spittle at the side of her mouth.

"All right." Sick dread churned in her belly. She knew her mother would humiliate them both. What she didn't know was how to deal with it. As a child, she'd begged, hidden, run away. But she wasn't a child any longer, and her mother was now her responsibility.

"A daughter would have come to see me by now. You know I'm all alone. You know I needed you. But no. You're too good for that, aren't you?"

"You have my number," Emma reasoned. "You could have—" No. Emma stopped herself. She knew from long experience that there was no reasoning with her mother in this condition. It would be a waste of breath to even try, and would only prolong the uncomfortable confrontation. "Why don't I take you home?"

"Oh no, missy. I don't damn well wanna go home now." She took an unsteady step forward. "I want you to take me to the store, and then we're goin' to the hospital to see Dell."

Emma's heart nearly stopped. Take her mother to the hospital? Not while she was drunk. "I won't buy you alcohol." She didn't bother to reply to her other request.

Her mother looked stunned at that direct refusal. Her eyes widened, her mouth moved. Finally, she yelled, "You just get me there and I'll buy it myself. I'm worried about your father and sick at heart and God knows my only daughter doesn't give a damn." As she spoke, she tottered around the table toward Emma. Ashes fell from the cigarette, which was now little more than a butt.

Just as she'd done so many times in the past, Emma

braced herself, emotionally, physically. Even so, she had a hard time staying upright when her mother's free hand knotted in the front of her shirt and she stumbled into her. "You'll take me," she hissed, her breath tainted with the sickly sweet scent of booze and the thickness of smoke, "or I'll tell everyone what you did."

A layer of ice fell over Emma's heart. It was now or never, and she simply couldn't take it anymore. "What *you* did, you mean."

The shock at her defiance only lasted a moment. "No one will believe that." Her mother laughed, and tugged harder on Emma's shirt. "You, with your damn reputation. You don't have any friends around here. Even that nosy sheriff was always checking up on you. He'll believe whatever I tell him. And you'll go to jail—"

"I'll take my chances."

Enraged, her mother drew back to strike Emma, but her hand was still in the air when Casey pulled Emma back and into his side. Her mother's swing, which would have left a bruise, given the force she'd put behind it, missed the mark by over a foot and threw her off balance. She turned a half circle and landed hard on her hands and knees in the rough gravel. Her cigarette fell to the side, still smoldering.

Emma had automatically reached out to break her fall, but she pulled back. She could feel Casey breathing hard beside her, knew he was disgusted and shocked at the scene—a scene he'd probably never witnessed in his entire life, but that was all too familiar to Emma.

B.B. went berserk, barking and snarling, and

Emma, feeling numb, caught his collar to restrain him. She whispered to the dog, soothing him while staring down at the woman who'd birthed her. She waited to see what else she'd do. Her mother could be so unpredictable at times like this.

But she stayed there, her head drooping forward while she gathered herself. Eight years had apparently taken a toll on her too. When she twisted around to look up at Casey, it was with confusion and anger. "Who the hell are you?"

Thinking to protect Casey, Emma said, "He's the sheriff's nephew."

"And," Casey added, his own anger barely under control, "I heard everything you just said."

Slumping back on her behind, slack-jawed, her mother stared from Casey to Emma and back again. Slowly, her lips curled and she pointed at Emma. "Did she tell you what she did? Do you know?" She hunted for her cigarette, picking it up and using it to light another that she fetched from her pocket. She took a long draw, looking at Casey through a stream of smoke. "She tried to burn down the diner."

Emma closed her eyes on a wave of stark pain. She'd held a faint, ridiculous hope that her mother wouldn't take it that far, that she'd only been blustering. That somehow she'd care just a little about her only child.

Barely aware of Casey taking her hand, Emma sorted through her hurt, pushing aside what she could to deal with the situation at hand. Mrs. Reider didn't deserve this scene. She ran a respectable business in a dry county. Having a drunken argument in her lot would probably go down as one of the worst things imaginable.

Slowly, Ceily came up to Emma's other side. She wasn't looking at Mrs. Clark, but at Emma. "You're the one who called and reported the fire that night, aren't you?"

It was so damn difficult, but Emma forced herself to face Ceily. When she spoke, she was pleased that she sounded strong, despite her suffocating guilt. "Yes. I'm sorry. It's all very complicated and I didn't mean for any of it to happen…"

"Your mother started it?"

Amazed that Ceily had come to that conclusion without further explanation, it took Emma a few moments to finally nod.

"That's a lie!"

Ceily ignored her mother's loud denials, speaking only to Emma. "Why? I barely knew your folks."

It would help, Emma thought, if she had a good solid reason to give, some explanation that would make sense. She didn't have one. "You weren't a target, Ceily. The diner is just the first place she came to where she thought she might find either a drink or money to go get a drink."

Ceily shook her head. "But I don't serve alcohol, and I cash out every night before closing up."

"I know. And if she'd been thinking straight, she might have realized it too. But alcoholism…it's a sickness and when you want to drink, nothing else matters…"

Her mother began protesting again, her every word scraping along Emma's nerves until she wanted to cover her ears, run away again. But she no longer had that luxury. She had to deal with this. "She broke in, and things went from bad to worse... I didn't know what to do."

Damon stepped up and looped his arms around Ceily so that she leaned into his chest. It dawned on Emma that Ceily didn't look accusatory as much as curious. Of course, her reaction would have been vastly different eight years ago, the night it had all happened. The shock, the anger and hurt had likely been blunted by time.

"How did you find her?" Ominous overtones clouded Casey's softly asked question.

Emma winced. Because the fire and Emma's visit to his house had happened on the same night, Casey had a right to his suspicions. "Earlier that day, I'd convinced my father that we had to stand together, to get her help. It was the worst argument we'd ever had. She was furious, and...I couldn't take it. So I went out. But I always cut through town coming home." Here Emma gave an apologetic shrug to Casey. "Your uncle had warned me that he'd run me into juvenile if he caught me out so late again."

"He worried about you," Casey told her with a frown.

"I know." Emma smiled, though she felt very sad that only a stranger had worried, and only because it had been his job. "I came home behind the businesses, as usual, because that way I was less likely to be seen from the street. I found my mom coming out of the back of the diner, and I realized what she was doing. Then I smelled the smoke."

"She'd already started the fire?"

"Not on purpose. It was her cigarette, but..."

Wanting to finish it, Emma rushed through the rest of her words. "The fire was small at first and I tried to put it out. But she kept fighting me, wanting us to leave before we got caught."

"Dear God," Casey muttered, and he glared at her mother, who gave him a mutinous look back.

Emma spoke to Ceily. "I knew I couldn't do that. I told her she needed help and that I thought you might let her just pay for the damages if she agreed to go to the hospital for treatment. But she didn't believe me and when I finally got the call through, she..."

"She threatened to blame you?" Casey asked.

Emma turned to him. "Yes. She said she'd tell everyone that I did it. I was...scared. I wasn't sure who might believe her."

"No one would have."

"You might not have blamed me, but—"

"I wouldn't have either," Ceily said.

Damon leaned around to look at Ceily, slowly smiled at her, then gave her a tight squeeze.

Emma couldn't believe they were being so nice. In so many ways, it might have been easier for her if they'd hated her and what she'd done. "I'm doubly sorry then, because I was a coward. The fire was already out of control. I made the call anonymously, went home with my mother and...things got out of control."

"That's how you got beat up that night, isn't it?"

He sounded furious and pained and...hurt? Because she'd been hurt? She glanced at him, but didn't reply because she didn't want to involve him further. "I made plans to leave."

"You came to me."

She shook her head at Casey. He couldn't seem to get beyond that, and she was beginning to think he put far too much emphasis on that one small fact. "With the intent of only staying one night."

"If I'd known that, you never would have gotten away."

"I had to leave. If I'd stayed until morning when everyone started talking about the fire, well, someone would have figured it out. Then I wouldn't have had the option to go."

He scowled, crossing his arms over his chest and appearing very displeased with her assessment. "How the hell did you get out of town so fast anyway?"

Knowing he wouldn't like the answer, Emma winced again. "I hitchhiked once I got on the main road. Neither Morgan nor his deputy saw me, of course, because they were still busy with the fire. With a lift from two different drivers, I got as far as Cincinnati, then caught a bus the rest of the way into Chicago."

Ceily stared at her in horror. "Dear God. You could have been—"

Damon interrupted Ceily. "But she wasn't. Instead, she found my family and she's now a part of us." He reached out and touched Emma's chin. "And she's suffered a lot over this."

"Damon, don't make excuses for me, please. I should have told the truth long ago. I should never have lied in the first place."

Damon, still holding Ceily at his side, addressed both her and Casey. "It took her a few years to get her life in order. After that, she thought about coming home and confessing all—she honestly did. But her father would beg her not to, and with so much time already passed…''

Emma laced her hands together. ''I couldn't bear the thought of my mother going to jail.''

Her mother shoved to her feet, outraged by the mere suggestion. ''No one is taking me anywhere! I didn't do anything. It was you.''

Casey shared a look with Ceily, then received her nod. ''No, you won't be going to jail. It was an accident, not arson. And even with the breaking and entering, well, it's been eight years. I'm sure the limitations on that have run out.''

Emma was agog, her mother smug.

''But…won't the insurance company want their money back? I know there was a lot of internal damage.''

Her mother grabbed Emma's arm in a viselike grip. ''Shut your mouth, girl.''

Casey stepped forward, but Emma stopped him with one look. She had avoided dealing with her mother for too long. When she'd been a child, she'd had an excuse. But as an adult… It was past time she took responsibility for what she'd done, and forced her mother to do the same. ''You're going to get help.''

''I don't need any help.''

For the very first time in over a decade, Emma felt nothing. Not hurt, not need, not even compassion. ''It's possible that legal charges might not apply anymore. But there are other things to consider now. Daddy's stroke is serious. If and when he's able to leave the hospital, I'm taking him with me.''

"Whaddya mean, 'with you'? He's my husband!"

"And he's my father. He needs someone who can take care of him, not the other way around. He'll need therapy and supervision and encouragement. You're not capable of any of that, so until you get help, get sober, and stay that way, you're on your own."

The fingers on her arm grew slack, then fell away. "You can't do that." Her whisper was rough with shock.

"Of course I can." Emma swept her arm around the lot. "Thanks to this visit, there are more than enough people who now know that you're incapable of taking care of yourself, much less someone in need of medical attention."

Damon, Ceily and Casey, along with Mrs. Reider and a half-dozen motel guests made up an audience. Two cars had stopped on the road, having also noticed the spectacle unfolding in the motel lot. In a town as quiet as Buckhorn, it didn't take too much to get the gossip going. She wouldn't be surprised to see the whole thing written up as front-page news in the Buckhorn press tomorrow morning. In the past, that would have devastated her, leaving her curled up with shame. Now, she just wanted things resolved.

"Emma?" Ceily smiled at her. "There was never an insurance claim made. I didn't want my premium to go up, and I'd been planning to renovate anyway, after Granddad turned the place over to me completely. So I used the money I'd saved and fixed it up with a lot of help from Gabe and volunteers from the town."

Nodding, Emma said, "I'll reimburse you."

"No, you won't." She turned to Mrs. Clark, who

stared blankly down at her feet. "But your mother can pay me one fourth of the money I spent, since there were some things I wouldn't have replaced if it hadn't been for the smoke and fire damage."

"I don't have that kind of money," her mother whispered, looking very lost and confused by it all.

Ceily shrugged. "So get a job. I'll let you make installments."

Her mother's look of horror was almost comical.

"They have a drug abuse and alcohol treatment facility at the hospital," Casey offered, speaking to Emma, not her mother. "We can take her there now." He looked as though he wanted to rid himself of her as fast as possible.

Sadly, Emma now felt the same. Years ago, she'd have done anything to help forge a normal relationship with her mother. She'd begged her, during her sober moments, to get professional assistance. But whenever she was sober, her mother always thought she had control over her drinking. She'd agree to quit, and mean it. But her resolve never lasted and Emma had long since grown tired of her mother's refusal to admit to her sickness.

However, what Emma had said was true—this time she would take her father away if her mother didn't get help. "Mother? What do you say? And before you agree or disagree, you should know I'm either taking you to the rehab facility, or leaving you here. Those are your options. If you stay, I have no doubt Mrs. Reider will give the sheriff a call, and you may well end up with court-ordered rehab anyway."

Her mother stared at her, looking much like a lost child. She was breathing hard, fighting tears, but

Emma also knew an excess of emotion came with alcoholism, so she stiffened her spine and waited. Finally her mother nodded, surprising Emma, giving her hope.

"Listen, doll," Damon said quietly, "she's nothing to you now."

Emma knew that wasn't true. A parent was a parent, good or bad, and she would make the best of this. She turned to Damon and offered him a slight smile. "She's my mother." Then she added with a sigh, "And she got us kicked out of here. Mrs. Reider wants us gone as soon as possible."

Damon groaned. Her mother looked away. Mrs. Reider hovered in the doorway, appearing impatient—and curious since she couldn't hear what was being said.

Ceily and Casey spoke at the same time. "You can stay with me." Then they both blinked, and Casey added, "Ceily, honey, you're more than welcome to Damon. By all means, take him. But Emma and B.B. are coming with me."

Ceily hugged onto Damon's arm. "Works for me."

Emma looked at Damon, who grinned and shrugged. "Sounds like it's all planned out, doll. That is, if you're okay with it."

Casey waited with a sort of tense anticipation they could all feel. But Emma had few choices, and she wanted to be with him. So she nodded. "Thank you."

EMMA WAS SO QUIET Casey couldn't help but worry. Getting her mother to the rehab center had taken far longer, and been more complicated, than he'd anticipated. But throughout it all, Emma had kept her shoulders squared, her emotions in check, and her determination at the fore. She was amazing.

After her mother had willingly signed herself in, Emma made plans to bring some of her things to her. She'd be at the facility for an undetermined length of time, but she'd start dependency counseling right away. Because leaving meant she'd likely lose her husband, she looked resigned to staying. She'd also asked, in a small, fretful voice, if Emma would visit her.

Emma had agreed, but there'd been no embrace between mother and daughter. For her part, Emma appeared motivated by pity for the woman who'd never been a real mother to her. She'd also been so distant, not touching Casey, hardly even looking at him. Casey didn't push her. She needed some private time to come to grips with everything, but under the circumstances that was tough to find. Mrs. Reider's was the only motel in Buckhorn, and any other lodging would put her too far away from her father. Though he wished this were easier on her, Casey was glad she'd be with him, even if it wasn't by choice.

It hadn't taken them long to pack her and Damon's things. While Emma stood by without saying a word, Casey had called ahead to his father to fill him in on the situation. Emma's silence hurt him, because he knew she was hurting. Dealing with her troubles was hard enough, but broadcasting those troubles to the whole town would be nearly impossible to take. Casey feared he'd just lost a lot of headway in convincing her to stay in Buckhorn.

Damon and Ceily were there when Casey pulled down the long driveway. Damon had used the excuse of bringing Emma's car to her, but Casey suspected he also wanted to see her settled. Thankfully, the kids were out of sight, but Sawyer and Morgan, Misty and Honey all waited for them. When Casey stopped the car at the side of the house, his relatives moseyed inside to give them some privacy.

Casey turned off the engine. "You okay?"

It took her a moment, then she said, "It's strange, but mostly what I feel is relief that it's all out in the open. At least now I can deal with it."

Casey nodded. He could understand that. "It'll be okay."

Her laugh sounded a little watery, too close to tears, before she rubbed her face and drew herself together. "Looks like I'll be spending even more time visiting hospitals, huh?"

Jaw locked, Casey reached for her hand. "You owe her nothing." Far as he could tell, all her mother had ever given her was grief.

"I owe this town. I owe Ceily."

"You didn't cause the damage."

"No, but I kept quiet about it. That's a crime in itself."

"You were a kid, damn it."

She raised a hand. "No, Casey. Don't coddle me by making excuses. I'm fine really. Just... exhausted."

Christ, she'd been seventeen years old, burdened with more than most adults could handle. He had no intention of letting her wallow in guilt, but he let it go for now. "We'll go to bed early," he promised her.

That had her laughing again. "*We* will, huh? Does

it bother you that your whole family will know I'm with you?''

Casey gave her a long look before stepping out of the car. B.B. jumped out with him and followed him as he circled the hood. Emma had already opened her own door before they could reach her. With Casey and Emma both carrying bags, they started toward the garage apartment. B.B., now very familiar with the Hudson household, followed along.

Finally Casey couldn't keep his mouth shut, and he said, ''It's been a long day for me too, Emma. Don't piss me off.''

She abruptly stopped, but since he and the dog didn't, she hurried to catch up. ''What are you talking about?''

He'd kept his turbulent emotions tamped down all day—not an easy feat when he damn well loved her and it killed him to see her hurt. Now it felt as if he was imploding, his anger shot up so fast. Dropping her luggage, he whirled on her and gripped her shoulders. ''I damn well want everyone to know you're with me, Emma. The whole town, preferably.''

Eyes huge, she asked, ''There's going to be so much talk. You have to know that Lois and Kristin and probably a dozen of their friends are saying awful things—''

Casey gave her a tiny shake. ''I remember being behind the garage with you eight years ago. You were tempting me, driving me nuts, and you even accused me of being a virgin, then had the nerve to act surprised when I didn't deny it.''

Her eyes softened. ''Any other guy would have, especially since it wasn't true.''

"I told you then that I didn't give a damn what people thought. So, why should I care now, especially when the alternative is not having you nearby? I'm not going to suffer a single moment of discomfort over it."

Some of the tension eased out of her and she gave him a genuine smile.

He pulled her into his chest. "Hell, Emma. I'm so proud of you. Don't you know that?"

"Proud?"

"God, yes." He held her back a little. "Look at you, at everything you've dealt with, all that you've accomplished. I don't know another person who could have handled that scene at Mrs. Reider's with so much grace and dignity."

"It was all I could do not to cry."

"Even if you had, so what? You sure had reason enough. But you didn't. You didn't cave in either. You've taken every rotten thing that's been thrown at you and somehow..." His own eyes grew damp, making him curse, making his voice hoarse. "Somehow you've stayed one of the most beautiful people I've ever known."

Breathing a little shakily, Emma moved back into his embrace. They stood there like that a long time, until Emma finally whispered, "Thank you."

Laughing with exasperation at the way she was forever thanking him for one thing or another, Casey locked his arms around her and hugged her right off her feet. "Baby, it wouldn't matter to me if your mother had burned down three buildings. She's not you." He nuzzled her ear. "I'm just glad that you're home."

Once he said it, Casey was afraid she'd again deny that Buckhorn was her home, so he kissed her, making any rebuttals impossible. It wasn't a lusty kiss, though he was more than ready for one of those too. Instead, he tried to kiss her with all the love he felt. It had been a day of emotional upheavals. She wasn't ready to have him start an overflow of declarations. Soon, he'd let her know how he felt. For now, touching her, holding her, having her close, would be enough.

"Come on," he said against her mouth. "We'll get you settled so you can get some rest."

Emma didn't argue, but when they turned around, they saw that B.B. had run off. They located him quickly enough, on the porch with Sawyer and Shohn. Both Hudson males wore wide, satisfied smiles.

Sawyer yelled out, "He was scratching at the door. Seems he wants to come in."

Emma started to apologize, but Casey cut her off. "He can visit with you for a while if he wants."

Shohn gave a whoop. "Can he sleep with me tonight? I'll take good care of him."

Casey said, "Dad?"

"Sure." Sawyer put one hand on Shohn's shoulder. "Fine by me if Emma doesn't mind."

Emma laughed. "He likes to hog the middle of the bed."

"That's okay." Shohn hung on the dog like a long-lost friend.

"He's liable to want to find me before the night is through," Emma warned.

Sawyer rubbed the dog's ears. "If he does, I'll

walk him over to you. But you never know, so we might as well let him try it.''

Since Casey wanted Emma to himself without the dog in the middle of them, he wrapped up the discussion and hurried Emma on her way. Once they were in the garage apartment, Emma dropped her luggage. ''I can unpack tomorrow.''

Casey glanced up at her. She'd gone straight through to the bedroom and stood next to his bed, her arms at her sides, her expression watchful. ''All right.'' He smiled. ''Are you hungry?''

She shook her head, then licked her lips. ''I'd just like to take a quick shower.''

Visions of her naked, wet, teased through his mind. ''Yeah.'' He cleared his throat. ''Let me get you a towel.''

Ten minutes later, he was stretched out on the bed with his back propped against the headboard. He'd removed his shoes and socks and unbuttoned his shirt, but he was still uncomfortably hot. And uncomfortably aroused.

Yet, he knew sex wasn't what she needed right now.

He tried turning on the television, but he couldn't block the sounds of running water in the bathroom. He felt tortured. Even after the sexual excesses of the past week where they'd spent several hours a day at the cabin making love, the need he felt for her hadn't diminished. Hell, if anything, he wanted her more now than ever.

When the water stopped, that only heightened his awareness. But when Emma stepped out with her hair pinned atop her head and her sweet body wrapped only in a towel, he nearly groaned. She was home. She was with him. She was his.

In the face of so much progress in their relationship, he would be patient.

"Don't get up," she told him as she strolled toward the bed and seated herself on the side of the mattress, near his hip.

Casey stared at her, unsure what she wanted at that particular moment, unwilling to do anything that might make her ill at ease with him.

"Your apartment is fabulous." She stared at his abdomen as she spoke. "I knew Jordan used to live here, but I didn't know it was so nice."

Casey nodded absently while noticing the water droplets that clung to her shoulders. The apartment was open and spacious, located directly over the three-car garage. The kitchen, breakfast nook and living room all flowed into each other, with only the bedroom and bath private. "It suits me."

She rested one slim hand on his naked abdomen. "Will your folks expect to see us tonight?"

Casey almost choked on his indrawn breath. She had to have noticed his erection, given that his cock strained against his jeans, leaving a long ridge beneath the material. But the little tease said nothing. "No. That is, they'll understand if we wait till morning."

"They don't object to me being here?"

His dad had probably already figured out that Emma was special to him. As to that, everyone might know, since he hadn't exactly tried to keep it secret. "No, they're glad to have you here."

Using just her fingertips, she traced the line of hair

from his navel down to the waistband of his jeans, making him shudder. "Did you lock the front door?"

With Shohn used to visiting whenever he chose, and all his young cousins forever underfoot, he'd taken care of that first thing. "Yeah."

"Good." She unsnapped his jeans and slipped her soft, cool hand inside.

Casey groaned. "Emma..."

Without a single reply, she freed his erection from the restriction of his jeans. Casey shifted, then groaned again when she leaned forward and brushed her cheek against him. He put one hand on her head, racked with mixed sensations. Lust was prominent because he could feel her breath on the head of his cock. But he also felt tenderness, because this was Emma, and with every second came the realization that she was his other half, the one woman meant for him.

She made a small hungry sound, and licked him from the base of his shaft to the very tip.

His hand clenched in her hair, his control fast evaporating. "Babe, wait."

Lifting her head, her dark eyes soft and heavy, Emma said, "Mmm?"

Could a woman possibly be more appealing than Emma was at that moment? He'd never get used to the way she looked at him with so much love in her eyes.

Love? God, he hoped so.

Casey closed his eyes and struggled for a deep enough breath so he could be coherent. "Let me get out of these jeans, okay?"

"All right." She agreed readily enough, stood—and then dropped the towel.

Casey lost it.

"Ah, damn, Em." Catching her about the waist, he tumbled her down into the bed and moved over her. The touch of her naked breasts on his chest, her belly on his abdomen, had him in a frenzy of need.

"Your jeans."

"In a second." Hell, if he shucked his jeans off now, he'd be inside her in the next second. He took her mouth, long and leisurely and deep until they were both panting, then slowly worked his way down her body. Kissing wasn't enough, and he indulged in a few gentle yet hungry love bites that had her gasping and squirming under him. She smelled of his soap, and strangely enough even that enticed him. He suckled her nipples until they were tight and straining, put small kisses on her ribs, dipped his tongue in her navel...

"Casey."

Where seconds before he'd been desperate to sink into her, to feel the clasp of her body tight around his shaft, now he wanted her to be desperate. Kneeling between her thighs, he growled, "I want to taste you."

Offering a soft moan for reply, Emma braced herself, legs stiffening, hands knotted in the sheets. Smiling, Casey bent and nuzzled through the springy curls, breathed in her rich scent, and after carefully opening her with his thumbs, covered her with his mouth.

They both groaned, Emma with a sinuous twisting of her body, Casey with the need to take more and more. He moved her legs to brace her feet against his

shoulders, cupped her hips in his hands, and held her
still for the thrust of his tongue, the careful nipping
of his teeth. He found her small, swollen clitoris and
drew it gently into his mouth for the softest suckling,
the demanding rasp of his tongue.

Within minutes she was ready to come, but like
him, she wanted more. "Casey, wait."

Her breathless plea barely reached him with the
taste and scent of her pushing him over the edge. He
felt her silky thigh on his jaw, felt her heels pressing
into his shoulders…

Her fingers tangled in his hair. "Casey, *wait*. I want
you inside me. Please."

Breathing hard, he looked up the length of her
body. Their eyes met, his glittering, hers dark and
vague.

He took one last, lingering taste of her, then lunged
to his feet. After hurriedly stripping off his jeans, he
found a condom in the bedside drawer and rolled it
on. All the while, he watched her, appreciating the
sight she made sprawled in his bed, how right she
looked there.

Emma came up to her elbows, but fell flat to the
mattress again when he moved over her, hooked her
thighs in his arms to spread her legs wide, and slid
smoothly inside her body. He felt her tightening with
that first stroke and pushed her legs higher so that he
was deep, so damn deep. She couldn't choose the
rhythm, couldn't alter the depth of his thrusts or
change the angle. He was in control.

He heard her broken cry on the second stroke, and
shuddered at the sharp bite of her nails on his shoulders as she tried to urge him even closer. On the third

stroke, harder, deeper, he relished the start of her release. "That's it, Em. Come for me, sweetheart. Come for me."

Her body arched beautifully, her breasts shivered with the strength of her orgasm, her expression was arrested, her breath low and guttural.

Teeth clenched, muscles straining as he held himself deep, Casey joined her, and as they both went boneless, he found the strength to murmur, "You're mine, Emma. Now...and always."

To his relief, she didn't deny it.

But then Emma was already sound asleep.

CHAPTER FOURTEEN

DAMON HAD BECOME as much a regular fixture around the Hudson household as Emma. For two weeks now, he and Ceily had been almost inseparable, which meant when Damon stopped in to visit, Ceily was there too. And more often than not, their visits seemed to be at dinnertime.

It was the first time Emma could remember seeing Damon so taken with a woman. That he should be taken with Ceily was nothing short of supreme irony. But she was happy for him, and for Ceily.

Honey and Misty had grown up with an austere father, which meant their dinners had always been rather subdued events. Now they both relished the boisterous, busy meals spent with friends and family. Since they lived so close, with Morgan and Misty just up the hill, and were best friends as well as sisters, they were often together. They claimed to enjoy the extra *rational* female company in Ceily and Emma, which Emma took to mean a woman not mooning over the brothers or Casey.

Certainly, Ceily was too straightforward to moon, but Emma? She merely hid her mooning. Truth was, she couldn't go five minutes without thinking about Casey—and smiling in absolute happiness. He occupied her every waking moment. The past month spent with him had been, well, the stuff of dreams... because she loved Casey with all her heart.

The more time she spent with him, the more she accepted that she'd actually fallen in love with him as a teenager, and never really stopped. Neither time nor distance apart had lessened the emotion one bit.

But being with him, making love to him every night, waking with him every morning, had strengthened that love until she couldn't imagine how she'd survive when she had to leave him.

Yet she knew that eventually she'd have to do just that.

While Casey was at work, Emma visited her parents at the hospital. Her father was now much improved, and her mother was, if not pleasant, at least sober. Dell had been thrilled to find out his wife had willingly gone into rehab for help. As far as Emma was concerned, that, more than anything, had helped revive his spirit. Her mother was allowed to visit him, and they'd talk for hours. Most of their conversations centered around her mother's complaints, but in his commiseration, Dell's speech had gotten much better, as had his motor control.

Her mother was determined to be there for him. It wasn't easy, and she had a lot of difficult times, but she was trying. Losing her daughter hadn't done the trick, but the possibility of losing her husband was too much.

They were both healing and, for once, Emma thought she might be able to be part of her own family. It would never be the ideal—it would never be the Hudson household—but it was an improvement.

She'd spoken with them about the future, and because they both relied on her now, they were willing to adjust.

Casey had gotten home a half hour ago and, after greeting Emma with a kiss, went straight to the apartment for a shower. With Damon and Ceily visiting again, he knew they'd have dinner with the family, rather than slipping off to the cabin with sandwiches, as they often preferred.

He'd just stepped back into the kitchen, hair still damp, casual clothes now in place of his suit, when Honey announced the fried chicken was ready. Morgan stood to call in the kids, but Casey said, "I wanted to tell you all something first."

Into that breaking silence, Emma's phone rang. She jumped, considered ignoring it, but Casey gave her a crooked smile. "Go ahead. This'll wait."

A little embarrassed, she made her apologies and answered the wireless phone while stepping out of the kitchen for privacy. With so many people in for dinner, the buzz of conversation still reached her.

Her first reaction to hearing Dr. Wagner's voice was alarm. Because she visited the hospital each day to be apprised of improvements, he had never found it necessary to call her. But at his jovial greeting, she relaxed...until he announced that he'd be sending her father home in the morning.

It was the signal of the end, her last remaining excuse for lingering in Buckhorn. She'd already contacted a Chicago hospital about her father's physical therapy once he left the hospital. It was located close to her home and could provide everything he needed. She'd also made plans with a rehab facility for her mother.

Unaware of her melancholy, Dr. Wagner continued. "You can take a copy of his chart with you, but I've already faxed one to the hospital you specified. Take a day or two to get him settled, then set up routine appointments."

"Thank you, I will." Emma squeezed her eyes shut, but couldn't resist asking, "You're sure he's ready to come home?"

"He's shown marked improvement over the last week. Yes, I'd say he's ready—and anxious. Everyone tires of the hospital in a very short time. And being home with his family is a good therapy in its own way, too."

The quiet drone of conversation in the kitchen had died and Emma wondered if everyone had paused to listen to her. "Thanks, Dr. Wagner. Is there a specific time I should be there in the morning?"

They made arrangements, and while Emma made mental note of all things pertinent, her heart ached. She didn't want to go, didn't want to leave Casey. Didn't want to leave her home.

But how impossible would it be for her to tend her parents here where everyone now knew of her mother's transgressions—and her own. She had to be reasonable, not emotional. She had a thriving business, which had been neglected for almost a month. She had a life, friends, family in Chicago. All she had in Buckhorn was a reputation, and some bad history.

With an invisible vise on her heart, and a lump in her throat, she reentered the kitchen and managed to dredge up a smile. Everyone looked up from the dinner table. "My dad is getting out of the hospital tomorrow."

The expressions varied from surprise, concern, to expectation. Casey merely looked detached, and that confused her.

Emma folded her hands together over her waist. "I'm taking him, and my mother, of course, home to Chicago with me."

Sawyer tossed down his napkin. Unlike his son, he looked far from indifferent. "You're what?"

Honey's eyes were wide. "Oh, but..." She glanced at everyone else, as if seeking help.

Morgan rubbed his forehead and muttered something under his breath. Misty fretted.

But Damon, damn him, looked at Casey with one eyebrow raised. "Well?"

Casey, sighing with long-suffering forbearance, left his seat to stand beside her. "I suppose I'll be going to Chicago too."

"What?" Sawyer pushed back his chair.

Morgan snorted. "Since when?"

"You can't be serious," Honey and Misty said in unison.

Emma gaped at him. "You're not moving to Chicago!"

"Why not?" Casey shrugged, disregarding her shock. "I'd already decided that I wanted to switch jobs—which is what I was about to announce when you got your call."

Everyone started to protest at once, but Casey didn't let it stop him. He held up a hand, silencing one and all. "No, just hear me out. I enjoyed what I was doing up to a point, but now it just isn't enough." He winked at Emma. "Having Emma around helped me to realize what I really want to do."

All eyes turned to Emma, making her gulp.

"Just what is that?" Sawyer finally asked.

"Financial planning. I had thought to open something up here, but…" He shrugged again. "Looks like it'll have to be in Chicago."

Emma's mouth fell open.

Ceily pushed back her chair and joined those who were already standing, which was just about everyone. "I'm going to Chicago too."

Damon dropped his fork and leaned back in his seat. "What the hell for?"

She blinked down at him. "Why, to be with you."

"But I'm staying here."

Emma and Ceily said at the same time, "You are?"

He scowled. "Yes, I am. I like it here." He cleared his throat and, though Emma had rarely seen him this way, he looked uncertain. "I spoke to Jesse about buying his land. We're working out a deal."

Ceily's eyes narrowed. "You spoke to *my* grandfather without telling me?" And then, with her eyes popping wide, added, "He agreed to sell to *you?*"

Damon joined the ranks of those standing. "Well, how else could we keep the land around and not have some city slicker throw a damn water park up?"

"You," Ceily pointed out, "are a city slicker."

"Not anymore," he told her with satisfaction. "I was thinking along the lines of some nice tidy little rental cabins that would blend with the woods. Maybe ten or twelve of them. They'd be unobtrusive but lucrative."

Everyone seemed to be holding their breath. Ceily

crossed her arms over her chest. "If you stay here, I'm going to fall in love with you."

Very slowly, Damon smiled. "Yeah?"

She gave a brisk nod. "And when I do, I'll damn well expect you to marry me."

His look so intimate, Emma blushed, Damon pulled Ceily close and kissed her. "It's a deal."

Casey threw up his arms. "Well, since that's settled... Emma, how soon do we need to leave?"

Emma rubbed her ear, utterly befuddled. "Casey..." She looked around at his family, but none of them appeared willing to help. "You can't leave here."

"Why not?"

Logic remained just out of reach. She shook her head. "This is your home."

"It's your home too. But what the hell? We can make a home anywhere, right?"

Sawyer covered his mouth and, Emma suspected, a smile. She groped behind her for a chair. Honey rushed to scoot one beneath her before she dropped. Morgan gave her an encouraging nod.

They were all nuts. When she finally found her voice, it emerged as a squeak. "Uh, *we?*"

Eyes intent on her face, his sensual mouth tipping in a slight smile, Casey nodded. "Me and you."

"But...it's not just me." He had to understand that. "It's my mother and father and..."

"And me," Damon said. He grinned. "I'm like a brother figure, don't you know."

Casey laughed. "And I'm not just me. Hell, Emma, this lunatic crowd—" he indicated the rapt faces of his family members "—is only a small part of the group."

Morgan scowled at him. "I changed your diapers, boy, so don't give me any lip."

Sawyer choked on a laugh. "Are you hinting that you want some privacy, Case?"

He rolled his shoulders, trying to look indifferent— and failing. "Not particularly. I just want Emma to admit that she loves me."

Her mouth fell open again. At this rate, she'd end up with a broken jaw.

Misty leaned over to put her arm around Emma. "Put him out of his misery, hon. Men hate to suffer, this bunch more than most."

Putting her head in her hands, Emma laughed, or maybe she was crying, or a little of both.

Honey wrung her hands. "I really would hate to see Casey move away. But more than that, I'd hate to see him brokenhearted."

They were all nuts. "Well, of course I love him."

Casey beamed at her. "Way to drag out the suspense, Em. Naturally, I love you too. So, where do you want to live?"

There was a time, Emma thought while she fought her smile, when this situation would have totally disconcerted her. She'd have felt out of place, conspicuous. But now she reveled in the open love exchanged between Casey and his family. She wanted to be with all of them. She wanted to have kids who would join the others in the yard, running and playing, happy and carefree and secure in a way she'd never been able to be. They were a good family to be around—a better family to be a part of.

Tears filled her eyes and clogged her throat, making her voice thick. "I'd like to stay here."

Until Sawyer and Morgan both slumped in relief, Emma hadn't known they were so tense waiting for her answer. But to her surprise, Casey didn't seem any more relieved with staying than he had seemed worried about leaving. He walked over to her and took her hand. "Now we could use some privacy. Feel like a boat ride?"

"Yes."

"But you haven't eaten!"

Casey kissed Honey on the top of the head. "Mind if we take it with us?"

Sawyer had already turned and begun packing food into a basket. "'Course she doesn't." He grinned at his son. "Leave B.B. here since he's still playing with the kids. I'll make sure he gets fed. And while you're gone, Honey and Misty can start planning the wedding."

Casey raised an eyebrow at Emma, and Emma laughed. They were overwhelming, wonderfully so. "Thank you."

Rolling his eyes, Casey said, "You say thanks more than anyone I know."

A mere half hour later, Emma found herself in the small cabin Casey owned, naked, beneath him, and thoroughly loved. Casey continued to nibble on her lips, her ear, her chin. The day was so warm, their flesh had melded together. Casey was still inside her.

"You will marry me, won't you, Em?"

She scoffed. "Like you ever had a doubt."

Raising himself up, Casey stared at her with such a serious expression she got worried. "Doubts?

You've filled me with more doubts than any man should ever have to suffer. You left here, when I never thought you would, leaving me to doubt if I'd ever see you again. You came back more wonderful than I thought possible, making me doubt I'd even still have a chance.''

''Casey.'' How could he have been so silly? She'd been his for as long as she could remember.

''Damn, Emma, I love you so much it's scary.''

''I love you too. I always have.''

''You did a very good job of hiding it.'' He kissed her, sweet and gentle, then deeper until he had to tear himself away. He cupped her face, rubbed her temples with his thumbs. ''I am so proud of you, Emma, but, God, it's unsettling to know you built this happy life somewhere else, and damned if you didn't constantly talk about running back to it. I kept wondering how long I could keep you here, if it'd be long enough to get you to fall in love with me again.'' He gave her another hard kiss and pressed his forehead to hers. ''Believe me, Em, I've had doubts.''

Emma squeezed him tight.

''Are you sure you're okay with staying here in Buckhorn?''

She grinned. More doubts? ''Yes. I love it here. I'd just convinced myself it didn't matter because I thought I couldn't stay.'' Then she felt compelled to ask, ''Aren't you happy to be staying here?''

''I'm happy to be with you. That's what matters most.''

''But,'' she said, insisting on the truth, ''you'd rather be here, wouldn't you?''

''Yes, I'd rather be here.''

"It won't be easy, you know. Kristin and Lois have spread a lot of gossip…"

Casey grinned. "Everyone already assumes they're just jealous—and understandably."

"Because I have you?"

He laughed, squeezed her, shook his head. "No, goose. Because you're so remarkable, beautiful inside and out."

Emma lowered her gaze to his tanned shoulders. "There's my mother and father to deal with."

"And your possessive dog and dumb-ass Damon and—"

She slugged him. "Hey!"

Laughing, Casey rolled so she was atop him. "Just teasing. I like your dog just fine."

She gave him a fierce scowl. "And Damon?"

Casey pretended to consider that, until Emma tweaked his chest hair. "Okay, okay! He's a good guy. I like him, now that I've gotten used to him."

"Really?"

"He loves you, and he's in love with Ceily, so he's okay in my book." His teasing over, Casey pressed her cheek to his heart and held her there. "No family is ever perfect, Emma. We'll make do with your folks, and you'll work at putting up with mine, and we'll have each other. Everything else will work itself out."

EPILOGUE

Two Months Later

CASEY PUSHED the recently repaired cabin door open and was nearly knocked off his feet by B.B.'s greeting. With his keen ears, the dog heard Casey's approach before his car had rounded the last bend. By the time he reached the porch, B.B. was always waiting.

"Hey, boy. Where's my better half?"

B.B. woofed, accepted a few more vigorous rubs, then ran outside to chase a squirrel. He seemed to enjoy the isolated surroundings as much as Emma.

Casey listened to the sound of running water and knew Emma was in the tiny shower. Since marrying her a week ago, he'd been about as happy as a man could get.

At her insistence, they'd moved into the remote cabin after renovating it a bit. Spotlessly clean, with walls, windows and roof repaired, it made cozy temporary quarters until Damon finished directing the builders on their modest house on the lake.

To Sawyer and Honey's delight, they'd been convinced to move nearby, only a few acres away from the main house on the land the family owned. With

Misty up the hill and Emma down, Honey claimed she had the perfect female company close by.

Casey tossed his suit coat aside, pulled his tie free and loosened his collar as he heard the shower shut off, replaced with the sounds of Emma humming. Seconds later she emerged from the bathroom in a long pink T-shirt, her hair wrapped in a towel. The second she saw him, her beautiful dark eyes lit up and she came to him for a kiss.

"I didn't hear you come in," she said, going on tiptoe to hug him.

It was the type of greeting he'd never tire of. Casey took her mouth in a long, deep kiss before slipping his hands beneath the bottom of the shirt and cuddling her bottom. "Mmm..." he said. But before he carried her off, they needed to talk. "How'd it go today?"

"Actually, it was great." She stepped away to the refrigerator and poured two glasses of iced tea. In silent agreement they wandered out to the screened porch and sat in the new pair of rattan rockers bought for just that purpose. B.B. took a leap off the dock— something he'd begun doing only days after they'd moved in, then waded up on the shore, shook himself off and plopped down in the sun to dry.

"The nurse is terrific and Dad really likes her. She's firm but friendly. Even Mom is grateful to her for the help. I think she still worries about Dad, even though he's doing better."

With Sawyer's help, they'd located a home health-care aide to take over Dell's physical therapy and keep him on a healthy diet by supplying both break-fast and dinner. Her presence freed up Emma's time, a necessity since she'd opened a massage therapy salon in Buckhorn, and found herself booked solid almost every day.

Emma's mother had stayed sober since that eventful day in Mrs. Reider's parking lot, much to Emma's relief. They were both trying to get along, though Casey doubted they'd ever be close. But now they were civil, and little by little they were building a tenuous relationship. It was a start.

Casey looked at her profile then set his tea aside. "Come here," he told her, catching her hand and pulling her into his lap. "You were too far away."

She smiled up at him. "Quit stalling. Tell me how things went with your grandfather."

He winced, but ended it with a grin. "We negotiated. I agreed to stay on as a consultant for the new hires in my department, and he agreed he wouldn't ask more than four days a month from me."

"Sounds doable. And like it might appease him. I know you didn't want any hurt feelings."

"He was so set on making me his heir."

Emma curled into him. "And you tried."

There was no refuting that. But he wasn't cut out for the corporate life, not when his roots were so entrenched in Buckhorn. "I think he's refocusing on Shohn." Casey laughed. "And if I know my little brother, he'll be running the business by the time he's twenty."

"I don't doubt he could if he set his mind to it."

Shohn had been the best man at their small wedding, and he'd also danced at the reception with every female in attendance. For a ten-year-old, he was an outrageous flirt and bursting with confidence. The women doted on him, calling him cute and audacious and adorable—a chip off the old block. Shohn just grinned throughout it all.

"You'll set your business up soon?"

"Yes." Since leaving Chicago, her life had been constant turmoil. Between the issues with her parents, relocating her home and work, the wedding, she'd barely had time to relax. More than anything, Casey wanted things to settle down into a calm routine. "I'll finish up two more weeks with Granddad so my replacement can make a smooth transition. My new office ought to be ready by then and all the advertisements will have been distributed. By the time the house is built we should be all set."

Resting her head on his shoulder, Emma said, "You don't need to make promises to me, Casey. The new house, the new jobs...they're a nice start, and I'm happy about them. But I'll always be happy, no matter what, as long as I have you."

Casey turned her face up to his so he could see her beautiful dark eyes. They were filled with love, all for him. Though Emma thought his life had always been blessed, he knew he'd just been passing time without her.

His grin started slow, but spread. "You know, sweetheart, though it's usually your line, I have to say thank you."

Tilting her head, she laughed. "What are you thanking me for?"

"You came back home to me, Em. You gave me a second chance to have the only woman I want. You gave me back *me*, because without you I was only half-alive."

Her eyes were enormous, sexy, shining with love. "Casey."

"I love you so damn much. Just as you are, just as you've always been, and however you'll be in the future. You're mine. Now and forever."

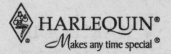